LOADED DICE

"Leaves us wanting more of this pulsing buoyant book."
—Los Angeles Times

"A poker novel with the punch of a royal flush . . . ought to be required reading." *—Chicago Sun-Times*

"Pure entertainment, building to a slam-bang ending."
—San Jose Mercury News

"Great fun with just the right amount of edge—sort of like a night out at the blackjack table." *—Booklist*

SUCKER BET

"Ingenious entertainment."
—The New York Times Book Review

"Great fun . . . Swain, an expert on card trickery and casino cheating, is an entertaining writer whose breezy style and flair for wise-guy dialogue make the story zoom by." *—Boston Globe*

"A vivid insider's look at casinos [that] hits the jackpot . . . *Sucker Bet* is a sure thing." *—Chicago Tribune*

"Swain has come up with a doozy. . . . The gambling details are a treat [and] the banter is worthy of a place at Elmore Leonard's table." *—Booklist*

FUNNY MONEY

"Fascinating . . . dazzling . . . entertaining . . . I can't think of a novel I've enjoyed more this year."
—*Los Angeles Times*

"There's a certain intelligence to a book that teaches you something—even something as esoteric as how to spot a casino cheat—and Swain juggles that mix of learning and adventure perfectly."
—*Houston Chronicle*

"Smart, snappy . . . tremendously infectious."
—*St. Petersburg Times*

"Great fun—with oddball characters, a twisted plot, and scheming dreamers out for the big score."
—*Lansing State Journal*

GRIFT SENSE

"A well-plotted debut mystery that pays off handsomely . . . *Grift Sense* delivers a vivid and credible look at the gaming industry through eccentric yet believable characters."
—*Chicago Tribune*

"*Grift Sense* is one of the best debuts I've read in years. It has a great plot, wonderful characters, and a slick, subtle wit."
—*The Toronto Globe and Mail*

"The hard-nosed dialogue and the fast-paced, serpentine plot deliver a page-turner of a mystery. Just when readers start to relax, thinking it's clear sailing to the end, Swain throws yet another curve."
—*Canadian Press*

deadman's
BLUFF

A Novel

James Swain

BALLANTINE BOOKS • NEW YORK

A Ballantine Books Mass Market Original

Published in the United States by Ballantine Books, an imprint of The Random House Publishing Group, a division of Random House, Inc.

BALLANTINE and colophon are registered trademarks of Random House, Inc.

ISBN 0-345-47551-8

Cover illustration: Don Sipley

Printed in the United States of America

www.ballantinebooks.com

OPM   9   8   7   6   5   4   3   2   1

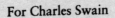

For Charles Swain

Luck ain't never paid the bills.

—PUG PEARSON, famous poker player

A Brief Glossary of Useful Cheating Terms

Action   Any gambling activity.

Agent   A cheater working with a casino employee while posing as a legitimate player.

BP   Big Player. The member of a cheating team who bets the big money. Also called the "take off man."

Brush off   A signal that says it's time to leave a casino.

Bug   A clip designed to secretly hold a card beneath the table. Also called a "thief."

Cold deck   A prestacked deck of cards.

Crossroader   A cheater who specializes in ripping off casinos.

Deadman's hand	Two black aces and two black eights. The poker hand held by Wild Bill Hickock the night he was murdered by a gang of cheaters in Deadwood, South Dakota.
Deal a deuce	To deal the second card from the top of the deck. Also called "dealing a blister."
Deal a plank	To deal off the bottom of the deck.
Doing business	Cheating.
Double heat	Intense scrutiny from casino security.
Feel a breeze	To know when cheating is going on, even if you don't know what it is.
Gaff	Any cheating device.
George	A signal among cheaters that everything is all right. Often done with an open hand on the chest or layout.
Giving the office	Signaling among cheaters.
Greed factor	Winning too much, too often.
Grift sense	An innate ability to spot a hustle or a scam. A compliment among hustlers.

Grind joint   A casino with low table minimums and small denomination slot machines.

Hairy leg   A moneyman who backs a game.

Herking and jerking   Distracting your opponent while cheating him.

Iggy   A cheater pretending to be a tourist.

Joint   A casino.

Kepplinger holdout   A hidden device that secretly switches playing cards.

Leaking   Exposing a secretly palmed card.

Local courtesy   An unwritten arrangement between local players in poker not to bet against each other.

Mechanic   A cheater skilled in sleight-of-hand.

Miracle move   A perfect cheating move. Also called a "million-dollar move."

Mortal lock   A sure thing.

Old moustache   A mobster.

On the square   To play a game honestly, without cheating.

Punch	A device used to create tiny indentations in cards.
Put the heavy on	To use force when dealing with an unpleasant situation.
Subs	Various types of cloth bags worn inside the clothing to hold stolen chips.
Suckers	Ninety-nine percent of the people who gamble. Also known as chumps, marks, pigeons, rubes, and vics (victims).
Steam	Unwanted attention. Also called "heat."
Swinging	To secretly switch cards during a game.
Texas Hold 'Em	A variation of poker invented by a dozen ranch hands who had only a single deck of cards among them.
Tokes	Tips.
Tom	A signal among cheaters that things look bad. Often done with a clenched fist on the chest or layout.
Wake the dead	A scam that is blatantly obvious.
Who shot John?	A ridiculous conversation among people who know better.

Part I

Driving the White Line

1

"I win," Rufus Steele said.

Tony Valentine could not believe his eyes. Steele, a seventy-year-old, whiskey-drinking Texas gambler, had just outrun a racehorse named Greased Lightning in the hundred-yard dash. The race had taken place on the manicured football field of the University of Nevada, the pulsating neon of the Las Vegas strip electrifying the night sky.

Valentine stood in the end zone with a mob of gamblers, many of whom had bet against Rufus. The gamblers were competing in the World Poker Showdown, the world's richest poker tournament. Valentine was there for a different reason. He'd been hired by the Nevada Gaming Control Board to figure out how a seeing-impaired player could be cheating the tournament, and he was trying to help his son avenge the murder of a childhood friend. The fact that he'd solved neither case to his satisfaction had made for a long four days, and watching Rufus fleece some suckers had provided a welcome distraction.

"I want to see the tape," declared a man known as the Greek.

The Greek had lost a half million bucks on the horse. He fancied himself a gambler, but had never swam with sharks as big as Rufus. The old cowboy sauntered over to where the Greek stood.

"Want to bet on the outcome again?" Rufus asked.

"Shut up!" the Greek roared.

Zack, the cameraman who'd filmed the event, rewound the tape, and the Greek and Rufus huddled behind him, staring at the camera's tiny screen. Valentine wanted to see the race again as well, and stared over the two men's shoulders.

Gloria Curtis brushed up beside him. In Vegas covering the poker tournament for a cable sports network, Gloria had filmed the race to be shown on her talk show. "Did you know Rufus was going to swindle the Greek like that?" she whispered to Valentine.

"Rufus didn't swindle him," he whispered back.

"He didn't?"

"No. Rufus *tricked* him."

"And how is that different?"

"Rufus told the Greek he could beat a horse in the hundred-yard dash. He never said the race would be run in a straight line."

She chewed her lower lip, thinking it over. "But Rufus put a plastic cone on the fifty-yard line, so the horse had to stop, turn around, and run back."

"It was a hundred-yard race, fair and square," Valentine said.

She smiled at him with her eyes, which were the prettiest Valentine had seen in a long time. She'd interviewed him about the cheating at the tournament, and they'd immediately hit it off. He had no idea where the relationship was going, or even if it was going anywhere, but the ride so far was enjoyable.

"I know it *looks* like Rufus swindled the Greek," he explained, "but the Greek went into the race with a gigantic edge, and he knew it."

"An edge?"

"An advantage. The Greek's advantage was that no human being can outrun a horse. The Greek *had* to know that Rufus would level the playing field to make the race competitive. And that's exactly what Rufus did."

"You still didn't answer my question. Did you know what Rufus was up to?"

"No." Valentine sensed Gloria didn't quite believe him. Normally it wouldn't have mattered, only she'd been in his thoughts these last few days. So he added, "Scout's honor."

She kissed him on the cheek. "Good."

"Here we go," said Zack.

The tiny screen on Zack's camera showed Rufus and Greased Lightning about to start their race. The horse's jockey stood in his saddle, clutching his crop. Valentine had been the starter, and the audio on the camera played back his voice intoning, "Take your marks . . . Get ready—go!" and the shot of the starter pistol.

Greased Lightning bolted, the jockey gripping the reins for dear life. The horse was out of control, and by the time the jockey managed to stop and turn around, he was ninety yards down the field. By then, Rufus had reached the cone, spun around, and was heading for the finish line.

"For the love of Christ," Valentine now said under his breath.

"What's wrong?" Gloria asked.

"Rufus tricked me."

"But I didn't think *anyone* could trick you," Gloria said.

Valentine shook his head, realizing what Rufus had done. The sound of the starter pistol had put Greased Lightning into a frenzy, and prevented the jockey from trotting to the cone, turning around, and galloping back.

"It happens," he said.

On the tiny screen, Rufus was huffing and puffing, his arms and legs working in unison, the horse coming up from behind like a runaway train. The ending was decided by inches, with Rufus throwing himself over the finish line as Greased Lightning thundered past. Zack froze the frame, and everyone leaned forward to see Rufus's hand break the plane of the end zone before the horse's nose did.

Rufus pounded the Greek on the back.

"I win," Rufus said.

Professional gamblers did not take IOUs or personal checks. They dealt in cold hard cash, and the Greek had brought an enormous bag of money with him to the football field. As the Greek paid Rufus off, he looked at him pleadingly.

"I want another chance," the Greek said.

There was weakness in his voice. Rufus glanced up from his counting.

"Want to win your money back, huh?"

The Greek nodded.

"I didn't bust you, did I?"

The Greek shook his head. "I have more," he said.

Rufus pulled the drawstring tight on the bag and gave it some thought. Sweat had started pouring off his body right after the race had ended. Valentine had tried to get him to drink water, but he'd refused.

"Well, I used to be pretty good at Ping-Pong," Rufus said. "How about this. I'll challenge anyone still playing in the tournament to a game of Ping-Pong, winner to reach twenty-one."

"How much money are we talking about?" the Greek asked.

Rufus pointed at the sack of money lying on the grass. "That much. Interested?"

The Greek smiled like he'd found sunken treasure. "Yeah, I'm interested."

"I've got one stipulation," Rufus said. "I supply the paddles. Your man can choose either one. If he wants to switch during the match, he can. I just don't want some guy showing up with one of those crazy rubber paddles that put so much spin on the ball that it's impossible to hit back."

"I'm agreeable to that," the Greek said.

"Tell Rufus not to go through with this," Gloria whispered in Valentine's ear.

"Why not?"

"Takarama is still playing in the tournament. I profiled him for my show the other day. He still practices table tennis three hours a day."

Shiego Takarama was a world table tennis champion

who'd retired to play tournament poker. He was still in tremendous shape, and Valentine envisioned him wiping up the floor with Rufus. He went over to Rufus and pulled him aside.

"You don't want to go through with this," Valentine said.

"Of course I do," Rufus replied.

"But you're going to lose."

"Tony, I can play Ping-Pong as good as the next fellow. I've got a table in my basement that I play my granddaughters on."

"But . . ."

"Did you hear what the Greek said? He has *money*. That's my money, Tony. The Greek is just holding it for me. Now, if you'll excuse me, I have some business to take care of."

There was no stopping a man when he wanted to gamble. Rufus went up to the Greek and shook hands, sealing the deal. Shaking his head, Valentine returned to where Gloria stood with her cameraman. "He'll never beat Takarama," he said.

A twinkle appeared in Gloria's eye. "So, you want to make a bet on that?"

"You mean bet *against* Rufus?"

"Yes."

Betting against a grifter was like betting against the sun rising. No matter how outlandish the proposition, the grifter was going to come out ahead.

"Never," he said.

2

Big Julie, a famous New York gambler, once said that the person who invented gambling was smart, but the person who invented chips was a genius.

Poker had a similar truism. The person who'd invented poker may have been smart, but the person who'd invented the hidden camera that allowed a television audience to see the players' hands was a genius.

George "the Tuna" Scalzo sat on his hotel suite's couch with his nephew beside him. It was ten o'clock in the evening, and the big-screen TV was on. They were watching the action from that day's World Poker Showdown, which was generating the highest ratings of any sporting event outside of the Super Bowl. His nephew, Skip DeMarco, was winning the tournament and had become an overnight sensation.

"Tell me what you're seeing, Uncle George," DeMarco said.

His nephew faced the TV, his handsome face bathed in the screen's artificial light. Skipper suffered from a degenerative eye disease that he'd had since birth. He could not see two inches past his nose, and so his uncle described the action.

"They're showing the different players you knocked out of the tournament today," Scalzo said. "Treetop Strauss, Mike 'Mad Dog' McCoy, Johnny 'the Wizard' Wang, and a bunch of other guys. It's beautiful, especially when you call their bluffs. They don't know what hit them."

Bluffing was what made poker exciting. A man could have worthless cards, yet if he bet aggressively, he'd win hand after hand. DeMarco had made a specialty of calling his opponents' bluffs, and had become the most feared player in the tournament.

"Is the camera showing me a lot?" DeMarco asked.

"All the time. You're the star."

"Do I look arrogant?"

Scalzo didn't know what arrogant meant. *Proud?* That word he understood. He glanced across the suite at Guido, who leaned against the wall. His bodyguard had a zipper scar down the side of his face and never smiled. Guido came from the streets of Newark, New Jersey, as did all the men who worked for Scalzo.

"Guido, how does Skipper look?"

"Calm, cool, and collected," Guido said, puffing on a cigarette.

"Is he a star?"

"Big star," Guido said.

"There you go." Scalzo elbowed his nephew in the ribs.

The show ended, and was followed by the local news. The broadcasters covered the day's headlines, then a story from the University of Nevada's football field came on.

"What's this?" his nephew asked.

Scalzo squinted at the screen. The story was about Rufus Steele challenging a racehorse to the hundred-yard dash. Rufus appeared on the screen dressed in track shorts. Beside him was Tony Valentine, the casino consultant who'd caused them so much trouble. Scalzo grabbed the remote and changed the channel.

"Put it back on, Uncle George," his nephew said.

"Why? He can't beat no fucking racehorse," Scalzo protested.

"I want to see it anyway. This is the old guy who challenged me to play him. I said I'd play him after the tournament was over if he could raise a million bucks."

The suite fell silent. "You're not going to play that son-of-a-bitch," Scalzo declared.

"If he raises the money, I'll have to, Uncle George," DeMarco said.

"Why?"

"Because this is poker. If I don't accept Rufus's challenge, he wins."

Scalzo did not like the direction the conversation was taking. He clicked his fingers, and Guido rose from his chair.

"Yes, Mr. Scalzo," the bodyguard said.

"A glass of cognac for me. What would you like, Skipper?"

"For you not to drink while we have this conversation," his nephew said.

Scalzo balled his hands into fists and stared at his nephew's profile. If someone who worked for him had said that, he would have had him killed. "You don't like when I drink?"

"You get mean. Doesn't he, Guido?"

Swallowing hard, the bodyguard said nothing. Scalzo made a twirling motion with his finger. Guido walked into the next room, shutting the door behind him.

Scalzo changed the channel with the remote, and watched Rufus beat Greased Lightning in the hundred-yard-dash while explaining it to his nephew. Then he killed the power and the room fell silent.

"This cowboy is the real thing," his nephew said.

"What's that supposed to mean?" Scalzo snapped.

"He's an old-time hustler, Uncle George. I can't scam him the way we're scamming the tournament. It won't work."

Skipper had won several dozen poker tournaments on the Internet. Live games were a different matter, with other players ganging up on him because of his handicap. Scalzo had wanted to level the playing field, and found a scammer in Atlantic City named Jack Donovan who'd invented a scam that would let Skipper win. Scalzo had Donovan murdered for the scam, then taught it to his nephew. Although Skipper had never cheated before, he'd gone along, wanting the recognition that winning brought, which he believed he deserved.

"But no one has figured out the scam so far," Scalzo said.

"Steele will. He'll feel a breeze."

"So let him put a sweater on."

"It's a gambler's expression, Uncle George. Steele will know *something* is wrong. Even if he doesn't know what it is, he'll figure it out eventually. I have to play him on the square. If I'm as good as I keep telling myself I am, then I should beat him."

"You want to play the cowboy legitimately?"

"Yes."

Scalzo scowled. Skipper was letting his mouth overload his ass. He wasn't going to play Steele head-to-head. The old cowboy knew too many damn tricks. Scalzo dropped the remote in his nephew's lap. "I'm going to bed," Scalzo said. "Let's talk again in the morning."

His nephew stared absently into space as if disappointed with his uncle.

"Good night, Uncle George," he said.

Scalzo entered the next room and was greeted by an unexpected guest. Karl Jasper, founder and president of the World Poker Showdown, stood at the bar, talking with Guido while drinking a beer. The face of the WPS, Jasper had black-dyed hair, whitened teeth, and shoulder pads in his jackets that made him look trimmer than he really was.

"Nice place," Jasper said.

Scalzo and his nephew were staying in a high-roller suite, compliments of the hotel. It had a fully stocked bar, pool table, Jacuzzi, and private theater with reclining leather chairs. It was the best digs in town, and wasn't costing them a dime. A snifter of cognac awaited Scalzo on the bar. They clinked glasses, and Scalzo raised the drink to his lips and sniffed.

"Did you see Rufus Steele on TV?" Jasper asked. "The man is becoming a menace."

Scalzo let the cognac swirl around in his mouth. It felt

good and strong and made him wake up. He liked how Jasper addressed things. He was a product of Madison Avenue, and had gone from account executive to founder and president of the World Poker Showdown in the blink of an eye. He was a smart guy who suffered from the same problem that a lot of smart guys suffered from: He didn't know how to run a business. Within six months of starting the WPS, he'd run out of cash. In desperation he'd gone to the mob, and Scalzo became his partner.

Scalzo could not have envisioned a more perfect setup. The biggest mistake the mob had ever made was letting themselves get pushed out of Las Vegas. No other town in the world had the same kind of action. By partnering with Jasper, Scalzo could run a card game inside a Las Vegas casino without the law breathing down his neck. It didn't get any better than that.

"Rufus Steele is a clown," Scalzo said. "The real problem is Tony Valentine. He wants to expose Skipper. He has a grudge with me."

The beer in Jasper's glass had disappeared. Guido popped the cap off a bottle and poured him another.

"You've dealt with Valentine before?" Jasper asked.

Scalzo nodded stiffly.

"Can he be bought off?"

"No," Scalzo said. "He was a casino cop for twenty years. They called him the squarest guy in Atlantic City."

"So what should we do?"

Scalzo stared across the suite at the picture window on the other side of the room. The curtains were pulled back, allowing him to see the pulsing neon spectacle that was the strip at night. For years he'd run a successful scam in Atlantic City that had made him a small fortune, but this was different. This was Las Vegas, and for as long as he could remember, he'd wanted a piece of it all for himself.

"We need to get rid of him," Scalzo said. "Once Valentine's gone, Steele will fade into the sunset, and we can go back to business."

"When you say get rid of him," Jasper said, "do you mean, run him out of town?"

Scalzo put his snifter down, and coldly stared at his guest. Jasper's face and hands were evenly tanned from playing golf three times a week. They'd been partners for over a year, and so far, Jasper had shown no regrets for having jumped in bed with the devil.

"I mean we need to kill the bastard," Scalzo said.

"You're serious."

"Yeah. If you wanna get somethin' done, you need to do it yourself."

Jasper blinked, and then he blinked again. *Making a Madison Avenue decision,* Scalzo thought. He placed his hand on Jasper's arm, and squeezed the younger man's biceps. "We need to do it right now," Scalzo added.

3

Old age was mean.

Valentine had discovered that a few years ago, the week he'd turned sixty. He'd gotten up one morning, and half the bones in his body felt broken. He'd tried to remember what he'd done to deserve such punishment, and realized his body was paying him back for a judo class he'd taken two days before.

A two-day-old payback. That was just plain mean.

Old age also turned cruel on Rufus right after the football field cleared out. Rufus was putting his winnings into a rented Wells Fargo truck when both legs cramped and his face turned blue. Valentine had thrown the last bag of money into the truck, then gotten his head under Rufus's armpit, dragged him to his rental, and poured Rufus into the passenger seat.

Gloria and Zack had already left. Valentine got the rental started, and drove across the field to the break in the chain-link fence that led to the parking lot, then on to Las Vegas Boulevard. As the tires hit pavement, Rufus's eyes snapped open.

"I need whiskey," the old cowboy muttered.

"You need to see a doctor first."

"Whiskey's cheaper and it works faster." Rufus pointed at a casino up ahead, a run-down joint called the Laughing Jackalope. "That place will do."

"You sure?" Valentine asked.

"Yessir."

Valentine found a space in the Jackalope's dusty parking lot. Killing the engine, he stared at the peeling paint and decay on the building. There were three types of casinos in Las Vegas: carpet joints, sawdust joints, and toilets. The Jackalope was on the low end of the toilet scale. Opening the door, Rufus practically fell out of the car.

"See you inside," he said.

Valentine watched Rufus lurch across the lot like a drunk on ice skates. At the front door he threw his shoulders back and snapped to attention, then marched inside.

The sound of a shot glass slamming the bar greeted Valentine upon entering the poorly lit, mirrored cocktail lounge. Rufus was at the bar, getting served. The bartender, a cross-eyed albino wearing a faded purple tuxedo shirt, held a bottle of Johnny Walker at the ready.

"Another?" the albino asked.

"I'd sure appreciate it," Rufus replied.

The albino poured and Rufus drank. The color had returned to his cheeks, and he no longer looked ready to keel over. Wiping his lips, he glanced through an open doorway into the next room where a couple of construction workers wearing coveralls were shooting pool. Rufus pointed at the halfway mark on the shot glass.

"To there, if you don't mind," he said.

The albino half-filled the glass. Rufus staggered into the next room, doing his drunk act, and started baiting the construction workers. The albino placed another shot glass on the bar and filled it with whiskey.

"No thanks," Valentine said.

"Who said it was for you?" the albino snorted.

The albino slammed the drink back, then returned the bottle to its slot on the mirrored display behind him. When he turned around, he gave Valentine a hard look.

"I remember you now," the albino said. "You came in here a few days ago, asking a lot of questions. Your name's Gerry, isn't it?"

Valentine and his thirty-six-year-old son, Gerry, bore a strong physical resemblance, and the crummy bar light was a good equalizer. Gerry had been with him until a few hours ago when Valentine sent him to Atlantic City to chase down a lead. He guessed the albino was one of his son's local sources, and said, "That's right. How's it going?"

"Shitty," the albino said. "What do you want?"

"You always so warm and fuzzy?"

"Just call me Mister Fucking Sunshine."

"You must really bring in the customers."

"You came in, didn't you?"

There was no use arguing with a guy like this, and Valentine decided to leave. Pulling out his wallet, he asked, "How much do I owe you?"

"Same as before," the albino said.

"Refresh my memory."

The albino reached into Valentine's wallet and gingerly removed a C-note. He put his elbows on the bar in a friendly fashion and said, "You want to see the notebook? I just got the updates last night. Lots of new dealers."

Valentine played back everything that had just happened. The albino knew his son, and had just taken a hundred-dollar bill from his wallet. "Sure," he said.

The albino removed a plastic three-ring notebook from beneath the bar. Valentine flipped it open and scanned the neatly typed pages. After a few moments, he realized what he was looking at. The notebook contained the names and physical descriptions of several dozen blackjack dealers in Las Vegas, their work hours, and how many times per hour they mistakenly "flashed" their hole card to the players. Reading a flashed card was called front-loading, and a perfectly legal way to beat the house.

Valentine shut the notebook. "Actually there was something else I wanted to ask you. What's the story with the World Poker Showdown?"

"I hear it's rigged for the blind guy to win," the albino said.

"Any idea how?"

"Rumor is, they're using touch cards."

Touch cards were a popular way among cheaters to mark cards. The cheater would use a sharp device called a punch to create an indentation in the card that could be felt by the thumb during the deal. This indentation let the dealer know when certain cards were coming off the top. Other variations used sandpaper and nail polish to scuff the back of the card.

"Thanks," Valentine said, rising from his stool.

"You know, you've aged a lot since the last time I saw you," the albino said.

Valentine was twenty-seven years older than his son. He wanted to tell the albino to get his eyes checked, but had a feeling the comment might be taken the wrong way. He said good night, and walked into the next room to watch Rufus shoot pool.

They left the bar with Rufus holding a handful of the construction workers' money. As Valentine drove away, Rufus took several hundred-dollar bills and shoved them into Valentine's shirt pocket.

"What's that for?" Valentine asked.

"Saving me from getting whacked over the head with a pool cue," Rufus said.

"You tell those guys I was a cop?"

"I sure did. That and those broad shoulders of yours kept those boys honest."

"Were they hustlers?"

Rufus nodded. "Their hands gave them away. They were wearing dirty construction clothes, but didn't have any calluses and their fingernails were clean."

Valentine took Las Vegas Boulevard to the freeway, then headed north toward their hotel. The Celebrity, two exits away, was hosting the World Poker Showdown. A giant billboard in front of the hotel resembled a movie marquee, on which a video clip was being shown.

"Is that who I *think* it is?" Rufus asked.

Skip DeMarco's handsome face had appeared on the marquee. DeMarco had knocked several famous players out of the tournament that day, just as he had since the beginning of the tournament four days ago, each time by calling their bluffs. DeMarco had "read" his opponents' hands, even though he could not see their faces.

"That boy's getting famous," Rufus said. "Too bad he's a cheat."

"The bartender at the Jackalope said DeMarco is in collusion with the dealer," Valentine said.

"Doing what?"

"Touch cards."

Rufus shook his head. "I don't think so."

"Why not?"

"There's a tell with touch cards. The thumb of the dealer's hand scrapes across the top card. It wouldn't fly."

The traffic started to move and Valentine goosed the accelerator. On the marquee, DeMarco was dragging his opponent's chips across the table with a gleeful look on his face. Rufus let out a disapproving snort.

"I can't wait to play that boy once the tournament's over," Rufus said.

"You really dislike him, don't you?"

"Kid's got no class. You can tell he's never driven the white line."

"What's that?"

"Looking for action. You drive a couple hundred miles to a game you've heard about. Sometimes the town isn't even on a map. If the game looks beatable, you play. You do this forty weeks a year, and spend the rest of the time at home, getting reacquainted with your wife and kids. It's a hard way to make a living. And the hardest part is driving the white line, not knowing what lays in store for you."

"Sounds dangerous," Valentine said.

"It is. One time down in Austin, I was playing in a tent on this rich guy's cattle ranch. It was Saturday night, and there's a hundred guys playing poker. Not just ordinary guys, either. There were billionaire oilmen, richer-than-God cattle barons, the crème de la crème of high society, if Texas has such a thing.

"A car pulled up, and four hooded guys with machine guns jumped out. They shot up the tent and made everyone lie down, then robbed us. They were slick, and everyone knew not to mess with them. I was the last person they got to. One of the robbers stared at me. Then he winked."

"A friend?" Valentine asked.

"Yup. We'd run together for a year. I'd heard he'd fallen on hard times."

"What did you say to him?"

"Nothing. I didn't want anyone in that tent knowing we were acquainted. I gave him everything I had, including my late father's watch."

"That must have been hard."

"I got it all back in the mail a week later. He hadn't even touched my bankroll."

They reached their exit. A minute later, Valentine was pulling up a winding front entrance lined with palm trees.

"That was awful nice of him," Valentine said.

Rufus frowned, as though being nice had nothing to do with it. "He wasn't going to rob me, even if I was the last person on the face of the earth. We drove the white line together."

People who gambled for a living lived on a roller-coaster: one day they were up, the next day they were hurtling down. When Valentine had first gotten together with Rufus four days ago, the old cowboy, one of the first victims of Skip DeMarco, had been poorer than a church mouse, and Valentine had offered the couch in his suite for Rufus to sleep on. Even though Rufus's fortunes had changed dramatically since then, he'd not asked Rufus to leave. He enjoyed the old cowboy's company.

They walked through the hotel's main lobby, which had a jungle motif. It reminded Valentine of an old Tarzan movie, and at any moment he half-expected a guy wearing a loincloth to come swinging through the lobby.

They got on an elevator, Valentine hitting the button for the fourth floor. As the doors closed, two guys hopped on. Late thirties, one black, the other white, they argued over who was the best golfer of all time—Nicklaus or Woods—neither man willing to back down.

Everyone got out on the fourth floor. Still arguing, the men went in one direction, Valentine and Rufus in the other. "I happened to personally know the best golfer in the world, and it wasn't Jack Nicklaus or Tiger Woods," Rufus said. "It was Titanic Thompson."

Valentine had heard of Thompson. He was a famous hustler who the character Nathan Detroit in *Guys and Dolls* was based on. "I thought Thompson's games were cards and dice."

"And golf," Rufus said. "Ti was the best. He taught me all the angles. I can beat any golfer in the world, if the money's right."

They reached the suite and Valentine stuck his plastic key into the door. He rarely stayed up late, and the long hours he'd been keeping were taking their toll. The security light flashed green, and he pushed the door open.

"Home sweet home," Rufus said, sailing his Stetson into the room as he went in. "I'll tell you a little secret about Ti. He always practiced his golf shots in the shade. That way, when suckers played him, they assumed he didn't get out much."

As Valentine turned to shut the door, it slammed open in his face. Pools of black appeared before his eyes and he staggered backward into a wall.

The men from the elevator rushed into the suite. The white guy was holding a nylon rope stretched between his hands, the black guy a pipe. The black guy ran across the suite and tried to smack Rufus over the head. Rufus fell on the couch.

"Don't hurt me," the old cowboy said. "Please don't hurt me."

The white guy wrapped his rope around Valentine's neck, then spun him around and put his knee into Valentine's back. Valentine tried to wiggle his fingers between the rope and his windpipe. It was no good.

"I'll pay you twenty grand, cash," Rufus said to his attacker.

"You got that much?" his attacker asked.

"Yeah, in the wall safe."

The black guy looked at his partner, then back at Rufus. "Double it, and I won't kill you."

"Deal," Rufus said.

"What about your friend?"

"What about him?" Rufus asked.

The black guy laughed harshly.

Valentine felt the fight leave his body and his legs begin to buckle. From across the room, Celebrity's garish neon flashed through the partially open blinds. Las Vegas was built on losers, and he realized he was about to become one of them.

4

Valentine was sinking in a bottomless lake. He felt weightless and surprisingly calm. *Dying isn't so bad,* he thought.

He heard a sharp *crack!* that sounded like thunder. The rope strangling him went slack, and fell to the floor. He took a deep breath, then spun around. His attacker was holding his arm, cursing in pain. Valentine kicked the man's legs out from under him. Called the sweep, it was the best way to take someone down. As the man fell forward, Valentine kneed him in the face for good measure.

He heard another *crack!* from across the suite. Rufus stood in the middle of the living room, brandishing a bullwhip. He cracked the whip like a pro, repeatedly hitting the black guy in places that were hard to defend: his ankle, face, and crotch. Valentine had seen Rufus slip something beneath the couch a few nights before, and had assumed it was a pair of shoes.

"Look out behind you," Rufus said.

Valentine spun around. The effort made his head

throb and the room spin. The white guy had gotten up and was staggering out the door, his face a bloody mess.

"Tony, behind you again," Rufus called out.

Valentine turned again, this time a little more slowly. Rufus's attacker ran past him. He joined up with his partner, and their pounding footsteps reverberated down the hallway. Cracking his whip, Rufus followed the two men into the hall. His Stetson was back on his head, and he looked as regal as any cowboy had the right to look.

"Anytime, girls," Rufus yelled, standing in the hallway. "Come back anytime."

Valentine got his wits back, then searched the suite for a weapon. He settled on a brass flower vase sitting on the TV. It was shaped like a woman in a floor-length dress. He went into the hall with the vase clutched in his hand.

"Call hotel security," he told Rufus.

"Sure. You okay?"

"Never better," Valentine said.

Like Hansel and Gretel in the forest, their attackers had left a trail. Instead of bread crumbs, they'd left drops of blood. He followed them to the hallway's end, stopping at the doorway to the emergency exit stairwell. Opening the door cautiously, he stuck his head in, staring into semidarkness.

From down below came voices. His adrenaline had burned off, and the bridge of his nose felt as wide as his head. The smart move was to retreat. He'd escaped, and that was the important thing. Only Valentine wanted to pay these jokers back. When it came to killers, he believed in the Old Testament's advice: "An eye for an eye, a tooth for a tooth." He went into the stairwell, and listened some more.

When Valentine returned to the suite a minute later, Rufus handed him a towel wrapped around some ice cubes. Sitting on the couch, he pressed the towel to his nose.

"I called hotel security," Rufus said. "They're dealing with a problem in the casino, and will be up in a few. Hey, Tony, you've got blood on your shirt. You okay?"

Valentine looked down at his shirt. The lower half was soaked in red.

"I'm fine," he said.

"Well, you don't look fine," Rufus said.

"Okay, so I'm lousy."

Rufus pulled a suitcase from the closet. He unzipped a pocket, removed a glass pint of bourbon, and offered it to him. "This is the finest bourbon known to man, brewed in a Mississippi bathtub by the great-grandson of Jack Daniels himself."

"No thanks," Valentine said. "But go ahead yourself."

Rufus unscrewed the top and took a long pull, smacking his lips when done. Some men, like Valentine's father, could not drink without turning into monsters. Others, like Rufus, seemed better for the experience.

Rufus retrieved the coiled bullwhip from the floor. It looked like a thick black snake whose head was hidden within its coils, and he tucked it beneath the couch.

"You always carry that around?" Valentine asked.

"Used to carry a gun," Rufus said. "After 9/11, I

started carrying the whip. In some ways, it's better than a gun. You should learn how to use one."

"You think so?"

"It's like fly casting a fishing rod. Ever try that?"

"I fly-fished once on vacation," Valentine said. "I caught the hook on my earlobe. Had to go to the emergency room at the hospital to have it removed."

"Maybe you should stick with beating people up."

"Thanks."

Rufus returned his pint to the suitcase, then consulted his wristwatch. It was an old silver dollar that had been turned into a timepiece. The coin needed polishing, but probably wouldn't see any in Rufus's lifetime.

"Those hotel guards are mighty damn slow," he said.

Valentine shifted the icepack on his face. A five-minute response time in a Vegas hotel was normal. Although their casinos had state-of-the-art surveillance systems, they were largely ineffective when it came to crimes against guests. There were simply too many rooms.

"They'll show up eventually," he said. "Since neither of us were killed, they're not hurrying. It's how things work. Everything gets prioritized. Especially guests."

"And since you and I aren't whales, we get the pooch treatment."

"Exactly."

Rufus removed his Stetson and patted down his hair like he was expecting company. He fitted his hat back on, and looked Valentine in the eye.

"I'd hate this crummy town if I didn't like to gamble so much," Rufus said.

* * *

In the bathroom, Valentine changed shirts, downed four ibuprofens, then appraised his profile in the mirror. He'd gotten his nose broken twice as a cop, plus a couple times in judo competition, yet it had never flattened. Good genes, he guessed. He returned to the suite, sat on the couch with Rufus.

"Come straight with me about something," Rufus said.

"Sure."

"When that guy was threatening me with the pipe, you thought I was selling you out, didn't you?"

Valentine considered denying it, then decided not to lie. "Afraid I did."

"Sorry. It was the only ruse I could think of."

There was a commotion in the hallway. Four uniformed cops entered the suite, followed by Pete Longo, chief detective with the Metro Las Vegas Police Department's Homicide Division. As Valentine rose from the couch, the cops drew their weapons.

"Stay seated," a cop ordered him.

Valentine dropped back into his seat.

"Where are your guns?" the cop asked.

"We don't have any," Valentine said.

The cops searched the suite anyway. Valentine glanced at Longo, whom he'd known for many years. Longo had recently lost a lot of weight, but hadn't changed his wardrobe. His rumpled suit swam on his body.

"Can't you help us, Pete?" Valentine asked.

Longo shot him a skeptical look. "You don't have any firearms in the suite?"

"There's a bullwhip lying beneath the couch, but that's it."

The cops finished their search. The one who'd been doing the talking approached the couch and said, "You better be telling the truth."

"Ain't no reason to lie," Rufus replied.

"Come with me," Longo said. "I want to show you something."

Valentine and Rufus followed Longo out the door, happy to be away from the uniforms. They took an elevator to the lobby, which was swarming with more cops, some in uniform, some plainclothes. Yellow police tape cordoned off an area around a door with an emergency exit sign above it. Longo lifted up the police tape and they walked beneath it. The detective pointed to a door propped open with a metal chair.

"Take a look," Longo said.

Rufus went first, and came away shaking his head. Then Valentine stuck his head in. The light inside the stairwell was muted, and he let his eyes adjust. When they did, he saw their two attackers lying at the bottom. Their faces looked eerily peaceful, save for the bullet holes in their foreheads.

"Recognize them?" Longo asked, now behind him.

"Those are the guys who just attacked us in our room," Valentine said.

"Did Rufus Steele shoot them?"

"No."

"Did *you* shoot them?"

"No."

"I'd like to do a paraffin test for gunshot residue."

"Be my guest."

"I also want to talk to your son. Last time I checked,

he had a grudge against some mobsters in town. Maybe this was his way of paying them back."

"Gerry isn't in Las Vegas, " Valentine said. "I put him on a plane to Philadelphia four hours ago."

"Why did you do that?" the detective asked.

He almost told Longo it was none of his business, then reminded himself he was a suspect in a double homicide and *everything* was Longo's business. "The World Poker Showdown is being scammed, and nobody knows how. The secret is in a hospital in Atlantic City."

"And you sent your son there to figure it out."

"That's right."

Longo's face was stoic. *He doesn't believe me,* Valentine thought. Gerry's stay in Vegas had been rough, and Valentine didn't want his son getting dragged back here.

"If you don't believe me, call him," Valentine said.

Longo dug his cell phone from his pocket.

"Give me your son's number," the detective said.

5

Stepping off the Delta 767 at Philadelphia Airport, Gerry Valentine spotted an undercover detective standing in the terminal. The detective was a handsome guy, black, six one, athletic, and pushing forty. What blew his cover were his cheap threads. That was where most detectives disguising themselves screwed up. They dressed like schleps.

Up until last year, Gerry'd been a bookie, and had done his fair share of business with underworld types. But then his life had changed. He'd gotten married and had a beautiful little daughter. His priorities had shifted, and he'd decided he didn't want his kid to have a criminal father. So he'd shut down his bookmaking operation and gone to work in his father's consulting business. It hadn't been easy. Sometimes, Gerry's past came back to haunt him, and he now considered walking back onto the plane.

He decided against it. Better to walk past the detective and see if anything happened. He'd always been good with his mouth, and could talk his way out of most situations. As he got close, the detective stuck his hand out.

"You must be Gerry. I'm Detective Eddie Davis."

Gerry had heard Davis's name before. Davis had helped his father track down his partner's killers a few years back. Gerry shook his hand.

"Let me guess. My father sent you."

Davis scowled. "He asked me to look out for you. Something wrong with that?"

"I don't need a babysitter."

Davis followed Gerry to baggage claim, where they watched some misbehaving kids ride around on the carousel. "Your father said you had a bad experience in Las Vegas, and that George Scalzo was involved," Davis said. "Hearing that, I figured I'd better meet you at the airport."

Gerry checked the tags of the garment bags on the carousel. He needed to get rid of this guy. He was going to Atlantic City to learn how Jack Donovan's poker scam worked, and expected to run into his friends from the old days. What was he going to say, "Hey Vinny, this here is Eddie Davis. Keep your mouth shut, he's a cop"? No, that wasn't going to work.

"Your father said Scalzo murdered a guy named Jack Donovan, and you and some buddies went to Vegas gunning for him, and nearly got yourselves killed," Davis said.

"Dad likes to exaggerate," Gerry said.

"Your father said one of your buddies got the hair on his face burned off by a flamethrower. That an exaggeration?"

His garment bag appeared. Gerry pulled a strap out of

a side pocket, attached it to the bag, then threw it over his shoulder. He knew the Philly airport like the back of his hand, and would give Davis the slip once he got downstairs. He couldn't have a cop playing Me and My Shadow with him on this trip. Not even a well-intentioned one.

"Ready to roll," he said.

Going downstairs, Gerry excused himself and headed for the men's room. Davis tagged him on the shoulder like they were playing touch football.

"I once had a suspect duck out through the side entrance," Davis said. "You weren't thinking of doing that, were you?"

"I'll tell you after I take a leak," Gerry said.

Davis shot him a disapproving look. "For Christ's sake man, I'm here to help *you*. I know about your background with the rackets. I won't hassle any of your friends if we run into them."

Davis sounded sincere, which made Gerry suspicious.

"Why would you do that?"

"Because I need your help with a cheating case I'm working on," Davis said.

Gerry considered Davis's offer. Having a cop watching his back wasn't such a bad idea. He'd made an enemy out of George Scalzo in Vegas, and suspected Scalzo would pay him back someday soon.

"Okay," Gerry said.

They sped along the scenic New Jersey Expressway in Davis's souped-up '78 Mustang, the four-lane, pencil-straight highway bordered by lush berms and mature oaks. Atlantic City had been created as a summer playground for rich people from Philadelphia, the expressway being the shortest distance from that city to the sea.

"This case has been driving me crazy," Davis said. "There's a retirement condo on the south end of the island where a resident is cheating other residents at cards. This guy is stealing retirement money. I want to nail him, but none of the residents will cooperate. He's local, they're local, and none of the cops working the case are."

"How much is the guy stealing?"

"A couple grand a week. He's done this to hundreds of elderly people."

Gerry got the picture. The cheater was what his father called a public menace—someone who enjoyed hurting people as much as stealing. "What's the guy doing?"

"He plays cards in the same restaurant every day, and that's where he fleeces his victims," Davis said. "He doesn't play for cash, but keeps a running tally of points on a sheet of paper. That way, we can't bust him for an illegal card game. I got my hands on the cards and they're normal. No marks, bends, or gaffs. I also filmed him through a window, and watched the video. He isn't doing any sleight-of-hand."

"Describe the restaurant where he plays cards."

"It's a mom-and-pop beachfront joint with some booths lining the walls and a half dozen round tables. Most of the customers live on social security or pensions. Nothing on the menu is too pricey."

"How long has he played there?"

"Years," Davis said.

"So he's got an arrangement."

The Mustang slowed down almost imperceptibly, then sped back up.

"I'm not following you," Davis said.

"The guy's got an arrangement with the owner of the restaurant," Gerry said.

"The owner's hardly there."

"Then he's got an arrangement with the manager, or head waitress or whoever's running the place."

"It's a waitress," Davis said.

Gerry wasn't his father's son for nothing, and said, "The guy cheats his opponent and gives the waitress a cut, probably twenty percent. More if she's involved in his scam."

Davis briefly took his eyes off the road. "Would you mind telling me how you came to that conclusion?"

"Sure. You said the cards weren't marked and the guy wasn't using sleight-of-hand. Well, that leaves only one more thing. They're a team."

"They are?"

"Have to be. The waitress is peeking at the opponent's cards when she waits on the table, writes it on a paper napkin or a check, and slaps it on the table. The guy picks the napkin up, and reads what his opponent is holding."

A pained look crossed Davis's face, and he resumed staring at the expressway. Gerry guessed Davis had spent some time in the restaurant and gotten to know the waitress. He'd formed an opinion of her, and was experiencing the unsettling feeling that came when you found out someone you liked was really a piece of garbage.

"How do I prosecute this guy, and get a jury to believe my story?" Davis asked.

Gerry had seen his father handle cases similar to this. Prosecuting cheating wasn't easy, the crime difficult to prove. "Haul the waitress in, tell her you know what she's been doing, and you're going to report her to the Internal Revenue Service for income tax evasion if she doesn't cooperate."

"I should turn her against her partner?"

"Yes."

Davis considered it. Like most cops, he rarely saw justice, and when he did, it usually had a pair of horns attached to it.

"That's one of your father's tricks, isn't it?" he asked.

"Sure is," Gerry said.

Atlantic City was a thirteen-mile-long island, and their arrival on its north end was greeted by the brilliant neon of half a dozen names synonymous with gambling. Casinos had sucked the lifeblood out of Atlantic City, and Gerry stared down the Monopoly-named streets he'd once played on, seeing poverty and despair.

At a traffic light Davis hit the brakes. "You hungry?" he asked.

Gerry was thirty-six, and could still eat an extra meal and not have trouble getting into his pants. His father had warned him that someday he would pay, but so far, he wasn't sweating it.

"What do you have in mind?"

"Sacco's Sack O' Subs."

Sacco's made the best submarine sandwiches in the

world, and was located on the southern end of the island, in the town of Ventnor where Gerry had grown up.

"You're on," Gerry said.

The restaurant was hopping when they arrived. Taking a booth in the back, they ordered the signature sandwich, an Italian hot sausage sub, then waited for their food. A couple in the next booth were talking with Jersey accents so thick that an outsider would have needed an interpreter to understand them. Gerry felt right at home.

Their sandwiches arrived. A TV set above the counter was turned on, showing Skip DeMarco playing at the World Poker Showdown.

"DeMarco used to come into the card rooms here." Davis sprinkled grated cheese over his sandwich. He wasn't sweating the calories either and took a big bite.

"How did he do?" Gerry asked.

"Lost his shirt. He filed a beef with the police, claimed the other players were taking advantage of his blindness and cheating him. It never went anywhere."

Gerry lowered his voice. "DeMarco is George Scalzo's nephew. He's scamming the World Poker Showdown."

Davis's eyes grew wide. "Well, I'll be. How's he doing it?"

"That's what I came to Atlantic City to find out," Gerry said. "My father thinks the scam's secret is at the Atlantic City Medical Center where my buddy Jack Donovan just died. He wants me to snoop around the hospital, see what I can find."

Davis chewed reflectively, perhaps familiar with Gerry's friend's shady past. "Most of the staff at the hospital know me pretty well. Maybe I can help you."

"You'd do that?" Gerry asked.

"Sure. I'd like nothing better than to see George Scalzo and his cheating nephew in jail."

Gerry lowered his sub to his plate. The distrust he'd felt for Eddie when he'd stepped off the plane had vanished. He started to say okay, then stopped himself. His father did not like having outsiders help with jobs, even when they were friends. Gerry needed to run this by the old man, make sure he was okay with it.

"I'll be right back," he said, sliding out of the booth.

He powered up his cell phone in the parking lot. He could taste the salt air coming off the ocean, could remember all the summers he'd spent playing on the beach. Growing up, he'd assumed that he'd raise a family here, but the arrival of casinos had changed that. Now, he could no more imagine living in Atlantic City than in Baghdad.

His phone's message icon was blinking, and he went into voice mail. Detective Pete Longo, head of homicide for the Metro Las Vegas Police Department, had called two hours ago. Saying he needed to talk to Gerry urgently, he left his number. Gerry had met Longo in Vegas and considered him a stand-up guy. He punched in Longo's number.

Longo picked up after two rings. His voice was all business.

"Your father tells me you're in Atlantic City," Longo said.

"That's right. I arrived a couple of hours ago," Gerry said.

"Can you prove that?"

"Why should I?"

"Because you're a suspect in a double homicide, that's why," Longo snapped.

Gerry felt the hair on his neck stand up. He'd been crosswise with the law many times, and knew that cooperation was the key to staying out of trouble. He asked Longo to hold, then went back into Sacco's, and found Davis working on his gums with a toothpick.

"I need a favor," he said, sliding into the booth.

"Name it," Davis said.

Gerry handed Davis his cell phone.

"Talk to this guy," he said.

6

"**Y**our son's alibi checks out," Longo said, folding his cell phone.

"I told you he was in Atlantic City doing a job," Valentine said.

"Never hurts to check."

Longo and Valentine sat on stiff-backed chairs in a stuffy detention room behind Celebrity's casino. Longo had given him a paraffin test to check for gunshot residue. Finding Valentine clean, he then peppered him with questions about the two men who'd attacked him and Rufus in the suite.

Valentine answered the questions, feeling sorry for Longo. The detective had a thankless job. The clearance rate for homicides in Las Vegas was the worst of any major U.S. city—with less than one in four murders ever being solved. If the cops didn't catch the criminals right away, chances were, they never would.

"Which brings us right back to you," Longo said.

"It does?" Valentine said.

"Yes. Right now, you're my main suspect in the murders, Tony."

Valentine stared into space. Hotel security had furnished Longo with a surveillance tape taken in the hallway near the emergency stairwell during the time of the attack. It showed his two attackers running into the stairwell, followed by Valentine clutching a metal flower vase. Valentine reappeared a minute later, and went back to his room.

"What happened in that stairwell?" Longo asked.

"Nothing," Valentine said.

"You didn't run downstairs and shoot those guys?"

"I didn't have a gun."

"Maybe you disarmed them. You were a judo champ, weren't you?"

"That was a long time ago."

"You didn't answer the question."

Valentine took a deep breath. Longo was getting on his nerves, the way good cops were supposed to. "I didn't shoot them. I stood at the top of the stairwell, decided it was too risky, and went back to my suite to lick my wounds."

Something resembling a smile crossed Longo's face. "The Tony Valentine I know would have run those assholes down, and made them pay for their transgressions."

"Sorry to disappoint you," Valentine said.

"Any idea who gave them the head ornaments?"

"If I knew, I'd tell you."

Longo crossed his arms in front of his chest. He'd gone through personal hell during the past twelve months because of an affair he'd had with a stripper. He'd done the smart thing, falling on his sword and confessing. It had made a better man out of him, and when he spoke again, his voice was softer. "I have enough circumstantial evidence to book you for manslaughter, only I'm not going to do that," he said.

Shifting his gaze, Valentine looked at the detective.

"You're a brother cop, and someone I respect," Longo went on. "I'm going to let you go, with the understanding that if I need to talk to you again, you'll drop whatever you're doing and cooperate."

Valentine rose from the chair. "Of course. Thanks, Pete."

"I want to tell you something else. There are seven bodies in the Las Vegas morgue connected to you and this fricking poker tournament. If I find out you're holding back in any way, I'll nail your ass to a board. Understood?"

He nodded stiffly.

"Have a nice night," Longo said.

He returned to his suite to find Rufus lying on the couch, staring at the mute TV.

"That detective finally come to his senses?" Rufus asked him.

"Sort of. I'll see you in the morning," Valentine said.

In his bedroom the phone's message light was blinking. He went into voice mail, heard Gloria Curtis request the pleasure of his company over breakfast, nine sharp in the hotel restaurant. He'd been late the last two times they'd gotten together, and heard an edge to her voice that said she wouldn't tolerate another infraction.

He brushed his teeth, threw on his pajamas, and realized he wasn't tired anymore. In the living room he got a soda from the minibar, asked Rufus if he wanted anything.

"Just some company," the old cowboy said.

Valentine pulled a chair next to the couch. On the TV was Skip DeMarco's heroics at the tournament. Poker was a boring game, with most hands decided by everyone dropping out, and one player stealing the pot. But the people running the WPS had figured something out. They focused on a handful of players, filmed them exclusively, then edited their play down to the exciting footage. The magic of television was turning DeMarco into a star.

Rufus killed the power with the remote. "Watching this kid reminds me of the time I got cheated in jolly old England."

"You got cheated?"

Rufus nodded. Valentine had learned that hustlers didn't like to talk about scams they'd pulled, but loved to talk about the times they'd gotten swindled. He supposed it was their way of explaining their own behavior.

"What happened?"

"One day I got a phone call asking me to fly to London to play cards with some British aristocrats, Sir This and Lord That. They sounded like suckers, so I hopped on a plane.

"When I arrived, they rolled out the red carpet. I stayed at a four-star hotel with a uniformed doorman and a suite with all the trimmings. Everyone I bumped into knew my name. Let me tell you, Tony, they buttered me up real good.

"That night, I went across the street to play cards. It was a private club, lots of polished brass and mahogany.

I met my opponents, and we retired to the card room for a little action.

"There's three of them, and one of me. One of them says, 'How about a game of Texas Hold 'Em, Mr. Steele?' Right then, I knew I was in trouble."

"Why?"

"At the time, I was the best Texas Hold 'Em player in the world. When some hoity-toity aristocrat says he wants to challenge me, my radar went up."

"So you left."

"Naw. If I'd quit every time someone was trying to cheat me, I'd have missed some great opportunities. I threw my money in the pot, and let them deal the cards.

"Now, I'm familiar with most methods of card cheating. I guessed these boys were going to signal each other, what most amateurs do. So I studied them real good." Rufus stretched his legs and yawned prodigiously. "Come to find out, they weren't signaling. So, I played."

"Did you lose?"

"Oh yeah. They bled me real good. Whenever I had good cards, they dropped out like they had a train to catch. When I tried to bluff, one of them would call me, and I'd get beat. Finally, I figured out what was going on."

"Let me guess," Valentine said. "There was a hole in the ceiling."

Rufus pulled his cowboy boots off and massaged the soles of his feet, which were rubbed raw from his footrace with Greased Lightning. "You got it. Someone was using a telescope to spot my cards, then relaying the information to a waiter, who passed the information to my opponents. It was a fancy setup.

"Then I got an idea. I excused myself and went to the coat check. I borrowed an umbrella, and went back to the card room. When I sat down, I opened the umbrella and held it over my head. Then I told them to shuffle up and deal."

"What did they say?"

"They summoned the club manager. He told me it was against house rules to play with an open umbrella. I told him it was raining outside, and I was afraid I'd get wet being there was a hole in the ceiling. I told him that if their doctors were as bad as their dentists, I'd just as soon not get sick."

Valentine slapped his hand on his leg. "Is that when the game stopped?"

Rufus shook his head. "That's when it got started."

"What do you mean?"

"That's when I *really* got cheated," Rufus said.

Rufus took out his wallet. It was a hand-stitched piece of rawhide he'd been carrying in his pocket for decades. From it, he produced a faded snapshot and passed it Valentine's way. It showed Rufus wearing a snappy brown jacket with suede shoulders, the crown of his Stetson encircled by dead rattlesnake. To round out the bizarre picture, he was holding an umbrella over his head.

"Who took the picture?" Valentine asked.

"One of my opponents. I should have realized I was about to get greased, but I was so full of myself, it just blew right by me."

He handed the snapshot back. "What happened?"

"I won a few hands, and pulled even. Then I got a

monster hand. Pocket kings. The best cards I'd had all night, so I bet twenty grand. Two of the Brits dropped out. The flop comes ace, king, four. I've got three kings, a set. I bet fifty grand, and the guy who stayed in leans forward and studies the table. The waiter brings him a drink. I start twirling my umbrella like Mary Poppins, just to piss him off. He puts his drink down, says he's betting one hundred grand. I figure he's got two pair. I call him. He flips his cards over, and I see he's got two aces in the hole. The flop and fifth street are meaningless. His three aces beats my three kings. End of night."

"Did you figure out how they cheated you?"

"Yeah, after I got home."

"It must have been real clever."

"It was," the old cowboy said.

Valentine sipped his soda. Rufus was not going to tell him how the scam worked unless he begged him. That was how it worked with these old-timers. You had to beg. Only Valentine had never been good at begging, so he gave it some thought. Rufus had said that his opponents knew what cards he was holding. That had led Rufus to conclude there was a hole in the ceiling, and somebody was watching him. But that wasn't the only use for a hole in the ceiling, and he said, "They were using luminous readers."

Rufus's face sagged. "You're not slowing down, are you?"

"Not so you'll notice. Want me to explain the rest?"

"Be my guest."

"The cards were marked with luminous paint," Valentine said. "The paint is invisible to the naked eye, and can only be read by someone with tinted glasses.

Only in this scam, the tinted glass was in the ceiling. The guy upstairs was reading the cards as they were being dealt. He passed the information to the waiter, who told your opponents. When you got dealt kings, and your host aces, and the flop turned ace, king, four, the guy upstairs knew you were in trouble. That's when they trapped you."

Rufus stopped rubbing his feet to give him a round of applause. It would have seemed sarcastic coming from anyone else, but from this old codger it meant something.

"That's damn good," Rufus said, clapping.

"Here's my theory about DeMarco," Rufus said. "I know the cards in the game are being checked every night, and so far nothing's come up, but maybe DeMarco's using a special luminous paint that grows invisible after a few hours."

"No such thing exists," Valentine said.

"Maybe someone invented it."

The snapshot of Rufus was lying on the coffee table. Valentine thought over what Rufus had told him about the scam in London.

"You think there's a hole in the ceiling of the poker room, and someone is reading the cards, and signaling their values to DeMarco," Valentine said.

"It would make sense, don't you think?"

"But how many times could they do that without people noticing?" Valentine asked, having seen enough scams to know that what eventually doomed them was repetition. "It would become obvious."

"Yes, it would." Rufus stretched his arms and made

the bones crack. "But I learned a good lesson in jolly old England. You only have to cheat a man once in a poker game to get his money. I've checked the ceiling of every poker room I've ever played in since that little episode." He paused. "Except here."

"Checked how?"

"With a flashlight."

"Do you have one with you?"

Rufus flashed his best cowboy smile. "I thought you'd never ask."

7

Casinos never slept. It was the greatest thing they offered people who liked to gamble. At any hour of the day or night, you could enter one and make a wager. Old-timers called it the itch for play.

Casinos' surveillance departments never slept, either. They watched the floor of the casino every minute of every hour, every day of the year. When President Kennedy was assassinated, one Las Vegas casino had stopped play for an hour in his memory, but the surveillance department had not stopped watching the casino.

Valentine knew he was taking a risk searching Celebrity's poker room for holes in the ceiling, but it was a risk he was willing to take. Celebrity had surveillance cameras covering the poker room, but that didn't necessarily mean those cameras were being used. Surveillance technicians were trained to watch the money. Places where money didn't change hands were often neglected, or ignored.

Celebrity's poker room was a good example. Tournament play ended at six o'clock each night, with everyone's chips stored in a safe and the room locked down until the next day. Since the opportunity for theft no longer existed, the technicians stopped watching the room. They might glance in from time to time, but chances were, they probably wouldn't.

Valentine and Rufus stood in the lobby in front of the poker room. Valentine had decided to pick the door and he eyeballed the lock. He'd used lock picks as a cop, and had kept them after he'd gone to work for himself. His lock pick kit looked like an ordinary car key case, and contained a dozen picks made from tungsten steel. He unzipped the case, and chose the appropriate pick.

"You're a man after my own heart," Rufus said.

Valentine heard a whirring noise and stopped what he was doing.

"What the heck's that?" Rufus asked.

Acoustics in casinos could be deceiving. The lobby was empty, and Valentine decided the noise had come from behind the door. He grasped the door's handle, and to his surprise, found that it was unlocked.

"This is our lucky day," Rufus said.

Putting his picks away, Valentine stuck his head inside. In the old days, casino poker rooms had been toilets, reeking of ashtrays and body odor. Televised poker tournaments had changed that. Celebrity's poker room had thick carpet and cut-glass chandeliers the size of wrecking balls. He spied a team of Hispanic cleaning men vacuuming the floor with a level of enthusiasm you hardly saw anymore.

"Follow me, and take off your hat," Valentine said.

"Why?"

"Because I don't want anyone in surveillance who might be watching to see it and recognize you."

"Got it." Rufus removed his Stetson.

Walking to the room's center, Valentine took from his pocket Rufus's flashlight and twisted it on. He shone the light at the ceiling, then moved it back and forth in a slow, steady pattern. If what Rufus had alleged was true—and the cards at Skip DeMarco's table were marked with luminous paint—then someone was reading them while looking down from above. That someone had to be looking through red-tinted lenses, which would become reflective the moment his flashlight shone against them. The hidden accomplice in the ceiling trick. An old scam but still a good one.

After a minute his hopes came crashing to earth. No glitters had appeared in the ceiling, the pure white alabaster not showing a single crack or imperfection.

"Damn," he muttered.

"No luck?" Rufus asked from several tables away.

Valentine's neck hurt from looking up, but he kept looking anyway.

"No, and it's pissing me off."

He twisted the flashlight off, returned it to his pocket. The cleaning men were racing around the room on their machines, making a game out of who could finish first. He saw Rufus take out a pack of cigarettes and light up.

"You want one?" Rufus asked.

"I'm trying to quit."

"I tried to quit once. Enrolled in one of those special progams."

"Did it work?"

"Yeah. Every time I wanted a smoke, I called a special

phone number, and a guy came over and got drunk with me." Rufus laughed through a mouthful of smoke. His pack fell from his hand, and he bent over to pick it up. As he did, he glanced beneath one of the poker tables.

"Well, lookee here," he said.

He pulled something from beneath the table, then held it on his palm for Valentine to see. It was pink and looked like it had been thoroughly chewed.

"Know what this is?"

"Gum?"

"Silly Putty."

Valentine came over for a closer look. "You think it's a bug?"

"Uh-huh."

"So we've got a mucker in the tournament."

"Sure looks that way," Rufus said.

A mucker specialized in switching cards during play. The bug was his assistant, and used to secretly hide a card beneath the table. When the mucker needed the card, he brought it up, switched it with a card in his hand, then put the extra card back in the bug. The switch required terrific timing, skill, and plenty of nerve.

"There's also a paper clip involved," Rufus said. "The paper clip is wedged into the Silly Putty, and the card is stuck in the clip."

"Did you see a paper clip on the floor?"

"No, but there has to be one."

Valentine searched the floor beneath the table. The carpet was sticking up after being vacuumed, and he walked over to the cleaning men and took out his wallet. They instantly silenced their machines.

"Which one of you cleaned that table?" he asked, pointing.

None of the men spoke English, but their eyes said they were eager to help. Rufus came over and asked them in Spanish, which he spoke without an accent. One of the cleaning men stepped forward and raised his hand.

"I clean," the man said haltingly.

Rufus asked him to open the bag on his vacuum. The man obliged, and Valentine handed him a twenty-dollar bill. The man's face lit up.

Rufus glanced into the bag, then stuck his hand in up to the elbow, and twirled his long fingers around. Moments later he pulled out an object, and held it up to the light. It was a paper clip painted black. Mucking cards during play was the hardest cheating known to man. No matter how good a mucker was, he never drew attention to himself, and played under the radar. This wasn't Skip DeMarco's scam; it was somebody else's.

"Looks like we've got another cheater working the tournament," Valentine said.

8

Hanging out with Eddie Davis was a step back in time. Outside of being an undercover detective, Davis was like a lot of guys Gerry had grown up with. He was single, liked to frequent clubs and singles bars, and drove a souped-up car. He was an eighteen-year-old kid in a forty-year-old body, and enjoying every minute of it.

Davis was also a night owl, and they did a loop of the island, eventually returning to the Atlantic City Expressway entrance. Gerry found himself remembering the housing development that once stood there, and the park with a statue of Christopher Columbus. The park had been one of his father's favorite places; his mother's, too.

Davis's cell phone began to play the theme song from the TV show *Cops. Bad boys, bad boys, what'cha gonna do, what'cha gonna do when they come for you?* He ripped the phone from the Velcro pad on the dash.

"Davis here."

"Eddie, it's Joey," his caller said. "I need help. I'm at Bally's with our friends."

Davis's brow knotted. "You got them pinned down?"

"Yeah."

"I'll be right over." Davis closed the phone. His tires ripped the macadam as they took off.

"Trouble?" Gerry asked.

"There's a gang of blackjack cheaters we've been trying to nail for a month. Two men, one woman. My partner spotted them at Bally's."

"Is the woman nicking cards?"

Davis's head jerked in his direction. "How did you know that?"

Nail-nicking cards in blackjack was a speciality among female cheaters. The woman would put in the work with her fingernails while no one was looking, then her partner would read the cards before they were dealt from the shoe, and signal them to the gang's third member, who did the heavy betting—organized cheating at its best.

"Lucky guess," Gerry said.

Davis got onto Atlantic Avenue, put his foot to the floor, and sped south.

"Not that it's any of my business," Gerry said, "but why haven't you arrested them before now? It sounds like you know them pretty well."

"We've tried to arrest them," Davis said. "They always seem to know when we're coming, and which door we're coming through."

"Psychic cheaters?"

"It's starting to feel that way," Davis said.

Gerry's mind raced. The hardest part about cheating a casino was avoiding the police, who were always present on the casino floor. It occurred to him that Davis's blackjack cheaters weren't psychic, they were just smart.

Bally's neon sign blinked gloomily in the pale night sky. The front entrance was jammed with stretch limousines, and Davis pulled down a side street and parked his car. He grabbed his cell phone off the dash, then turned to Gerry. "Sorry, but I need to leave you here."

Gerry pointed at the cell phone in Davis's hand. "You going to call your partner and tell him you're coming?"

"Sure am," Davis said, his hand on the door.

"That's how the cheaters know you're coming," Gerry said.

Davis took his hand off the door. "Say what?"

"The cheaters are picking up your calls. That's why you can't catch them."

The look on Davis's face was pained, but he didn't let it slow him down. "How are they doing that?"

"They're using a police scanner."

"Keep going."

"A member of the gang sits outside in a car with the scanner, and monitors the casino's in-house security frequency," Gerry said. "Whenever the police want to make a bust inside a casino, they have to alert the casino's security department. The security department calls the guards on the floor to avoid any confusion or problems. The guy in the car intercepts the call and alerts the gang. It gives them enough time to run."

Davis held up his cell phone. "By law, I have to call Bally's security department before I make a bust. What do you suggest I do?"

"Find the guy with the scanner," Gerry said. "They're good for about a hundred yards. Either the car is on a side street, or near the entrance."

"You sound like you know all about this," Davis said.

Gerry reddened. There were a lot of things he knew about the rackets. He hadn't planned on spilling the beans to Davis, but sometimes these things just happened.

"I've been to the carnival a couple of times," Gerry admitted.

Davis took Gerry's advice, and checked the side streets on the north and south side of Bally's casino. To the south was Michigan Avenue. The detective parked his Mustang at the end of the street, then strolled down the sidewalk while shining a flashlight into each parked vehicle. He returned with a smile on his face.

"What's so funny?" Gerry asked.

"I just saw a couple of kids tearing each other's clothes off," he said.

The northside street was Park Place, and Davis turned down it while staring at his cell phone. Gerry could tell that he wanted to call his partner inside the casino.

"I sure hope you're right about this," Davis said.

Park Place dead-ended at the beach. As Davis drove to the end of the block, Gerry glanced into the vehicles parked on either side of the street.

"I think I saw him," Gerry said.

"Which car?" Davis asked.

"The black Audi. There was a guy smoking a cigarette and talking on a cell phone."

"Telling his buddies inside the coast is clear."

"Probably," Gerry said. "Gangs that use scanners keep a constant dialogue with the man outside, just to make sure the scanner hasn't malfunctioned and stopped picking up the frequency."

"Never can be too careful, huh?" Davis said.

"It's part of the business," Gerry said.

Davis turned the car around, and parked so he was facing Bally's instead of the ocean. It allowed him to watch the guy in the Audi several cars away.

Gerry didn't particularly like the view, but didn't say anything. Bally's was located where the magnificent Marlborough-Blenheim hotel had once stood, considered by many to be the island's single greatest contribution to architecture. It was hard to look at the ugly building that had replaced it and not get depressed.

Davis took binoculars from the glove compartment, brought them to his face. The street was well lit, and Gerry realized the detective was reading the Audi's license plate.

"How good's your memory?" Davis asked.

"Photographic."

"Okay. Remember this license. RFG 4M6."

Gerry repeated the license number three times to himself.

"Is that a local plate?"

"That's a good question," Davis said, adjusting the binoculars. "Let's see. It's from Newark."

Davis put the binoculars away, then called the station house and got transferred to a desk sergeant. He asked to have a vehicle checked out, then cupped his hand over the mouthpiece. "The license, Mr. Memory."

Gerry repeated the license, and Davis gave it to the desk sergeant. He was put on hold, and turned to Gerry. "I'm going to find out who the owner of the Audi is, and have his name run through NICAP and see what pops up. If the guy is part of a gang, chances are he's got a rap sheet."

Gerry leaned back in his seat. Chances were better than good that the guy in the Audi had a record. You couldn't be a professional scammer and not get caught at least once. It was part of the business.

The desk sergeant returned a few minutes later. Davis pulled a notepad and pen out of the glove compartment, and started writing. He wrote in furious script, and covered two pages with notes. Done, he thanked the desk sergeant and hung up.

"Do you believe in fate?" Davis asked.

"Not really," Gerry said.

"Well, maybe you should start. The owner of the Audi is Kenny "the Clown" Abruzzi, age fifty-two, born and raised in Newark, his father, brother, and three uncles all mobsters. Kenny was inducted into the Mafia at age twenty, has been arrested nine times, and gone to prison three."

"Sounds like a real charmer," Gerry said. "What does that have to do with fate?"

"He works for George Scalzo," Davis said.

Gerry felt the blood drain from his head. "You're kidding, right?"

"Not about something like that," Davis said.

Gerry heard the sound of a car door opening. Davis heard it as well, and jerked his head. Together they stared through the windshield. Kenny Abruzzi had climbed out of his Audi, and was coming directly toward them. He was built like a refrigerator, his face cast in stone. Something long and dark was clutched in his hand.

9

Canada Bob Jones, a famous card cheater who'd specialized in fleecing the clergy on America's railroads during the early twentieth century, had once said that it was morally wrong to let suckers keep money. This was also Rufus Steele's mantra, and Valentine sat in Celebrity's sports bar, watching Rufus fleece a couple of suckers at darts.

It was three A.M. and the bar was mobbed with the day's losers from the tournament. Every single one had a sob story to tell about how or why he'd gotten knocked out. It was like listening to fishermen talk about the big one that got away.

The bar had a retro motif, and posters of half-naked starlets who were now card-carrying members of AARP hung from the walls. Valentine removed the Silly Putty they'd found in the poker room and started to play with it. It wasn't unusual to find a mucker in a poker tournament, but there was something not right about finding one in *this* tournament. Maybe after a good night's sleep, he'd figure out what it was.

"Hey Tony, come here and take a look at this," Rufus said.

Valentine slipped out of his chair and went to where Rufus stood at the dartboard, attaching a hundred-dollar bill to the cork with colored toothpicks. Finished, Rufus stepped back and studied his handiwork. "Pretty big target, wouldn't you say?"

"Looks big from here," Valentine said.

The suckers came over to stare at the bill. Their names were Larry and Earl, and they'd gotten knocked out of the World Poker Showdown on the first day. Each had won a satellite event in his hometown, and believed he was a world-class player. In fact, they both knew little about cards, and had simply beaten a bunch of guys who knew less than they did. Each man ran his fingers across the bill's face.

"Explain the rules again," Earl said.

"Be more than happy to," Rufus replied. Picking up three darts from the holder beneath the board, he stepped back to the blue line on the floor, toed it, and lined up to throw a dart. "First, you have to throw a dart from the blue line, and hit the bill."

"Anywhere?" Earl asked.

"That's right," Rufus said. He tossed the dart, and it did a graceful arc through the air and hit the board with a loud *plunk*, impaling the bill. "Then, you have to step forward, stop, throw a second dart, and hit the bill."

"A giant step or a baby step?" Earl asked.

"A moderate step," Rufus replied. Taking a moderate step forward, he lined up his shot and threw the dart, hitting the bill in its center with another *plunk*. "Last but not least, you have to return to the blue line, take a moderate step backward, and throw the last dart." Suiting action to words, Rufus returned to the blue line, took a moderate step backward, and lined up his shot. The dart flew gracefully through the air, and hit Benjamin Franklin in the center of his forehead. Rufus smiled, obviously pleased with himself. "That's all there is to it, boys. Hit the hundred-dollar bill three times, and it's yours. If you don't, you have to pay me a hundred dollars. It's that simple."

Larry and Earl stepped away to talk it over. Valentine knew plenty of bar room hustles and saw nothing transparent with Rufus's proposition. Throw three darts, hit the bill, and win a hundred dollars. Rufus lowered his voice.

"You know this one?"

"No. Is it a scam?"

The old cowboy chuckled under his breath. "Of course."

"What's the trick?"

"Just watch, pardner."

"You're on!" Earl called out.

"This handsome fellow has agreed to referee," Rufus said, pointing to Valentine. "He's an ex-cop, so you can trust him with your money."

Earl and Larry each gave Valentine a hundred dollars for safekeeping. Earl pulled the three darts out of the board, and went to the blue line. He let the first dart fly, and it landed in the center of the bill. "Bingo!" Earl exclaimed.

"One down, two to go," Larry exhorted him.

Earl took a moderate step forward, lined up his shot, and threw his second dart. The dart seemed to take on a life of its own, and sailed over the dartboard and hit the wall, pocking it in the process. The dart fell to the floor with Earl staring at it.

"Must be the beer," Earl said.

Taking out a money clip stuffed with cash, Earl peeled off another hundred and handed it to Valentine. "I want to try again," he said.

"Be my guest," Rufus replied.

The first dart was easy; the second again went high. Earl cursed like he'd hit his thumb with a hammer and threw another hundred Valentine's way. "Again," he said.

"Of course," Rufus said.

Earl's first dart hit the bill. He stepped forward for the second shot, lifted his leg like a dog watering a bush, and let the second dart fly. It hit the hundred-dollar bill, but just barely. Earl let out a war whoop.

"One more to go," Larry said encouragingly. "Come on, Earl, you can do it."

Earl returned to the blue line and took a moderate step backward. His beer was sitting on the corner of the pool table. He stared at it, then shook his head like he wanted to have nothing to do with it. He lined up his shot and let the dart fly. It flew over the board and hit a poster of a bikini-clad Farrah Fawcett squarely in her navel.

"God damn!" Earl screamed.

"Let me have a try," Larry said.

Ten minutes later, Valentine and Rufus left the bar with most of Larry's and Earl's money. The suckers had not gone quietly, and were demanding a rematch on the golf course. Rufus had politely declined and bid them good night.

"I thought you were good at golf," Valentine said.

"Only when the price is right," Rufus replied.

On the elevator ride to their room, Valentine finally broke down and asked Rufus to explain how he'd managed the dart trick.

"Ain't no trick," Rufus said, smothering a yawn.

"You didn't put something in their drinks?"

"Naw."

"Then how does it work?"

"Throwing a dart is harder than you think," Rufus explained. "Even the best players have to take a few practice throws before they play. The arm's muscles have a memory, and it takes a while for the memory to kick in. By changing the distance for each throw, the muscles in the thrower's arm get confused, and the darts miss the target."

"You made it look easy when you threw the darts."

"That comes from years of practice and self-denial."

The elevator reached their floor and they got out. Valentine took the Silly Putty and paper clip from his pocket, and stared at them while walking down the hallway to his suite.

"That bug's still bothering you, huh?" Rufus said.

"It sure is," Valentine said.

"Sort of makes you wonder what kind of tournament they're running."

"How do you mean?"

"First DeMarco cheats me, and now this."

Valentine was tired, and the old cowboy's words were slow to sink in. The World Poker Showdown had already had one allegation of cheating, and the tournament should have gone out of its way to ensure that no more took place. Yet more cheating *was* taking place, and he had the evidence right in his hand. He stopped at the door to his suite and fitted the plastic key into the lock. Then he looked Rufus square in the eye.

"You think the people running the tournament are crooked, don't you?"

Rufus nodded grimly. "Cheaters don't like to expose other cheaters. It makes them uneasy."

"It that why the tournament isn't regulating itself?"

"That would be my guess."

The light on the lock flashed green. Valentine removed the key and pushed the door open. He could hear his bed calling to him, but it wasn't as loud as his conscience.

"Then I guess I'll just have to shut the tournament down," he said.

10

As Kenny "the Clown" Abruzzi walked up to the car, Davis reached into his sports jacket and drew a .40 mini-Glock, the same gun Gerry's father had carried up until the day he'd retired from the Atlantic City Police Department.

"Get ready to hit the floor," Davis said.

Gerry stiffened. Bally's unfriendly neon sign offered enough light to let him see Abruzzi's face. The guy looked lost.

"I think he wants to ask us something," Gerry said.

"With a gun in his hand?"

"I think it's a flashlight."

"Your vision that good?"

"Twenty/twenty."

The flashlight in Abruzzi's hand came on, proving Gerry right. It shone a sharp beam of light onto a piece of paper in his other hand that looked like directions. Davis slipped the Glock back into his shoulder harness, then rolled down his window.

Abruzzi flashed a sheepish grin. For a big guy, his face was small, with a hawk nose, smallish eyes, and dark hair slicked back on both sides. He held the instructions up to Davis's open window, the familiar MapQuest symbol at the top of the page.

"Hey buddy, can you help me?" Abruzzi asked. "I think I'm lost. I'm looking for a Days Inn."

Davis looked at the instructions while watching Abruzzi, then pointed out his window. "The Days Inn is five-and-a-half miles south on Atlantic Avenue. Hang a left, and go straight. You can't miss it."

Abruzzi said thanks, then hustled back to the Audi and climbed in. Gerry sensed he had made Davis as an undercover cop, and was going to run. Davis guessed the same thing, and redrew his Glock while opening his car door.

"You going to arrest him?" Gerry asked.

"I will if I find a police scanner in his car," Davis replied.

"What can I do, besides stay out of your way?"

Davis had one foot on the macadam, and he turned to look at him. "Get behind the wheel. When I go up to Abruzzi's car, I'll give you a sign. Turn the headlights on so I can see what I'm dealing with."

"Sounds like a plan," Gerry said.

Davis got out and silently shut the door.

Gerry climbed across the front seats. Growing up a cop's son, he knew that there was a science to handling a bust. If the bust was to go right, the first few seconds of the suspect learning his freedom was about to be taken away were critical. Anything could happen if the arresting officer didn't handle the suspect properly.

Gerry got behind the wheel and found the switch for the headlights.

Then he watched Abruzzi. The mobster had fired up a cigarette and was blowing smoke out his window. Davis came up to the window and identified himself as a police officer, then ordered Abruzzi to step out of the car while keeping his hands visible. Stepping back, Davis made the okay sign to Gerry.

Gerry hit the headlights and flooded the Audi in light.

Abruzzi didn't get out. Instead, he stuck his head through the open window and started talking. He was playing dumb, and Gerry guessed this was where he'd gotten the nickname the Clown. Davis again ordered him out of the car.

Abruzzi kept up the idiot routine, and Gerry found himself thinking how Abruzzi had approached them with the instructions. It had allowed him to see what he was up against, and Gerry sensed Abruzzi was going to put up a fight. Gerry flashed the car's brights, and Davis glanced in his direction.

"What?" Davis said loudly.

"Signal 30," Gerry called out.

A Signal 30 was used by the Atlantic City police dispatchers when there was trouble and they needed to round up officers.

"I won't say it again," Davis said to Abruzzi. "Out of the car."

"All right already," Abruzzi said.

Quickly drawing a gun from a hiding place in his door, Abruzzi fired it at Davis, a sharp *bang!* ripping the night air. Davis instinctively went backward, the bullet from Abruzzi's gun taking out the headlight of a car parked across the street. Twisting his ankle, Davis fell to the pavement, and lay on his side with a dazed look in his eyes.

"Throw your gun away," Abruzzi said.

"You're under arrest."

"Like hell I am. Throw it away or I'll clip you."

Davis reluctantly tossed his Glock across the macadam.

"You're real smart for a spade," Abruzzi said sarcastically.

Gerry sensed that Abruzzi was going to shoot Davis in cold blood, then drive away. Abruzzi had sized them up. Davis was the threat, and Gerry wasn't.

Gerry twisted the key in the ignition and heard the Mustang's engine roar. Abruzzi jerked his head and stared just as Gerry threw the Mustang into drive.

Big mistake, Gerry thought.

Gerry hit the rear of the Audi doing forty-five mph, throwing it into the street. The impact, making a horrible crunching sound, buckled the Mustang's hood, and a mushroom cloud of black smoke hung ominously above the vehicle. Getting out, Gerry went to where Davis lay, saw a dark pool of blood swelling around the detective, and gagged.

"Jesus Christ, you're shot," Gerry said.

"I don't feel shot." Davis touched his back, then brought his hand to his face. It was covered with red, and he grimaced.

"Go make sure Abruzzi's disarmed," he said.

"But you're bleeding, Eddie."

"Just do as I say," Davis said.

Gerry ran over to the Audi. It no longer looked like a fancy forty-thousand-dollar sports car. The driver's seat was empty, the windshield disintegrated. Twenty feet up the street Abruzzi lay on the pavement with his head twisted at an unnatural angle. He'd killed a mobster. *A mobster.* Gerry staggered backward.

"Gerry!" Davis yelled at the top of his lungs.

"What . . . ?"

"Don't pass out on me, man."

"He's dead. . . ."

"Stop looking at him."

Gerry turned his gaze from the dead man and filled his lungs with air.

"Was there a police scanner inside the car?" Davis asked.

Gerry took a deep breath, tried to collect his wits, then went to the Audi, looked inside the crumpled car. An upside-down police scanner sat on the passenger seat, the multicolored lights on its control panel flashing wildly. Frantic voices came out of its speaker. The guy's partners inside the casino had heard the collision.

Gerry went back to where Davis lay on the pavement.

"Scanner's there," he said.

"Get on my cell phone, and call Joey inside the casino," Davis said. "Tell him to grab the guy's partners. Joey's number is in the phone's menu."

The pool of blood around Davis's body was expanding. The detective's voice sounded perfectly normal, but Gerry knew that people could get shot and never feel it.

He ran back to the Mustang and pulled the car's radio off the dashboard while praying it still worked. There was a crackle of static and a dispatcher came on.

"Officer down," Gerry said. "I have an officer down."

11

Valentine was sound asleep when the phone rang the next morning. He fumbled with the receiver, a word resembling *hello* spilling out of his mouth.

"You up?" Bill Higgins asked.

"I was writing my memoirs," Valentine mumbled.

"I heard what happened last night. Are you okay?"

"My neck's a little sore, but I'll live."

"I need to talk to you."

"I'm all ears."

"Face to face," Bill said. "Not over the phone."

Before going to sleep, Valentine had shut the room's curtains and turned the air-conditioning down to its coldest setting. Snuggled beneath the blankets was the place to be, and his body was fighting to go back to sleep.

"How about lunch?"

"How about right now?" Bill snapped.

Valentine opened his eyes and stared at the imaginary face of Bill hovering on the ceiling. One of his best friends, Bill was also director of the Nevada Gaming Control Board, and the most powerful law enforcement officer in the state of Nevada. Bill didn't have to ask nicely if he didn't want to.

"You're sure this can't wait?"

"George Scalzo sent those hitmen last night."

"Who told you that?"

"The FBI are wiretapping Scalzo's phones and over-heard him putting out the contract. He did it in code, though, so they can't arrest him."

The FBI ran a special operation in Las Vegas that did nothing but try to prevent contract killings. Murder-for-hire was prevalent in Sin City, and the bureau paid snitches to keep their ears to the ground to hear when a contract came up.

"Scalzo doesn't give up easily," Bill went on. "Mark my words, he's going to hire someone else to kill you."

Valentine's eyes had shut as his head sunk deeper into his pillow. Thirty more minutes of blessed sleep was all he wanted. "I'll change rooms and grow a moustache."

"Tony, I want to discuss this with you," Bill said, growing agitated. "It's my responsibility to make sure nothing happens to you while you're in Las Vegas. I hired you for this job, remember?"

His eyes remained shut. Thirty years ago, having two guys try to kill him would have resulted in a sleepless night. He'd had a wife and a kid and a mortgage to worry about. But time had changed his situation: his wife was dead, the house sold, and Gerry a grown man. Being threatened didn't have the same consequences anymore.

"I get it. This is one of those cover-your-ass phone calls."

"Eight-fifteen in front of your hotel," Bill said. "Be there."

Bill's shining Volvo C70 convertible was parked by the entrance when Valentine stepped through the hotel's front doors thirty minutes later. Bill had driven Volvos well before they'd become fashionable, claiming that Swedish engineering and Native American sensibilities shared a lot in common. He sat behind the wheel, his protruding chin marred by random specks of gray. Valentine climbed in and they sped away.

The Volvo raced across the flat, sun-baked desert, the engine starting to breathe around ninety. Valentine tilted his seat back and stared at the endless highway ahead. Years ago, he'd considered retiring out west with his wife, having often heard it referred to as God's country. Seeing it unfold in this morning light, he understood why.

Fifteen minutes later, they sat in the parking lot of a roadside gas station that sold hot coffee and fresh doughnuts. The woman behind the counter had made them out as law enforcement, and given them freebies. It made their day.

"Listen, I've got some bad news," Bill said.

Valentine stared into his friend's face while biting his doughnut. Bill was a Navajo, and kept his emotions well below the surface. "I hate to start the day with bad news. Tell me something funny first."

"Why does it have to be funny?"

"Because you're about to give me bad news. I'd like a good laugh first."

Bill scrunched up his face. "Okay. Here's a joke I

heard. How do you get an eighty-year-old woman to say 'Shit!' "

Valentine should know this one. He lived in Florida.

"I don't have a clue."

"Get another eighty-year-old woman to yell 'Bingo!' "

He laughed. Definitely a Floridian joke. He washed down his last bite of doughnut with a gulp of coffee. It hit his stomach like a bomb, and he felt himself wake up. "Okay, I'm ready for your bad news."

"I know this is going to sound harsh, but I'm taking you off the case," Bill said.

"You're firing me?"

"Yes," Bill said.

Valentine didn't know what to say. He stared out the windshield at the big, cloudless Nevada sky. Bill started the engine and pulled onto the highway, pointing the Volvo back toward town. A long minute passed.

"It's like this, Tony," his friend said. "Yesterday, I was given twenty-four hours by the governor of Nevada to produce hard evidence that there was cheating taking place at the World Poker Showdown. If I couldn't prove there was cheating, I was told in no uncertain terms to leave the tournament alone. That also meant letting you go."

"The governor told you to end the investigation?"

"That's right," Bill said.

"Is he being pressured?"

"Yes. The World Poker Showdown is helping every casino in town get business."

"So the casino owners asked the governor to squash the investigation."

"Bingo."

"Shit." Valentine's eyes shifted to the ruler-straight highway. It resembled a tunnel, the desert scenery compressed. If he left Las Vegas, George Scalzo won, and Valentine wasn't going to let that happen. He had never run away from a fight in his life.

"What if you could prove there *was* cheating at the tournament? Would the governor let the investigation continue?"

"He'd have to," Bill said.

"Would you keep me on the job?"

"Of course I'd keep you on the job."

From his jacket pocket Valentine removed the Silly Putty and paper clip he'd discovered in Celebrity's poker room the night before. Sticking the Silly Putty on the dashboard, he plunged the paper clip into it like a flag.

"I didn't know you were into toy figures," Bill said.

"They help pass the time," Valentine said. "Guess what this one is."

Bill stared at the dashboard. "A bug?"

"That's right. Rufus Steele found it stuck beneath a table in Celebrity's poker room last night. There's a mucker scamming the tournament."

The Volvo slowed so they were actually doing the speed limit. Bill removed the bug from the dash and held it in his hand.

"Skip DeMarco?" he asked.

"No, it's someone else. The folks running the World Poker Showdown should be watching for stuff like this, considering there's already been one allegation of foul play. But they're not. They're running a loose ship."

Bill frowned. He had joined the Nevada Gaming Control Board twenty-five years ago, and had spent much of that time changing Las Vegas's image from a mob-run town to a family-friendly destination. One bad incident could change that overnight.

"Are you suggesting I ask the governor to stop the tournament?" Bill asked.

"No. Tell him you want him to keep the tournament going so you can nail the mucker, and show everyone that Vegas doesn't tolerate cheating. It would be good for business, and there will also be another benefit."

"Which is?"

"While we're catching the mucker, we can scrutinize DeMarco's play, and figure out what the hell he's doing."

"What about Scalzo? I'd bet my paycheck he's going to hire another hitman to whack you."

"I've got a bodyguard, remember? Rufus cracks a mean bullwhip."

"Be serious."

Valentine *was* being serious. The truth was, Scalzo was afraid of him. That gave him the upper hand, and he planned to take full advantage of it.

"I'll deal with Scalzo," he said.

12

"**D**etective Davis wasn't seriously hurt," the doctor at the Atlantic City Medical Center emergency room told Gerry. "He landed on a piece of glass on the pavement that put a gash in his back. He'll be good to go once we stitch him up."

Gerry wanted to give the doctor a hug but instead just nodded. She was a fiftyish woman with steel gray hair and sunken eyes that had seen their share of heartache. She gently touched Gerry's sleeve. "You look pale. Are you going to be okay?"

"Just a little shook up," Gerry admitted.

"Here. Come with me."

She led him to a visitors' area where they sat on a small couch. An ambulance had shown up outside Bally's before any police cruisers, and Gerry had ridden to the hospital with Davis. Watching Davis bleed all over the back of the ambulance, Gerry had realized that he was partially responsible for what had happened. Davis had picked him up at the airport as a favor to his father. Davis should have been home, and not on the street.

"Did the sight of all that blood bother you?" the doctor asked.

"Yeah, how did you know?" Gerry said.

"It's a common reaction. The human body has a hundred quarts of blood. Eddie lost a tiny fraction of that. He'll be fine. Trust me."

Gerry gazed into her kind face, and found it in him to smile.

"You're a Valentine, aren't you?" she asked.

His smile grew. "That's right. Gerry Valentine."

"Faith Toperoff. I knew your parents. How are they doing?"

"My mom passed away two years ago," Gerry said. "My dad runs a consulting business out of Florida."

"I'm sorry for your loss. I always admired your parents for staying on the island after the casinos came," she said. "Not many people had the stomach for it, especially those first few years."

"How long have you been here?" Gerry asked.

"All my life."

There weren't many like her left on the island, and he said, "My folks talked about packing up and leaving, but my father couldn't do it. He said he'd be a traitor."

"It was especially hard on the local cops," she said. "The crime rate shot up every time a casino opened, and it was already the highest in the nation. I remember the night your father shot to death the man who'd shot his partner. Your father took it hard, even though he'd done the right thing. New Jersey struck a devil's bargain the day it decided to let casinos take over this island."

Gerry stared at the scuffed tile floor. He got depressed when locals talked about the old days. Atlantic City had been a decent place to live until the casinos had appeared. He'd been a teenager, and remembered hundreds of restaurants and retail stores closing down, while neighborhoods like South Inlet and Ducktown had disappeared altogether. A voice came over a public address, looking for Dr. Toperoff. She rose and slapped Gerry on the leg the way his mother used to do.

"Tell your father I said hello," she said.

Gerry stayed in the visitors' area until he saw the sun come up. He decided he was thirsty, and went downstairs to the basement and bought an iced tea from a humming soda machine. It tasted like the best thing he'd ever drunk.

He walked around, trying to collect his thoughts. Once the police found out he was responsible for sending Abruzzi to the big poker game in the sky, he was going to be put through endless questioning. He was in for a long day.

He came to the hospital cafeteria. It didn't open for another half hour, and he stared through the doorway into the darkness. Two weeks ago, while visiting Jack Donovan, he'd come downstairs to this same cafeteria to get sodas, then returned to Jack's room to find his friend's oxygen tubes ripped out. Jack had died trying to tell him about the amazing poker scam he'd invented.

Gerry continued to stare into the darkness. His father believed the secret to Jack's scam was hidden inside the hospital, and that if Gerry looked hard enough, he'd discover what it was. Jack had invented the scam while getting chemotherapy, and Gerry decided that would be the best place to start searching.

He found a hospital directory posted by the elevators, and located the floor on which cancer treatments were given. Getting on an elevator, he pushed the button for the floor. He finished his drink while the elevator creaked upward.

Even though Jack knew he was terminal, he'd still continued to get weekly chemotherapy, unwilling to give up the fight despite having already been counted out. It was the kind of courage that Gerry hoped he would summon when he faced the music.

The signs led him to a wing that looked brand new. A honey-blond nurse with the beginning of a double chin manned the nurses' station, a fat diamond ring and gold band sitting on her third finger. Her eyes said it was okay for Gerry to approach, so he did.

"Can I help you?" the nurse asked.

"Please." He took a business card from his wallet and placed it on the counter. His title was partner, a nice gift from his father. She stared at it indifferently.

"Grift Sense. What's that?"

"We help casinos catch cheaters."

"I thought it was the other way around."

Gerry started to put the card away, then thought better of it. "Sometimes it is. We nail those guys, too."

"What does 'grift sense' mean?"

"It's a hustler's expression, a compliment, really. It means you have a gift for spotting grift."

"Sounds like fun. What can I do for you?"

There were charts spread all over her work area and a pen stuck behind her ear. Working alone and working hard. Gerry found himself liking her, despite her coolness.

"A friend of mine was getting chemotherapy here," Gerry said. "His name was Jack Donovan. I was wondering if I could ask you some questions."

She stiffened. "Jack Donovan is dead."

"Yes. I know that."

"I can't talk to you about his death," she said. "There's an ongoing criminal investigation being conducted by the homicide division of the Atlantic City Police Department. I was interviewed by two detectives, along with practically everyone else on the floor who was in contact with Jack."

"I don't want to talk to you about his death," Gerry said. "I want to talk to you about his therapy."

She pushed her chair back a foot from the desk. "What about it?"

"Jack invented a way to cheat at poker during his therapy. So far, it's got all the experts fooled."

"How do you cheat at poker?"

"In this case, marked cards."

"Marked how?"

"That's the sixty-four-thousand-dollar question."

From his wallet, Gerry removed the playing card that Jack had given him before he'd died. It was an ace of spades from Celebrity's casino in Las Vegas. The card had been scrutinized by an FBI forensic lab and found to be clean. Yet it was marked, and could be read if you knew the secret. She examined the card and handed it back.

"So you think Jack Donovan devised some special

way to mark cards while getting treatment in this hospital," she said.

"That's right," Gerry said.

Her face changed, and so did her tone. "What do you want me to do, Gerry Valentine, vice president of Grift Sense, let you search the place? Get real."

This was a real Jersey girl, filled with piss and vinegar and capable of intimidating a three-hundred-pound NFL lineman.

"Of course not," he replied.

"Then what do you want?"

"Jack Donovan stole something from this hospital," Gerry said.

"He did?"

"Yes. It was in a metal strongbox in a bag under his bed. I saw it. Whatever was in that strongbox can be used to mark cards, but also happens to be dangerous."

"Dangerous how?"

"I don't know."

"How can you be looking for something if you don't know what it is?"

"I'm guessing there has to be a record of the theft. If I know what was taken, I'll know what the scam is."

"It's that easy?" she asked.

Gerry nodded. He would take the mystery substance and coat a few dozen playing cards with it, and the rest would explain itself. To his surprise, she picked up his business card, and slipped it into her breast pocket.

"And it will go no further than that?" she asked.

"That's right. No one will ever hear about it."

She pulled out her lower lip and let it snap back, deep in thought. "I liked Jack. He was always cracking jokes, even when he knew what his situation was. I'll look through the computer, let you know what turns up."

"Thanks a lot," Gerry said.

The phone on her desk had several buttons. The red one lit up and rang at the same time. She picked it up and said, "Cancer ward nurses' station, Gladwell here."

She listened for a moment, then looked at Gerry a little differently than before. "There are some homicide detectives in ER searching the hospital for you. They want to question you about a dead guy they think you sent through the windshield of a car."

It was not the way Gerry had hoped to end their conversation.

"Tell them I'll be right down," he said.

Part II

George and Tom

13

Skip DeMarco stood naked at the bedroom window in his suite, imagining the world he could not see. Although his vision was limited to a few inches in front of his face, DeMarco had a keen sense of light and dark, and imagined the sun climbing over the tall, bluish mountains that ringed Las Vegas, a city his uncle had described to him in great detail. His uncle made the casino-lined streets sound like something out of *The Wizard of Oz,* but DeMarco didn't picture them that way. Vegas was a cutthroat town, designed to separate suckers from their money. That was why his uncle liked it here so much.

The room's air-conditioning rose with the intrusion of natural light. Shutting the blinds, he walked to the closet and went through the slow, painstaking process of picking out today's outfit, holding each garment in front of his face to determine its color. He decided on a flowing black silk shirt, black linen pants, two gold necklaces, and shades. The tiny inner-canal earpiece he'd worn each day of the tournament lay on his bureau. As he fitted it into his ear, he heard his uncle's soft tapping on the door.

"Come in, Uncle George."

His uncle entered, shutting the door behind him.

"You sleep good?" the older man asked.

"Like a rock. How about you?"

"Fine. Show me what you're wearing."

DeMarco stood in the center of the bedroom, and let his uncle appraise his selection of clothes. It was a routine they'd followed since he'd gone to live with Scalzo as a little boy.

"You look great, kid," his uncle said.

"The black isn't too ominous?"

"What's that supposed to mean?"

"Foreboding. Scary."

"You look like a man," his uncle bristled.

DeMarco pointed at the dresser. A radio transmitter lay on it, which was used to test the earpiece and make sure it was functioning properly. "Do the test, Uncle George."

His uncle picked up the transmitter and flipped the power on. Then he pressed the transmitter's main button. DeMarco heard a short click in his ear.

"Do it again," DeMarco said.

His uncle pushed the button twice. DeMarco heard two clicks.

"Perfect," he said.

"You're not leaving this out for the maid to see, are you?" his uncle asked.

"It goes in the wall safe," DeMarco said. "Put it away for me, Uncle George, would you?"

His uncle shuffled across the room and put the transmitter into the wall safe. A diabetic, he suffered from swollen feet. "It's like walking on marshmallows all the time," he often said. His uncle carried insulin with him, yet told everyone the insulin was for his nephew, not himself. DeMarco believed that little deception said a lot about his uncle.

"Now, look in my ear," DeMarco said.

"You clean it real good?" his uncle asked.

DeMarco smiled. Another standard line.

"Yes, I cleaned it real good."

His uncle examined his nephew's ear. When properly fitted, the earpiece was impossible to see. Earpieces had been used to cheat card games for years, with someone on the outside secretly reading everyone's hands, and passing the information to the cheater via a radio transmitter. But that scam was easy to detect. If an RF detector was pointed at the table during the transmission, the detector would pick up the radio frequency, and the cheater would be exposed. Nearly every casino and poker room in the world used RF detectors for this purpose.

But the scam his uncle had given DeMarco to cheat the World Poker Showdown was different. For starters, there was no outside person reading the other players' cards. And, if an RF detector was pointed at the table, the machine would hardly register, and the operator would think it was someone's cell phone. But the best part was that there was no evidence. The cards were clean, and so was everything else.

There was only one bad part about the scam. DeMarco didn't know how his opponent's cards were being read. It was a creepy feeling to hear clicks in his ear, and not know who was sending them, and several times he'd asked his uncle to explain the secret. Each time, his uncle had placed his hand on his nephew's shoulder and promised to tell him after he won the tournament.

Scalzo watched his nephew finish getting dressed, then looked at his watch. "Let's go downstairs. They're going to start playing soon."

"I need to brush my teeth and comb my hair," his nephew replied, heading toward the bathroom.

"Your hair looks fine, and no one's going to smell your breath."

"Come on, Uncle George. Appearances are important."

"Didn't you hear what I said? You look fine."

"It won't take two minutes. Is that so much to ask?"

The bathroom door closed before Scalzo could reply. His nephew was letting all the attention go to his head. Scalzo had adopted Skipper twenty years ago, expecting the boy to grow up to be like him. Instead, Skipper had turned into a big peacock.

Scalzo went into the next room, slamming the door behind him. He spied Karl Jasper standing in the center of the living room, talking with Guido. It was the second time in two days that Jasper had come to Scalzo's suite without being asked.

Guido hurried over to his boss.

"What the fuck is he doing here?" Scalzo asked under his breath.

"He demanded that I let him in," Guido said.

"He demanded?"

"Yeah. I figured it was important. You want, I'll throw him out."

Guido's job didn't involve making decisions. Going to the boss was the *only* right decision for Guido to make. Reaching down, Scalzo grabbed his bodyguard by the balls, and gave them a healthy squeeze. Guido's eyes nearly popped out of his head.

"Don't ever do something without asking me first," Scalzo said.

"*Yes, sir.*"

"*Never* do something without asking me first," he said, as if clarification were needed.

"*Yes, sir.*"

Scalzo released his death grip, and Guido slunk away. Then he walked up to Jasper. Jasper had been watching them, and his face had turned a sickly white.

"What the fuck do you want?" Scalzo said.

"We need to talk," Jasper said.

"About what?"

"About what happened last night with Valentine."

Scalzo pointed at the glass slider that led to a narrow balcony with a view of the desert. Only high-roller suites had windows that actually opened in Las Vegas hotels; everyone else was a prisoner of their room.

"Out there," Scalzo said.

Jasper opened the slider and let Scalzo go first. *Showing some respect,* Scalzo thought. They both went outside.

"What happened last night?" Jasper asked, closing the slider behind him.

Scalzo grasped the balcony's metal railing and stared at the mountains. He hated when people questioned him, hated it more when he had to answer. The mountains seemed close, and he tried to guess their distance.

"We had a problem," he said quietly.

Jasper edged up beside him, bumping shoulders, his voice a whisper. "A problem? You hire two goons to snuff Valentine, and they end up dead in the hotel stairwell. I'd call that a catastrophe."

Scalzo kept staring ahead. "You want to know what really happened?"

"Of course I want to know. We're partners, aren't we?"

"Valentine killed them."

"You sure?"

"Yes. I picked them up, brought them to the hotel, and sent them to Valentine's room. Twenty minutes later, one of them called my cell, said that Valentine and the cowboy had fought back. I waited by the elevators for them to come down. I heard two shots from the stairwell. I went and opened the door, saw them lying dead on the floor. I heard footsteps and looked up. Valentine was running up the stairs holding a gun."

Jasper swallowed hard, then opened and shut his eyes several times. When he spoke again, his voice was barely a whisper.

"So what do we? We can't have Valentine screwing things up for us."

A hundred miles, Scalzo decided. *The mountains were one hundred miles away.* He turned from the balcony and leaned against the railing, staring through the slider into the living room of the suite. Skipper hadn't come out yet. Still preening two inches in front of the vanity, he guessed.

"I already made arrangements for Valentine to be taken care of," Scalzo said.

"That was fast."

"I have a flag in every state."

A flag in every state meant Scalzo knew a mob guy in every state who would do him a favor. In this case, the favor came from a mob guy who had connections with the warden of a local prison. This warden had an inmate doing a life stretch, courtesy of Tony Valentine. By noon, that inmate would be on his way to Las Vegas.

"This man won't screw up," Scalzo added.

"How can you be sure?"

"He and Valentine have a history."

Through the slider Scalzo saw Skipper come in. His nephew had switched into a shiny gold shirt and looked like a fag. *This bullshit has to stop,* he thought.

"I sure hope you're right," Jasper said.

Scalzo shifted his gaze, and stared into Jasper's face. It was a look meant to inspire fear. He saw Jasper's lower lip tremble, and knew that it had worked.

"Don't ever question me again," Scalzo said. "Now, I'm going to tell you something, and I don't want you to forget it. Are you ready?"

"Sure," Jasper said.

"If you ever force your way into my suite again, I'll kill you. Understand?"

Jasper stepped backward and nearly fell over the railing. He quickly righted himself. "I understand," he said.

Scalzo opened the slider, and went into the suite.

14

Bill Higgins dropped Valentine at Celebrity at a few minutes before nine. As Valentine walked through the front doors, he remembered his breakfast date with Gloria Curtis, and hurried through the lobby toward the restaurant. A concierge dressed like Jungle Jim hurried toward him.

"Mr. Valentine?"

"What's up?" he said, not slowing down.

"I have a message from Ms. Gloria Curtis."

"What does it say?"

"It's a written message."

The concierge whipped a small white envelope from his outer breast pocket and presented it to him. Valentine dug for his wallet to tip the guy.

"No need, Mr. Valentine. My compliments."

The concierge walked away. The help got paid garbage in Las Vegas, and he chased the guy down and stuck a twenty in his hand, then walked to the elevators reading Gloria's note.

Tony, I heard what happened last night! I'm in my room. Please call me.

He found a house phone, and when an operator came on, asked for Gloria's room. She picked up the phone on the first ring.

"Tony, is that you?"

"Hello, Miss Curtis," he said, knowing that hotel operators often listened to calls.

"Where are you?"

"I just walked through the front doors."

"Zack called me earlier. He said you and Rufus Steele were attacked in your suite last night, and the men who did it were found dead in the stairwell."

"That's the *Reader's Digest* version," he said.

"Were you beat up? Did they damage that beautiful face?"

His cheeks burned. Never before had anyone called his face beautiful. "The face is fine. My neck is sore, but it will heal."

"Please come up to my room," Gloria said. "I'm in 842."

Valentine hesitated. The older he'd gotten, the more important mealtime had become, and he'd been looking forward to eating breakfast.

"Do you still want to eat?" he heard himself ask.

"I ordered breakfast through room service. I hope you like your eggs scrambled with cheese in them."

"That's exactly how I like them," he said.

"You've got a neck like a bull," Gloria said, examining the bruises on the back of Valentine's neck while he sat on the couch in her living room.

"I should. I stand on my head ten minutes every day."

"How long have you been doing that?"

"About twenty-five years."

She sat down beside him with a funny look on her face. She wore a powder blue suit, white blouse, and a Hermès scarf wrapped around her neck. She'd told him a few days ago that her network was putting her out to pasture because she was getting older, but to him, she looked just right.

"It's one of my judo exercises," he explained. "I took judo up when I started policing casinos. My boss didn't want us using our guns on the casino floor, so I got involved in the martial arts."

"Let me guess. Shootings are bad for business."

"Yes. It seems gamblers see it as a sign of bad luck, and stay away in droves."

"So you still practice?"

He stretched his neck and nodded. Normally he went to judo class three times a week, and could still throw around guys half his age. Telling her would only sound like bragging, so he kept quiet. Breakfast sat on a trestle tray in an alcove off the living room and smelled delicious. Gloria saw his eyes drift toward the food, and she brought her hand beneath his chin. She raised his face an inch and held his gaze.

"If I were to ask you a question, would you give me an honest answer?"

"I'd try," he said.

"Come on. Yes or no?"

"Yes."

"Did you shoot those two men in the stairwell last night? Everyone says you did."

"Who's everyone?"

"Please answer me," she said.

You couldn't be a television announcer for as long as Gloria and not have great eyes. Hers were a soft aqua that could melt your heart if you looked into them too long.

"No, I didn't shoot them," he said.

"Do you know who did?"

"No idea," he said.

Gloria stared deeply into his eyes. After a few intense moments, her face softened, and he guessed she believed him. She gave him a soft kiss on the lips, then led him to the food.

He pulled a chair out for her, then sat down to breakfast. He'd known Gloria four full days, and their relationship seemed to be forging ahead at warp speed. He liked her, she liked him, and they never ran out of things to talk about.

Below a metal tray a Bunsen burner kept the food warm. Everyday scrambled eggs with cheese, bacon, hash browns. She loaded up his plate, and as he bit into a strip of bacon, she gave him a look.

"Something wrong?"

"I was wondering about your sports jacket," she said, serving herself half the amount of food she'd served him. "You've worn it every day, yet it always looks fresh. No wrinkles or stains. Do you get it dry-cleaned each night?"

"I have several," he admitted.

"You alternate them?"

"Yes."

"Are they all black?"

"All black. My late wife used to call them my uniform, I guess because you can only wear a black sports jacket with a white shirt and dark pants."

"You been wearing them for a long time?"

He thought about it. "Twenty-eight years."

Her fork landed on her plate with a jarring clang. "You've worn the *same* make of black jacket for twenty-eight years?"

He suddenly realized the deep hole he'd dug for himself. If he'd learned anything since he'd started dating, it was that women were as interested in a man's personal habits as they were in his opinions. And he had just told her that he was a neanderthal.

"Maybe I should explain," he said.

She leaned forward. "Please do."

"It's sort of a long story."

"I like long stories."

His mouth had become dry, and he sipped ice water. "In the 1970s, New Jersey was going broke, so the politicians tried to convince the voters to legalize casinos, even though nobody wanted them. Our illustrious governor, a guy named Brendan Byrne, barnstormed the state, and told people that New Jersey's casinos would be different than Las Vegas, and would feature 'European-style' gambling."

"As in Monte Carlo?"

"Yes, as in Monte Carlo. Byrne made it sound like James Bond was going to be gambling, instead of some poor guy who hauled garbage."

"How funny."

"It was. When gambling was legalized, Byrne established a dress code. Men were supposed to wear jackets inside the casinos."

"Classy. Did it work?"

He smiled, the memory as fresh as the day it had happened. "It was a disaster. The first casino was Resorts International. It opened on Memorial Day weekend, and the line of people was a mile long. When the doors opened, they came in like a stampede. The casino had put five hundred black sports jackets in a cloak room near the entrance, with the idea being that men who didn't have a jacket would rent one. No one did.

"I was working inside the casino. One day, the floor manager comes up to me, and says, 'Tony, turn around.' I did, and I felt him run a tape measure across my back like a tailor in a clothing store. He said, 'Perfect, you're a size forty-two,' and he told me to follow him.

"He led me to the room where the sports jackets were, and pointed at a rack. He said, 'Tony, these jackets are forty-twos. Take what you want. We're throwing them out.' Well, they were all brand new, and my wife and I were barely scraping by, so I loaded up my car, took them home, and stored them in a spare closet. The next day, I loaded up the car again."

"How many did you take?"

"All of them."

"How many was that?"

He'd worn through two jackets a year for the past twenty-eight years, and still had a half dozen left. "Sixty-two," he said. Then added, "It saved us a lot of money."

"Did you ever consider retiring the jackets after you left the police force?"

"Yeah, but I decided against it. The jackets were Geoffrey Beene, who'd had a boutique at Resorts. They were the best clothes I'd ever worn."

"Your uniform," she said.

"Yeah. My uniform."

Gloria looked at her watch and stood up. "I need to run. I have an interview with one of the poker players in ten minutes. Stay and finish breakfast, if you like."

She grabbed her jacket off the couch and hurried to the door. He followed her, not certain what she thought of his story. He hoped it didn't make him sound too eccentric.

"Will I see you later?" she asked, stopping at the door.

They were the sweetest words she could have said. Valentine started to answer, then remembered what he'd wanted to talk to her about.

"I need to tell you something," he said.

She put her jacket on, and tossed back her hair. "What's that?"

"There may be another hitman gunning for me."

"That's awful, Tony. What are you going to do?"

"I need to change my room, maybe start wearing a disguise when I'm in the hotel. I wanted you to know in case—"

"In case what?"

"In case you didn't want to be around me."

"But I enjoy being around you," she said. "Do you think I invite every guy I meet up to my room for breakfast?"

He did not know what to say. She put her arm on his

shoulder and rested it there—something a good friend might do. She crinkled her nose. "Thank you for telling me. May I make a suggestion?"

"Sure."

"Move in with me. You can sleep on the couch."

His napkin escaped his fingers, and fell to the floor. Gloria was the nicest woman he'd met in years, but that didn't change the fact that he was investigating the tournament, and she was covering the tournament for her network. He never mixed business and pleasure, which was why the words that came out of his mouth surprised him.

"Okay."

"Just okay?"

"I mean, yeah, that's great."

She gave him a kiss, then consulted her watch again. "Now I'm late. Talk to you later."

She was out the door before he could say good-bye.

15

Al "Little Hands" Scarpi was pumping iron in the weight room at Ely State Penitentiary when an inmate named Big Juan came in. Six six and about three hundred pounds, Big Juan walked with a strut that came from having his way most of his life. Little Hands was six inches shorter and fifty pounds lighter, but not easily intimidated.

Sweat poured down Little Hands's face as he curled a pair of fifty-pound dumbbells. The weight room was quiet except for the belching guard reading a comic book in the corner. In exchange for additional time in the weight room, Little Hands waxed the guard's car every week, using nothing but a can of Turtle Wax and a rag. It was boring work, but got him out of his cell for a few hours. Sometimes, that was all a man needed to keep from going insane.

Big Juan came over to watch. He had a towel slung over his shoulder and a teardrop tattoo beside his left eye—meaning he'd killed someone. Little Hands had killed plenty of people, but had never done anything as stupid as write it in ink on his body. He continued to curl the dumbbells.

"You Little Hands?" Big Juan asked.

Was the guy blind? Al's hands were the size of a child's, the fingers thin and delicate, and had caused him undue hardships growing up. Kids in school had made fun of them, and as he'd gotten older, guys in bars had picked fights with him. The hands were his handicap, and why he'd taken up weightlifting.

"What do you think?" he replied.

Big Juan stared at his fingers, then over his shoulder at the guard.

"I need to talk to you," he said quietly.

"About what?"

"A deal."

Little Hands had gotten a head of steam going with the dumbbells, and his sweat made a small puddle on the floor. He started every day like this, sweating so hard that he was able to forget he was a prisoner, a man going nowhere for a very long time.

"I'm available next Tuesday morning at nine," Little Hands said.

Big Juan gave him a dead-eyed stare. Little Hands had tried to develop a sense of humor since coming to the joint. It made the day go quicker.

"What's that supposed to mean?"

"It's a joke. You like jokes?"

"Fuck no," Big Juan said.

Little Hands had run into a bunch of humorless guys in Ely. Nearly all came from the streets and acted like a different species. He kept pumping the dumbbells.

"You want to hear my deal or not?" Big Juan asked.

"Sure."

Big Juan lowered his voice. "I can get you out of here."

Little Hands didn't slow down or pause or do any of the things that inmates did when someone mentioned freedom to them. Lawyers did it all the time, as did wives and loved ones and cops who wanted you to cooperate with them. They talked about freedom like it was something that could be pulled out of a top hat, and handed back to you. Little Hands knew better. The system was the only thing that could give a man his freedom back.

"How much is it going to cost me?"

"That's the good part," Juan said. "It won't cost you nothing."

Little Hands put the dumbbells on a rack, then walked over to a weight bench. There was a barbell across the bench with three hundred pounds in weights fitted on it. He always ended his sessions doing bench presses with the barbell.

"Keep talking," he said.

Everything cost something in the joint, especially a favor. Little Hands suspected that Big Juan was playing him for a fool. He didn't like that.

He asked Big Juan if he lifted. It was a dumb question, but Little Hands liked to play stupid sometimes, just to see where it would get him.

Big Juan said yes, and Little Hands asked him to spot for him.

"Sure," Big Juan said.

Little Hands lay down on the weight bench. The

bench was made of steel, and had uprights to hold the barbell in place. He lifted the barbell off the uprights, and pressed it five times over his head. Finished, he asked Big Juan to help him, and the bigger man lifted the barbell off Little Hand's chest and fitted it into the uprights.

"Your turn," Little Hands said, rising from the bench.

Big Juan hesitated. Three hundred pounds was a lot of weight, even for someone who lifted every day. But Big Juan was a macho man. He wasn't going to take weight off the barbell and humiliate himself in front of Little Hands. He was the *bigger* man, so he lay on the bench and lifted the barbell off the uprights.

Big Juan pressed the barbell above his chest, and the effort made his face change color. Little Hands stood over him.

"Come on, you can do it. Four more."

Big Juan blew out his cheeks and strained to press the barbell again. His arms began to tremble, and Little Hands put his hands on the bar to help him.

"Thanks, man," Big Juan said.

Little Hands continued to hold the bar and let Big Juan catch his breath.

"How are you going to get me out of this fucking place?"

Big Juan looked up at him. "You know the conservation camp?"

Ely Conservation Camp was part of the prison and was run in conjunction with the Nevada Division of Forestry. The warden assigned camp operation support activities to model inmates. Working at the camp was the dream of every Ely inmate.

"What about it?" Little Hands asked.

"You're being assigned to it."

"When?"

"Today. This morning."

Little Hands released his grip on the barbell, and it sunk down to Big Juan's chest.

"Come on. Do another."

Big Juan strained with the barbell, barely lifting it a foot above his chest. When he could lift it no farther, panic set into his eyes. Little Hands picked up the barbell and held it a few inches above him.

"Then what happens?"

Big Juan was blowing out his cheeks, regretting every bad thing he'd ever done to his body. In a whisper he said, "You'll take a truck over to the conservation camp and check in. Another truck will take you out to a forest to do a clean-up job. You'll walk away from the job into a waiting car."

"Where am I going?"

"Las Vegas."

"Who's behind this? Someone in Las Vegas?"

"Yeah," Big Juan wheezed.

Little Hands was getting the picture. He'd lived in Las Vegas and knew how that town worked. When one of the casino bosses wanted something done, palms got greased, phone calls got made, and it got done. He made Big Juan do another press. The effort nearly killed him.

"Who does this person in Las Vegas want me to kill?"

Big Juan was opening and shutting his eyes while sucking down air. Each time he inhaled, cherry-sized lumps formed where his jaw met his sideburns.

"Who said this was a hit?" Big Juan asked.

Little Hands leaned down and breathed in Big Juan's face. "I was a hitman. Ain't no other reason someone is going to go to the trouble to spring me out of here."

"Some retired cop," Big Juan said.

"That's the hit?"

"Yeah. He's in Las Vegas."

Little Hands felt his brow tighten the way it did when his blood pressure rose. A retired cop was responsible for putting him in the slammer.

"What's his name?"

"Valentine."

"Tony Valentine?"

"Yeah. You know him?"

Little Hands lowered the barbell and forced Big Juan to do another press. He'd dreamed about snuffing Valentine ever since being locked up. Valentine had sucker-punched him in a Vegas motel while Little Hands was staring at a porno movie playing on the TV. The movie had reminded Little Hands of something he'd seen his mother doing when he was a little kid. It had messed Little Hands up real good.

Big Juan was shaking his head in defeat. He'd had enough. Little Hands lifted the bar off his chest, and Big Juan shut his eyes.

Little Hands crossed the weight room with a towel in his hands. He looked out the barred window that faced the yard. Ely housed over a thousand prisoners along with the state's Death Row inmates. Security was tight, with armed guards sitting in turrets on the two main buildings, watching the yard twenty-four hours a day. He'd heard lifers talk about "escaping" by running between the two main buildings, and going out in a blaze of gunfire. No one *had* ever escaped, and he imagined the glory of being the first.

"Get your hands off the bars," the guard called out.

Little Hands released the bars and turned to face the guard.

"Sorry."

Comic book in his lap, the guard fingered his double-barreled shotgun. He was a round kid with a moon face and flour-sack arms.

"Get away from the window," the guard said.

"I was just looking."

"You heard me, Hercules."

Little Hands walked back to the weight bench. Big Juan was still panting like he'd just run a four-minute mile. The guard picked up his comic book and emitted a loud belch as he flipped back to his spot.

"I want the job," Little Hands said.

Big Juan nodded, then tried to get up. He fell back hard on the bench and closed his eyes. When he re-opened them, there was a new appreciation in his face.

"Doesn't all that weight make you hurt?" Big Juan asked.

"Sure," Little Hands said.

"Why do you do it?"

Little Hands smiled to himself. Big Juan's muscles would be burning, his body going into shock. He would hurt for days, had maybe even damaged his joints or his heart. He did not understand pain the way Little Hands understood pain. Few people did.

"Because I like it," Little Hands said.

16

"**H**ave you ever seen one of these before?" Detective Joey Marconi asked.

Gerry Valentine tiredly shook his head. Late morning, and he was sitting in the hospital visitors' area with Eddie Davis's partner, having spent several hours going over what had happened outside Bally's.

Marconi was holding a New York Yankees baseball cap. He'd found the cap on the floor of Bally's while chasing the other members of Abruzzi's gang, who'd escaped out the casino's rear exit. The cap had a miniature receiver and three light-emitting diodes sewn into its rim, and had been used to rip Bally's off at blackjack.

Gerry had seen some sophisticated cheating equipment since going to work for his father, but the cap was unique. By looking upward into the cap's rim, a cheater could read signals being sent by another member of the crew. *Like looking at a tiny movie screen,* Gerry thought.

"Do you know how the cap works?" Marconi asked.

"I think so," Gerry said.

Marconi was on his sixth cup of coffee, and as animated as a five-year-old with a sugar buzz. He was small and wiry and so Italian he looked Greek. He wore the standard undercover detective's uniform: blue jeans and a sweatshirt with a pullover hood. Across the front of the sweatshirt were the words I'M BLIND, I'M DEAF, I WANT TO BE A REF!

"You have to do better than that, Gerry," Marconi said.

"I do?"

"Yes. Your story will determine how this case is handled."

"Handled by who?"

"The district attorney."

Gerry took a deep breath. This wasn't going right. Marconi was treating him like a suspect, instead of someone who'd saved his partner's life. He put his elbows on his knees, and gave Marconi a hard look.

"Excuse me, but what am I missing here? Abruzzi was going to shoot Eddie. I did the only thing I could."

"I believe you, but we have to make sure the district attorney believes you."

"Why wouldn't he? You have the gun, don't you?"

Marconi lowered his gaze, and stared at the floor. It was the quickest admission of guilt Gerry had ever seen.

"You don't have the gun?" Gerry asked.

"Couldn't find it," Marconi said, eyes still downcast. "I had two uniforms stay and search the area after daybreak. The gun is gone."

"Meaning what?"

"Meaning that we don't have evidence that the guy you killed actually took a shot at Eddie, as you and Eddie claim."

"What about the car across the street that got winged?" Gerry asked. "That's evidence, isn't it?"

"The car is gone, too," Marconi said, not enjoying the role reversal.

"Gone? How does that work? Mirrors?"

"We're not sure."

"Let me guess. One of the uniforms let the owner drive it away."

Marconi massaged his face with his hands. "Probably."

Gerry had grown up hearing about bone-headed mistakes made by cops. The average pay for a uniform on the AC police force was twenty-eight grand. As a result, the force didn't always attract the best and the brightest, and mistakes at crime scenes were common.

"So what you're saying is, I might be facing a manslaughter rap," Gerry said.

Marconi looked up. "That's not going to happen. You have my word."

"But it *could* happen."

"Let's not go there. We need to concentrate on your story. I want to explain to the DA that this was an organized gang of cheaters. Right now, all I've got is this baseball cap. If you can explain how it works, we're home free."

"Do you know what a crossroader is?" Gerry asked.

Marconi clutched a cup of machine-made coffee. "That's a cheater who specializes in ripping off casinos."

"Correct. The most important weapon in a crossroader's arsenal is signaling, or what crossroaders call giving the office. Here's an example." Gerry spread his fingers out wide. "This is called George, and is usually done on the table, or with the hand held flat against the chest. What do you think it means?"

Marconi shook his head.

"George means everything is okay. If five cheaters are spread out across a casino, they can use George to communicate that the coast is clear. Here's another example." Gerry made his hand into a fist. "This is called Tom. It's also done on the table, or against the chest. Tom means there's a problem, and everyone needs to clear out."

"Tom is also a criminal name for the police," Marconi said.

"Maybe that's where it came from," Gerry said. "My father busted a gang using George and Tom to cheat a blackjack game. The dealer was involved, and flashing cards to her accomplices as she dealt. The flashing was invisible to the eye-in-the-sky cameras, but could be spotted by a pit boss standing behind her. Her accomplices used George and Tom to tell her when the pit boss was there, and when he wasn't. They stole over a half million dollars using just two signals."

The baseball cap lay on a coffee table. Gerry pointed at the receiver and LEDs stitched into the rim. "The gang inside Bally's was using electronic signals. We know they had a woman nail-nicking cards at blackjack. Once the cards at a table were marked, two members of the gang used the information to beat the house."

"How?" Marconi asked.

"You play much blackjack?"

"No."

"It's a simple game. The dealer gets two cards, one face up, the other face down. The players also get two cards, and try to get a total closer to twenty-one than the dealer. Because the dealer goes last, the house has an edge of one and a half percent.

"When cheaters nail-nick cards, it allows them to read the dealer's face-down card, and know the dealer's total. This gives them a fifteen percent advantage. But, the cheaters must be careful. Staring at the dealer's hand is a dead giveaway that marked cards are in play."

"Makes sense," Marconi said.

"Here's what the gang in Bally's was doing. One member sat to the dealer's right. He read the nicks on the dealer's face-down card, and sent the information to his partner through a tiny transmitter strapped under his pant leg. His partner played the Iggy, or dumb tourist. He drank and smoked and horsed around. He also read the signals in his baseball cap, and beat the house silly."

Marconi thought it over. "Let me play devil's advocate for a minute. What if the district attorney says the LEDs inside the cap are decorative. Plenty of people wear lights and electronic doodads in baseball caps. What do I say then?"

"The cap has a receiver," Gerry said. "According to the New Jersey device law, no person shall possess any calculator, computer, or any other electronic, electrical, or mechanical device to assist in projecting or altering the game's outcome."

A thoughtful look crossed the Marconi's face.

"That will work," the detective said.

*   *   *

Gerry took out his cell phone. He needed to call his father, and get him up to speed. He wondered what his father would say upon hearing that Gerry had killed a member of George Scalzo's crime organization.

A female cop entered the visitors' area. The bland contours of her uniform could not hide her stunningly attractive figure. She pulled Marconi into a corner, spoke in a hushed voice, then handed him a thick Pendaflex file from under her arm. Marconi opened the file, his dark eyes scanning the page, then glanced nervously at Gerry.

"Thanks, Ellen," he said.

She left. Marconi came over to where Gerry was sitting, and dropped the folder in Gerry's lap. Then he sat down across from him.

"We need to talk," Marconi said.

Gerry put his cell phone back into his pocket. "What's wrong?"

Marconi pointed at the folder. "That."

Gerry opened the file, and found himself staring at a Xeroxed memo from the Atlantic City Casino Control Commission. His name was on the center of the page and highlighted in yellow marker. He glanced at the other memos beneath it. His name was highlighted in yellow on them as well.

"What are these?"

"Memos from the Atlantic City Casino Control Commission on which your name appears," Marconi said. "Out of curiosity, I had Ellen do a name search through the computer. That's how many files the CCC has on you. Your name is linked to more gambling scams in Atlantic City than anyone else in the computer. Tell me how I'm going to explain that to the district attorney."

Gerry dropped the folder on the coffee table. A few hours ago he'd killed a scammer; now Marconi had evidence that said he was also a scammer. It didn't paint a pretty picture, and he decided to come straight with the detective.

"Does it bother you that I was never arrested?" Gerry asked.

"So you were smart."

"My name's on fifty memos. That would make me a genius, don't you think?"

Marconi leaned back in his chair. "Okay, so what's your point?"

"Cops think that wherever there's smoke, there's fire," Gerry said. "But there isn't any fire here. Before I went to work for my father, I was a bookie. I did good business, and I'm not ashamed of it. I also had a reputation as being Tony Valentine's son. Every scammer in the Northeast knows who my father is. Guys would come to me and ask me my advice."

"What kind of advice?"

"They would be thinking about scamming a casino in Atlantic City. They would tell me what they were going to do, ask me if I thought my father had ever seen it before. When I was a kid, my father used to show us scams at the dinner table. I was exposed to a lot of amazing stuff when I was growing up. I also understand how my father thinks. I'd look at the scam, and tell them if I thought it would pass muster."

"You charge for this?"

"No."

"Then why did you do it?"

"The guys I helped out referred customers to me."

"That's sweet. How many guys did you tell not to bother?"

"Nearly all of them," Gerry said. "Most of the scams were old, stuff my father had seen before. To be honest, I think I saved the taxpayers a lot of money."

"How so?" Marconi asked.

"I kept those guys out of jail, and saved the taxpayers from having to pay for it."

Something resembling a smile crossed Marconi's face. He took the file and slapped it against Gerry's leg, then rose from his chair. "A regular public servant. I'm going to go have a talk with the DA. Don't go anywhere."

Gerry realized he was off the hook. Marconi left, and Gerry took out his cell phone and called his father.

17

"**Y**ou did *what*?" Tony Valentine asked, the cell phone pressed to his ear.

"I killed a guy who works for George Scalzo," his son said. "He was trying to shoot Eddie Davis outside Bally's. I rammed Eddie's car into the back of the guy's car, and sent him through the windshield."

Valentine closed his eyes. "Jesus, Gerry. You killed a mobster."

"I know, Pop. Think I should go into witness protection?"

"That's only for criminals," Valentine said.

"Bet I could tell the police a couple of things that would make me qualify."

Valentine found it in him to laugh. He was still in Gloria's suite, the sunlight splashing through the window. Over the years, he'd become convinced that casino hotels did everything imaginable to drive guests out of their rooms during the day, from having chambermaids come early to clean, to facing the rooms due east so they became flooded with light each morning.

"I do have some good news," his son said. "I talked to

a nurse at the cancer ward where Jack Donovan died. She remembered Jack, and said she'd search her computer to see if anything dangerous was stolen from the hospital."

"I'm not concerned about Jack right now," Valentine said, closing the blinds. "I'm concerned about you. Scalzo won't take this lying down. He already has a contract out on me."

"He does?"

"Yes. I'm having to watch my back," Valentine said. "So, here's what I want you to do. Catch the next plane home. Better yet, catch the next plane to San Juan, and meet up with Yolanda. Lay low for a while, so I can figure out what to do."

There was silence on the line. Valentine would have thought the connection had gone dead had he not heard his son cough. He went to the table where the breakfast he'd shared with Gloria still sat. A piece of cold bacon found its way to his mouth.

"I'm going to stay in Atlantic City," his son said.

Valentine nearly choked. "What are you talking about? You could get whacked."

"I owe it to Jack Donovan."

"What about your wife and daughter? What do you owe them?"

"Pop, remember the conversation we had before I left Vegas?"

Valentine thought back to the day before. So much had happened since, it seemed like last month. He picked up another piece of bacon and bit into it.

"I may be your son, but I'm also your partner," Gerry went on. "When things happen you don't like, you can't switch roles, and order me around because I'm your son."

"I can't?"

"No. I came to Atlantic City to find out how Jack's poker scam works. Just because I've got some mobster pissed off at me doesn't mean I should run."

"But your life's in danger."

"It's part of the business," Gerry said. "Look, Pop, what if every time *your* life was in danger, I called you up and told you to run back to Florida, hide in your house, and make Mabel answer the door. Think you'd like that?"

Valentine bristled. "This is different."

"Why it is different?"

"I'm your father."

"You're my sixty-three-year-old father, who probably shouldn't still be playing cops and robbers," Gerry said. "But you do, and I keep my mouth shut."

"You think I'm playing cops and robbers?"

"It's dangerous work, and you're not a kid anymore."

His son had a point. If last night was any indication, his ability to defend himself had diminished. He needed to be more realistic about what he could and couldn't do.

"Do you worry about me?" Valentine asked.

"All the time."

"Why haven't you said anything?"

"I saw where it got Mom," his son said.

When it came to catching crooks, Valentine had never let anything stop him. He couldn't scold Gerry for wanting the same thing.

"So you're staying in Atlantic City to figure out Jack's secret," he heard himself say.

"That's right."

"What about protection?"

"Eddie Davis and Joey Marconi said they'd help me out."

"That's only two guys."

"I'll be fine. Trust me."

Valentine started to argue, then thought better of it. Gerry had to make his own decisions, and he could only pray that none of them would get his son killed. He heard a knock on the door. "I've got company. I'll talk to you later."

"You're cool with my decision?"

"Yes. Just promise you'll watch your back."

"Love you, too, Pop," his son said.

Valentine stuck the last strip of bacon into his mouth as he went to the door. He still ate bacon and eggs and lots of other food that wasn't considered healthy, having decided that he'd rather exercise every day than not eat those foods. It was called living, and he was going to do it until the day he died.

He stuck his eye to the peephole. Rufus stood in the hallway dressed in a purple velour running suit and black high-top sneakers. He ushered the old cowboy in.

"How did you know where to find me?" Valentine asked.

"I had you paged in the casino and the restaurants," Rufus said. "Then I checked with the valet, and they said your car was still here. Since you and Ms. Curtis have been getting along so famously, I figured I'd find you here."

Valentine's cheeks burned. Hearing Rufus had found him so easily was unsettling.

"It's not what you think," he said.

Rufus flashed his best aw-shucks smile. His teeth, stained the color of mahogany from years of chewing tobacco, looked like pieces of antique furniture.

"Maybe not, but I bet it will be soon," Rufus said.

Valentine's cheeks burned some more. "So what can I do for you?"

"The Greek is taking me up on my Ping-Pong bet," Rufus said. "He paid the hotel to put a Ping-Pong table in the poker room, then talked some sucker into playing me during the break. They're waiting downstairs. I was hoping you'd act as my second."

"Sure," Valentine said.

Rufus removed a pack of cigarettes from his jacket pocket, banged one out, and tossed it into the air. The cigarette did a complete revolution, then landed on his outstretched tongue. He fired it up with a lighter.

"Who's the sucker?" Valentine asked.

"Some Japanese guy named Takarama."

Valentine had wanted to warn Rufus about Takarama the night before, but in all the excitement it had slipped his mind. "I hate to tell you this, but Takarama was the world table tennis champion a few years ago."

Rufus took off his Stetson and scratched his skull. "Is he still in the tournament? The deal was, I'd only play someone still in the tournament."

"Afraid so. Takarama's a helluva poker player, too."

Rufus smoothed the remains of his hair, covered it with his hat. "Let me ask you something, Tony. Would you bet against me? Hypothetically speaking, of course."

"I'd have to say yes," Valentine said.

"What kind of odds would you give me against Takarama?"

Valentine thought it over. He'd seen Takarama walking around the poker room the day before. The guy looked to be in tremendous shape.

"Twenty to one."

"Think I can get that downstairs with any of the hairy legs?"

Hairy legs were the money men who backed poker players, and often could be spotted in the audience during tournaments, gnashing their teeth like berserk fathers at a Little League game. Takarama could always fall down and break his ankle, and he said, "Maybe ten to one."

Rufus exhaled two purple plumes of smoke through his nostrils. It made him look like a fire-breathing dragon, and his eyes sparkled mischievously.

"Good," Rufus said. "Let's go downstairs and reel in some suckers."

18

Suckers made the gambling world go round.

They came from all walks of life. Some were smart, while others had not graduated high school. Some were wealthy, some poor. What they shared in common was a complete misunderstanding of the law of averages, and an unflappable belief in the laws of chance. Chance, suckers believed, was the god of gambling, and if they were in the right place at the right time, Chance would smile down on them, and they'd win.

Suckers made up 99 percent of the people who gambled. Each year, they invested billions of dollars in the lottery and at casinos, and had nothing to show for it. They also kept dog and horse tracks alive, and paid for thousands of bookies to run their businesses. They were the bottom line of every gambling operation's financial success.

And suckers were dependable. Even though they rarely won, they never stopped gambling, spurned on by the manufactured thrill that came from placing a wager. When they *did* win, they poured their winnings back into the game, convinced they'd finally hit a lucky streak, only to see their money and their dreams vanish like a puff of smoke.

Valentine followed Rufus into Celebrity's poker room to find the suckers crowded around the Ping-Pong table, eagerly awaiting the match. Nearly a hundred strong, they wore the disheveled look of men who weren't sleeping regularly. Rufus doffed his Stetson and gave them a big Texas wave.

"Good morning! How's everyone doing this fine morning?"

"Is it morning?" someone yelled back.

"Last time I checked," Rufus said. "Ready to see me play Ping-Pong?"

Several in the crowd guffawed. Rufus pulled off his running jacket to reveal his trademark Skivvies T-shirt. He began doing windmills while hacking violently.

"You okay?" Valentine asked.

"Never better." Rufus pounded his chest. "My lungs could use some help, though."

"Want me to get you something?"

"Shot of whiskey would hit the spot."

"That's going to help your lungs?"

"Who said it was going to help my lungs? I just like whiskey."

They were talking loud enough for the suckers to overhear. A handful had their wallets out, and were debating whether to get in on the action.

"Make that a double," Rufus said.

Valentine lowered his voice. "You want me to make that apple juice instead?"

"Apple juice is for old folks," Rufus said.

"A double it is."

Valentine crossed the poker room in search of alcohol. There was a cash bar beside the registration table, and he caught the eye of the female bartender. She was young enough to be his granddaughter, and shot him a disapproving look when he ordered Rufus's drink.

"It's a little early in the morning, don't you think?" she asked.

"And a Coke for me," he added.

She handed him the drinks with a grin on her face. "You're not in the tournament, are you?" she asked.

"No. How could you tell?"

"You look normal," she said.

He crossed the room with the drinks. A mob was gathered around Rufus, who continued to flail his arms like Indian clubs while giving his snake oil salesman spiel.

"Come on, boys, I'm about to play some Japanese world champion at Ping-Pong for a half million bucks, winner take all. If that ain't a safe bet, I don't know what is. Place your wagers now, or forever hold your peace."

"What kind of odds you offering?" one of the suckers asked.

"Ten to one," Rufus said.

"I'll bet you even money," the sucker said.

Rufus shot the sucker a murderous look. "You want even money, son? I've got one foot in the grave, and my opponent's a former champ. Ten to one, take it or leave it."

"Which foot?" the sucker asked.

"The one I'm not standing on," Rufus said.

The sucker took his money out. "You're on."

The doors to the poker room banged open, and the Greek and Takarama came in. A shade over six feet, Takarama wore black gym shorts and a matching polo shirt. He did not have an ounce of fat on his perfectly proportioned body. His shoulder-length hair was tied in a ponytail, giving his face a hawkish quality. His eyes scanned the room in search of his prey.

"Sure you want to go through with this?" Valentine asked.

"That pipsqueak can't lick me," Rufus said loudly.

The Greek sauntered over. He hadn't changed his clothes since the night before and looked like a bum's unmade bed. He fancied himself a professional gambler, but with every loss to Rufus, his true colors were increasingly clear. He was a sucker. What still made him special was his huge bankroll.

"Thanks for dressing up," Rufus said.

The Greek scowled. Curly black hair popped out of every part of his head. "You ready to play Takarama?" he asked.

"Of course," Rufus said. "The question is, is *he* ready to play *me*?"

"He sure is. A half million dollars to the first player to reach twenty-one?"

"Correct," Rufus said. "The only stipulation is, I supply the paddles. Your man gets to choose his weapon, and if he wants to switch at any time in the match, he can."

"Agreed," the Greek said.

Rufus and the Greek shook hands. Then Rufus turned to Valentine.

"Tony, I need to you to do me a little favor," Rufus said. "Go to the casino's main restaurant, ask for Chef Robert, and get the bag he's holding for me."

Valentine was nobody's caddy, but was willing to make an exception for Rufus.

"Sure," he said.

To reach the restaurant, Valentine had to walk through the casino. It was packed, the noise deafening. One of the great urban myths was that casinos pumped oxygen onto the floor to make people gamble. The truth was, they kept the air-conditioning down and made their cocktail waitresses wear tiny outfits, which accomplished the same thing.

The restaurant was called Auditions, and he walked past the empty hostess stand and looked around. It was decorated like a Hollywood sound stage, with fake movie sets and glossies of stars hanging on the walls. The kitchen was in back, and he cautiously pushed open a swinging door. A man wearing a chef's hat stood at an island.

"Can I help you?"

"I'm looking for Chef Robert," Valentine said.

"I'm Chef Robert. Are you with the health department?"

Once a cop, always a cop. "Rufus Steele sent me."

"Oh yes."

From beneath the island Chef Robert produced a canvas bag with Celebrity's logo splashed across the front. Valentine took the bag from his hands, and nearly dropped it on the floor.

"What's in it, bricks?"

"Cooking utensils, per Mr. Steele's request," Chef Robert said.

"How much do I owe you?"

"Mr. Steele has already compensated me."

Valentine tipped him anyway, then walked out of the kitchen, the bag pulling at his arm like a little kid. His curiosity was killing him, and he opened the bag and looked inside. It contained two cast-iron skillets. He thought Chef Robert had made a mistake. Then it dawned on him what Rufus was up to.

Pulling out his cell phone, he called Gloria Curtis.

"This is *bullshit*," the Greek said. "You can't play Ping-Pong with those!"

"Who says I can't?" Rufus replied, holding a cast-iron skillet in both hands. "I said I'd supply the paddles. Well, these are the paddles."

"I won't stand for this," the Greek replied.

"Are you welching on our bet?"

"You're damn right I am," the Greek said.

In a huff, the Greek started to walk out. Valentine was standing next to the Ping-Pong table, and as the Greek neared the doors, saw Gloria and Zack come in. She cornered the Greek, sticking a mike in his face. Zack started to film them.

"I hear you and Rufus Steele have an interesting wager going," she said.

The Greek raised his arms as if to strangle an imaginary victim. He quickly lowered them. "The bet's off," he said.

"Oh no," she said. "It sounded like it would make a wonderful piece."

"Didn't you hear me?" The Greek raised his voice. "The bet's off."

Gloria stepped back, unsure of what was happening. Takarama, who'd been leaning against the wall with a stoic look on his face, tapped the Greek on the shoulder.

"What?" the Greek said.

"You are dishonoring me," Takarama said.

"But he's trying to trick us," the Greek said.

"A man's word is his bond."

"But—"

"No exceptions," Takarama declared. He crossed the room to where Rufus was standing. "May I see one?"

Rufus handed him a skillet. Takarama pulled a Ping-Pong ball out of the pocket of his shorts, and bounced it on the flat side. The ball went up and down with the precision of a metronome. Takarama's eyes glanced into the Greek's unshaven face.

"I can beat him," he said.

The Greek's expression changed.

"Are you sure?"

Takarama nodded solemnly, the ball still going up and down.

"But you've never played with a skillet," the Greek said.

"It does not matter," Takarama said.

"Rufus *has*," the Greek said.

"He is not Takarama," the former world champion said.

19

Valentine's son knew a lot about sports. When it came to exceptionally gifted athletes, Gerry had a theory that he claimed most bookies shared: Great athletes were not normal. They were freaks.

His son's definition of a freak didn't match *Webster's*. According to Gerry, freaks could run faster, jump higher, and recuperate more quickly than the rest of us. They'd also been blessed with quick reflexes. Put simply, their bodies were more physically gifted, a fact that became apparent simply by looking at them.

Takarama was the perfect example of a freak. He had muscular calves, tree-trunk thighs, a girlish waist, and shoulders befitting a running back. There did not appear to be an ounce of wasted tissue on his body, and probably never had been. Walking over to the Ping-Pong table with the skillet in hand, he took several practice serves.

"Are you sure you can beat him?" the Greek asked, standing beside him.

"Yes," Takarama said confidently.

The Greek was sweating, the bright light of Zack's camera centered squarely on his face. Embarrassed by his decision to renege, the suckers had moved away from him. The Greek looked lost. In the poker world, your reputation was all you had.

The Greek turned to Rufus. "You're on," he said.

Gloria Curtis produced a shiny coin from her purse, tossed it into the air.

"Call it," she said to Rufus.

"Heads," Rufus said.

The coin landed on the floor. It was heads.

"Yee-haw," the old cowboy said.

Rufus and Takarama took their positions at opposite ends of the Ping-Pong table. As Rufus bent his knees and prepared to serve, Takarama went into a crouch and held the skillet in front of his body defensively. His eyes narrowed, seeing only the table.

Rufus held his skillet a foot from his head, the ball resting on the palm of his other hand. "Good luck, son," he said.

"I do not need luck," Takarama replied.

Rufus tossed the ball into the air and banged it with the skillet. It wasn't the kind of stroke that Valentine had thought would produce a deadly spin, but that was exactly what happened. The ball hopped over the net, then leaped a few feet into the air, hitting Takarama's skillet and flying behind him.

"My point," Rufus declared. "One-zip."

Rufus served four more unreturnable serves. With each lost point, Takarama shifted his grip on his skillet, and tried another method of stroking. Each change produced the same result. A wayward shot and a lost point.

"Five-zip," Rufus said, tossing him the ball.

Takarama went to the sideline and wiped his hands with a towel. When he returned to the table, Rufus was sipping whiskey.

"Not funny," Takarama said.

"You ought to try some." Rufus grinned.

Takarama prepared to serve. He tossed the ball into the air, and hit it with his skillet. As he did, the index finger on his serving hand struck the table edge. He yelped and dropped his skillet.

"Hope you didn't break it," Rufus said.

"Time out," the Greek called.

Takarama clutched his damaged finger and left the room to walk off the pain. When he returned, he'd regained his composure, and banged the table with the palm of his good hand.

"I get you now," he said.

It took Takarama a few points to figure out how to serve. When he finally did get the ball over the table, Rufus batted it back for a winner. Rufus had an unusual technique, and relied solely on his wrist to stroke the ball, his arm hardly coming into play.

Takarama copied the motion, and on Rufus's next service game, managed to win two points. The score was now thirteen to two, but a significant shift had occurred. Like all great athletes, Takarama had adjusted his game, and was forcing Rufus to work to win a point, making the old cowboy lunge from side to side. The toll on Rufus was immediate. His chest sagged, a hound-dog look appeared on his face, and after every point he stopped to catch his breath.

On his next serve, Rufus lost five points in a row,

making the score thirteen to seven. The whiskey had risen to his face and sprouted a thousand red blossoms. He looked like a dying man. Taking his Stetson off, he tossed it to the floor.

It was Takarama's turn to serve. Rufus made a motion to throw him the ball, only to drop it on the floor instead. There was a loud crunching sound.

"Shit! I stepped on it," Rufus said.

The Greek pulled a Ping-Pong ball from his pocket, and tossed it to Takarama.

"Here you go. Whip his ass."

Takarama won the next five points. He was effortlessly moving the ball around the table, making Rufus swing at air. What had started as a one-sided contest was still one, only the person getting the beating had changed. With the score thirteen to twelve, both sides decided to take a break.

"I'm open to suggestions," Rufus said, sucking on a bottle of water.

Valentine did not know what to say. Rufus had met his match, and everyone in the room knew it. Gloria stepped forward with an encouraging look on her face.

"I have an idea," she offered.

Rufus brightened. "Yes, Ms. Curtis."

"Moon-ball him."

"You want me to moon him?" Rufus said.

"No, I mean throw up some moon balls," she said.

"What are those?"

"Lobs, like they do in tennis. It's a great way to throw off your opponent's rhythm. I saw Tracy Austin lob Martina Navratilova in the final of the U.S. Open Tennis Championship. Martina won the first set and was rolling. Then Austin started throwing up moon balls. It threw Martina off, and she lost the match."

Rufus tossed away his empty water bottle. Then he retrieved his skillet from the floor, and pointed the flat side straight at the ceiling, visualizing the shot.

"I don't know," he said skeptically.

"What do you have to lose?" she asked.

It was Rufus's turn to serve. He sent the ball over the net, and Takarama shot it back. Rufus lunged to his right, and hit the ball straight into the air like he was sending up a missile. The ball went so high it nearly touched a chandelier, then fell back to earth and landed on Takarama's side of the table. It bounced so high that Takarama had to tap it back, giving Rufus a perfect kill shot.

Only Rufus didn't kill it. Instead, he lofted the ball into the air, then paused to watch its flight. He appeared to be thoroughly enjoying himself.

"Take that," the old cowboy said.

Takarama made a face that was part anger, part disgust. He had a lot of pride, and Valentine was not surprised when he took a step back from the table and changed his grip on the skillet. As the ball bounced on his side, he leaped into the air.

"Aieeee!" he screamed.

Takarama hit the ball on the rise, and sent it screaming past Rufus at a hundred miles an hour. His swing, loaded with top spin, finished with his arm coming up by the right side of his forehead. With a normal Ping-

Pong paddle it wouldn't have been a problem. With a skillet, it caused him to smack himself in the face.

The sound of the impact was awful. Takarama dropped the skillet on the floor, then brought his hands to his eyes, and staggered around the room muttering in Japanese. The Greek rushed to his aid.

"You okay?"

Takarama said something that sounded like a curse.

"Time out!" the Greek announced.

"For how long?" Rufus asked.

"How the hell should I know?" the Greek said.

Takarama walked in a serpentine pattern around the room, and Valentine guessed he'd given himself a concussion. Reaching the doors, Takarama pushed them open and staggered into the lobby. The Greek hurried after, followed by Rufus, Valentine, Gloria, and Zack, with the suckers bringing up the rear.

Takarama walked on rubber legs across the lobby and into the busy casino. He approached a roulette table surrounded by people. He pushed his way through to the table, and plucked the little white ball as it spun around the wheel.

"My serve," he said.

Then he fell face-first to the floor, taking a tray of colored chips with him. The crowd parted, and the croupier came around the table, looking down at Takarama in disgust.

The Greek stood several feet away, crying his eyes out. Rufus threw his arms triumphantly into the air.

"I win," Rufus said.

20

Mabel Struck was examining a Gucci handbag that had cost a casino in Reno a hundred thousand bucks, when the phone on Tony's desk lit up.

"Darn it," she said under her breath.

She'd come to work early that morning, wanting to play with the handbag that UPS had delivered the night before. The handbag was a gift from the Reno district attorney for Tony's testimony at trial. Mabel had several friends who liked to boast about how much they spent on handbags, and she couldn't wait to tell them that she had a Gucci bag that could actually *make* money. She snatched up the phone.

"Grift Sense," she answered cheerfully.

"Ms. Struck?" a man's voice asked.

"That's me."

"This is Special Agent Romero with the FBI."

"Good morning, Special Agent Romero. How are you today?"

"I'm fine. I wanted to thank you for your help the other day. The man we arrested was running crooked gambling parlors in twenty different locations. He's going to jail for a long time."

By looking at some photographs that Romero had sent, Mabel had determined that a craps game in the basement of a man's house was crooked, the table positioned against a wall with a large magnet hidden inside, the dice loaded with mercury. The information had allowed Romero to catch an elusive suspect, and had made Mabel a new friend.

"That's wonderful news," Mabel said.

"Something urgent has come up, and I wanted to get ahold of you. I need to tell you something which is extremely confidential."

Mabel leaned into the desk. Although she'd never met Romero, she'd formed a mental picture of him. Early fifties, with jet black hair, boyish features, and an engaging smile. "Is there something the matter?" she asked.

"Unfortunately, there is . . . I'm terribly sorry. Someone just walked into my office, and I need to speak with him. Will you excuse me for a moment?"

"Of course."

Romero put her on hold. Mabel took the handbag off the desk, and peered inside. It contained a video camera with a high-powered lens. The bag had a small hole in the fabric, and she thought back to what Tony had told her about the case.

Once, every casino in the world had let people playing blackjack cut the cards, the practice considered a common courtesy. Then, for security reasons, the practice had been discarded. Except at the Gold Rush casino in Reno, where old habits died hard. It was here that the crossroaders had struck.

The gang's members were a family, consisting of a husband, wife, and son. The scam happened during the cut. The husband would riffle up the center of the deck, and let four cards drop. He would then cut the cards. This placed the four cards he'd dropped on top of the deck. To anyone watching, his actions looked normal.

Using the camera inside the bag, his wife, who stood behind him, secretly filmed the four cards during the cut. The information was sent to her son, who sat outside the casino in a van and watched on a computer screen. The son then sent a text message to his father on a cell phone, and told him the cards' values. Since the father was playing heads-up with the dealer, he knew his first hand *and* the dealer's, and bet accordingly.

Romero returned to the line. "Sorry about that."

"So, how can I help you this morning?" Mabel asked.

"Well, I'm about to help you. The other day when we spoke, I passed along some confidential information about a mob boss named George Scalzo, who is presently under FBI surveillance."

"I remember," Mabel said.

"The agent handling the Scalzo case called me a short while ago, and informed me that George Scalzo put out a contract on your boss's life last night. The attempt failed. So, he's gone and put another contract on your boss."

"What a horrible man. Are you going to arrest him?"

"I wish we had the evidence to," Romero said. "Scalzo owns a contracting business, and uses a special code when he wants to talk to his underlings. The code uses building materials as passwords for criminal activity he wants done. When he orders a specific material, it means he wants a certain job done. In this case it was concrete, which means he wants a person killed."

"How clever."

"I figured you would know the best way to contact your boss, and give him a heads-up."

The receiver grew warm in Mabel's hand. Tony was always saying that the deeper he got into a case, the more dangerous it became. It sounded like it was time for him to come home.

"I'll call him once I hang up the phone," she said.

"I'm afraid there's more bad news," Romero said. "The agent who's handling the Scalzo case also informed me that Tony's son, Gerry, was responsible for the death of an associate of Scalzo's in Atlantic City."

"Gerry killed someone?"

"Yes. Gerry was protecting an undercover policeman, and won't face criminal charges. But that doesn't change the situation."

"Which is what?"

"That your boss and his son have gotten themselves into a blood feud with one of the most ruthless men in the United States. Your boss has a reputation for being a resourceful individual, and I'm sure his son is as well. But I'm afraid this is a fight that is stacked against them."

"Why do you say that?" Mabel asked.

"Scalzo has connections all over the country, especially in Las Vegas, where he is now. And he has a small army on his payroll in New Jersey. If Scalzo is gunning for someone, he'll usually get them."

Mabel sighed. If she'd learned anything working for

Tony, it was that her boss didn't know the meaning of the word *quit,* and neither did Gerry. They were stubborn males, and not inclined to run away from a fight. "Thank you, Special Agent Romero. I appreciate the call. I'll make sure Tony and Gerry are warned."

"You're welcome. May I ask a favor?"

"Certainly."

"Please keep this conversation between you and your boss."

"It will go no further."

"Good-bye, Ms. Struck."

Mabel nestled the receiver into its cradle. Pushing her chair back from the desk, she steepled her hands, and rested her chin on her fingertips. It was her thinking pose, and she sat silently, contemplating what to do.

When the phone rang fifteen minutes later, she was still absorbed in thought. She glanced at the Caller ID on the phone and saw that it was Gerry's wife, Yolanda, calling on her cell phone. Yolanda had gone to Puerto Rico to visit her family a week ago, and Mabel had missed her company. She picked up the phone.

"Hello, Yolanda. How is sunny Puerto Rico?"

"I left three hours ago," Yolanda replied. "I'm at the Miami airport, waiting for a connection to come home."

"Is everything all right?"

"No. I mean yes. Oh, I don't know."

"What's wrong?"

"I had this horrible dream last night," Yolanda said. "I wouldn't have given it any weight, only my mother had the exact same dream. So, I decided to come home."

Yolanda's eighty-year-old mother was psychic, and had premonitions when bad things were about to happen. Mabel said, "Tell me what happened in your dream."

"I was in a cemetery. It was freezing cold and pitch dark. I was looking at a tombstone with Gerry's name on it and I was sobbing. I laid flowers on Gerry's grave, then put flowers on a grave with a tombstone that had Tony's name on it."

"You saw both their names?"

"Yes," Yolanda said quietly.

"And your mother had this same dream?"

"Yes," Yolanda said. "She saw tombstones with Gerry's and Tony's names as well. Now, will you please tell me something?"

"Of course, my dear."

"Are Gerry and Tony all right? Please be truthful with me."

Mabel hesitated. Then her eyes fell on the frame hanging over Tony's desk. It contained five playing cards—two black aces, two black eights, and the five of diamonds. Wild Bill Hickock had been holding aces and eights the night he'd been shot in a poker game, murdered by a gang of cheaters who were afraid of being run out of town. They were known as a Deadman's Hand, and had been bought by Tony as a reminder that no job was worth getting killed over.

"I'm afraid they're up to their eyeballs in trouble," she blurted out.

"So my dream was a premonition," Yolanda said.

"I hope not," Mabel said.

There was a loud noise in the background, and

Yolanda said, "They're boarding my plane. I need to run. I'll be home soon."

The phone went dead in Mabel's hand. Identical dreams couldn't be a coincidence. Tony and Gerry were going to get hurt if they didn't do something. She stared at the Deadman's Hand, then shut her eyes and prayed, not wanting Wild Bill's fate to be Gerry's and Tony's as well.

21

"I owe you a big steak," Eddie Davis said.

"I might just take you up on that," Gerry replied.

Davis was signing paperwork so he could be released from the emergency room of Atlantic City Medical Center. The ER was relatively quiet, the groaning drunks and shooting victims and other casualties of the night having been treated and moved out. A bearded doctor stood beside Davis, holding a medicine bottle filled with white pills. He shoved them into Davis's hand.

"This is penicillin. Follow the instructions on the bottle," the doctor said. "The wound on your back could become infected. You need to watch it."

"I will," Davis said, pocketing the bottle.

The doctor handed Davis another sheet of paper to sign. It was printed in bold lettering, and stated that Davis had been given instructions from a doctor and fully understood them. Gerry guessed this freed the hospital from liability in case Davis got sick, and decided to sue. Davis scribbled his name across the bottom.

Outside in the parking lot they found Marconi sitting

in a Chevy Impala, fighting to stay awake. Gerry guessed Marconi would rather be home sleeping than sitting there, only there was an unwritten code that said if your partner got hurt, you hung with him. His father had done it many times. Marconi climbed out of the car and whacked Eddie on the arm.

"Hey brother, glad to see you're still in one piece. I spoke with the district attorney about Abruzzi getting killed outside Bally's. Everything's cool."

"Did you nail the guy's partners?" Davis asked.

"They escaped. I managed to grab a good piece of evidence, though." Opening the back door of the car, Marconi took the gaffed Yankees cap off the passenger seat and handed it to Davis. "Take a look at this."

Davis examined the cap, trying to hide his disappointment that Marconi hadn't nailed Abruzzi's partners. As he handed the cap back, Gerry stuck his hand out.

"Can I look at it again?"

Marconi handed him the cap. The cap had been bothering Gerry, only he hadn't known why. Turning the cap over, Gerry ran his finger over the LEDs and receiver sewn into the rim. Most cheating equipment was crudely made, with the main emphasis on getting the money. The niceties were almost always ignored. But this cap was different. It was new and looked liked a tailor had stitched it. The transmitter and LEDs were unusually thin, and he suspected they'd cost a lot of money.

Then it occurred to him what was wrong.

Cheating equipment was expensive. Several underground companies sold devices to rip off games, and the equipment often cost several thousand dollars. The markup was incredible, the reasoning being that a cheater would make the money back in one night. Gerry tried to imagine how much the baseball cap would cost from one of these companies. They charged through the nose for anything electronic, and he guessed the cap would cost ten grand. He handed the cap back to Marconi.

"Can I ask you a couple of questions?" Gerry asked.

"Go ahead."

"The gang you were chasing inside Bally's, how many members were there?"

Marconi stuck the cap on his head. It was several sizes too large, and made him look like a little kid. He counted on the fingers of one hand. "One woman was nicking the cards. A second guy was reading the nicks and transmitting the information. And there was the guy wearing the cap and doing the betting. Three members."

"Don't forget Abruzzi," Davis said.

"Correction. Four members."

"Okay," Gerry said. "Four members, but only one is actually stealing."

"That's right."

"How much was the gang winning?"

"Around fifteen hundred a night," Marconi said.

Gerry stared at the cap on Marconi's head. Now he knew what was bothering him.

"That's not enough money," Gerry said.

Marconi shot him a puzzled look. "What do you mean?"

"Look at the overhead the gang has," Gerry explained. "Four members, plus the cost of the cap and a police scanner. Oh, and there's George Scalzo's take to consider, since he's bankrolling this operation. Fifteen hundred a night hardly covers the cost of doing business."

"You've lost me," Marconi said. "If fifteen hundred isn't enough money, then why were they cheating Bally's? For laughs?"

Gerry asked to see the cap again, and turned it over. The expert tailoring job was the clue. A pro had stitched this cap, and if his hunch was correct, many more just like it.

"If my hunch is right, there are more members of this gang cheating Bally's, not just the ones you were after," Gerry said.

Marconi and Davis snapped to attention.

"Can you prove that?" Davis asked him.

"I sure can," Gerry said.

Marconi drove them to Bally's with the gaffed baseball cap on his head. During the drive, he broke the news to Davis that his prized Mustang had been totaled from Gerry ramming it into Abruzzi's car. Davis stared out the window and sulked.

"You'll find another one," Marconi said.

"Like hell I will," Davis replied.

Bally's entrance was jammed with tour buses. Marconi maneuvered around them and parked by the valet stand. As they got out, he said, "Boat people."

Boat people was casino slang for senior citizens. Like every other casino in Atlantic City, Bally's relied on seniors to make its nut. They were easy customers, staying long enough to squander their social security checks in slot and video poker machines. Inside they found a sea of white hair and polyester. They walked to the cashier's cage where Marconi cornered the casino's floor manager, a red-faced man wearing a purple sports jacket. Marconi explained why they were there.

"You want to do *what*?" the floor manager said.

"Go up to your surveillance control room and take a look at some tapes," Marconi said.

"Gaining entrance to that room takes a fricking act of Congress," the floor manager said. "I need to tell the people upstairs what this is about."

Marconi took off the cap, and showed the floor manager the rim. "This cap was used to scam your blackjack tables. We want to watch the tapes of the guy who was wearing it. Think you can arrange that?"

The floor manager muttered something unpleasant and left. Casino people were fiercely territorial, and tended to bang heads with cops as a matter of principle. They went into a coffee shop to wait.

"Do senior citizens rip off casinos?" Marconi asked a few minutes later.

Gerry had ordered coffee and was gulping it down to stay awake. "Seniors can be as bad as anyone else. My father nailed a gang who were stealing six figures a year."

"What were they doing, putting slugs in slot machines?" Marconi asked.

Gerry shook his head.

"Fudging their Keno cards?" Davis asked.

Gerry shook his head again. "It was a bus scam. The tour operator was in cahoots with them."

Cops liked to think they knew everything when it

came to crime. Davis and Marconi traded looks, then stared Gerry down.

"What the hell's a bus scam?" Davis asked.

Gerry put down his coffee. "The casino was paying a tour operator ten dollars a head to bus seniors in twice a week. The seniors had a larcenous streak, and told the tour operator they'd inflate the count if he'd split the money with them."

"They stole six figures doing this?" Marconi asked incredulously.

"Yeah. The tour operator was bringing in ten buses, twice a week. The count on each bus was being inflated by ten heads. That's two grand a week."

Marconi and Davis dealt with bad people every day, but this seemed to bother them. If Gerry had learned anything working for his father, it was that gambling made people do things that they wouldn't ordinarily do. He finished his drink.

"How did your father nail them?" Davis asked.

"My father was working the casino on another case," Gerry said. "He happened to walk outside, and saw the tour operator throwing unopened box lunches into a Dumpster. He mentioned it to management, and was told the casino gave each senior a boxed lunch as part of the deal. My father went outside, and counted all the boxes in the Dumpster. That's when he figured out what they were doing."

"Did the seniors go to jail?" Davis asked.

"No one went to jail," Gerry said. "The tour operator gave his share back, and did community service. The seniors had spent theirs, so they worked it off at the casino."

"That your father's idea?" Davis asked.

Gerry nodded. His father believed in giving first-time offenders a pass, provided they were truly repentant. Everyone involved in this case had been. The floor manager appeared at the entrance to the restaurant, and motioned to them impatiently. They settled the bill, then came out to where the floor manager waited.

"You've got clearance," the floor manager said.

Bally's surveillance control room was the heart and soul of its security operation. Housed on the third floor, it was a windowless, claustrophobic room filled with the finest snooping equipment money could buy. The room was kept at a chilly sixty degrees, and each technician wore several layers of clothing. The floor manager led them past a wall of video monitors to a master console in the rear of the room, where a short, bespectacled man wearing a gray turtleneck sat with his fingers clutched around a joystick.

"They're all yours," the floor manager said.

The floor manager left, and Marconi introduced himself, Davis, and Gerry. The man at the console removed his glasses and quizzed Gerry with a glance.

"You Tony Valentine's son?"

"Sure am," Gerry said.

"Your father taught me the ropes," the man said. "We used to say your father could see a gnat's ass and hear a mouse piss. How's he doing?"

"Great," Gerry said.

"Glad to hear it. My name's Lou Preston. I hear you want to watch some tapes."

Gerry explained the blackjack scam with the baseball

cap to Lou Preston. When he was finished, Preston's head was bobbing up and down.

"So you think there might have been more cheaters wearing these caps," Preston said. "Can you give me an approximate time when this took place?"

"Around four o'clock this morning," Marconi said.

"What exactly did the caps look like?" Preston asked.

Marconi took the cap off his head and gave it to Preston. Preston placed the cap beneath the reading light on his console, and spent a few moments examining it.

"Let's see if we can find this cap in our digital library," he said.

Preston began to type on the keyboard on his console. Like most large casinos, Bally's used digital video recorders to continuously tape the action on the floor. It was a far cry from the old days, when the tapes in VCRs had to be switched every hour. Within seconds, four tapes appeared on a matrix on Preston's computer screen. Each tape showed a different man in the casino wearing a baseball cap while playing blackjack.

"These four gentlemen were playing blackjack in our casino at four o'clock this morning," Preston said. "Is one of them your guy?"

Marconi pointed at the guy in the right-hand corner of the matrix. "That's him."

Preston dragged the cursor over the picture and clicked on it. The picture enlarged to show a guy in his early fifties wearing a Yankees cap and smoking a cigar. He wore his shirt open, and hanging around his neck were several thick gold chains.

Preston did some more magic with his cursor, and the

baseball cap became the only thing on the screen. He struck the ENTER key, then leaned back in his chair.

"In sixty seconds we'll know if your hunch is correct," he told Gerry.

The hard drive on Preston's console made a whirring sound. Marconi and Davis looked confused, and Gerry guessed they weren't up to speed on the latest technology being employed by casinos to track cheaters. Pointing at the baseball cap, he said, "Lou just burned an image of this cap into his computer. He's asked the computer to take a look at all recent tapes, and see how many similar caps turn up. Within a minute we'll know how many there were."

"I thought that took hours," Davis said.

"*Used* to take hours," Preston corrected him. "We now use Kalatel DVRs to record digitally. It's light years faster than before. We can search the tapes for anything we want."

"Beats using a catwalk, huh?" Gerry said.

"Personally, I liked the catwalks," Preston said. "Gave me plenty of exercise. They did have their drawbacks, though. One time, I was on the catwalk with a camera with a zoom lens, trying to photograph a cheater switching dice. There was a two-way mirror in the ceiling, and as I tried to photograph the switch, the cheater stared straight up at me. I must have leaned on the mirror, because dust was falling down on his head. Needless to say, he ran like hell."

The hard drive had stopped whirring, and Preston hit ENTER again.

"Bingo," he said. "Four matches."

They huddled behind his chair, and Preston pulled up

each match the computer had made. Four men, all Italian, with ages ranging from late forties to late fifties, wearing jewelry around their necks or hands, and wearing Yankees baseball caps.

"Looks like a casting call for *The Sopranos*," Marconi said.

Gerry felt a hand on his shoulder, and glanced at Davis.

"Good job," Davis said.

Preston e-mailed copies of each man's image to the Atlantic City Police Department to be checked against its database of known criminals. Then he escorted his guests through the surveillance control room to the door. As Marconi and Davis walked into the hall, Preston turned to Gerry.

"One thing's bothering me," Preston said. "Why me?"

Gerry didn't understand the question.

"Let me rephrase that. Why *my* casino?" Preston said. "There are a dozen casinos on the island; why did these guys pick mine? It's a question I always ask myself when we get ripped off. Is there a flaw in our system, or did a security person on the floor get paid to look the other way? Or is there another reason?"

"Such as?"

"Maybe your hunch is correct," Preston said. "Maybe the scam *is* bigger than everyone thought. Makes sense, don't you think?"

Gerry realized he was nodding. Talking to Lou Preston was like talking to his old man. Lou knew how cheaters thought, and had grift sense. "You think this gang might be hitting *all* the casinos on the island?" Gerry asked.

"I don't see why not."

"How can we check?"

"Easy," Preston said. "Atlantic City's casinos are connected through a system called SIN. Stands for Secure Internal Network. We use it primarily to alert each other about teams of card counters. I'll use SIN to alert them about the Yankees caps, and ask the casinos to run the same check that I ran. Who knows? We might hit gold."

Lou was smiling, and Gerry realized why. Lou knew the outcome of what that check would be. They were going to find mobsters with Yankees caps in other casinos.

"Just one second," Gerry said.

Going into the hall, Gerry went to where Davis and Marconi waited by the elevators. They looked ready to call it a day, and Gerry put a hand on each of their shoulders.

"Sorry, guys, but we're not done yet," he said.

22

Within sixty seconds of Takarama being dragged out of Celebrity's casino, the mess around the roulette table was cleaned up and the croupier was back spinning the little white ball while happily exhorting the crowd to "Place your bets! Place your bets!"

Flush with cash, Rufus Steele threw a fan of hundred-dollar bills on the layout. He had collected his winnings from the Greek and the other suckers who'd bet against him, and his pockets were overflowing with money. "Five thousand on the black," he said.

The ball rolled around the wheel and dropped on a black number. A number of bystanders broke into wild applause and Rufus bowed to them.

"Is he always so lucky?" Gloria Curtis asked.

Valentine stood off to the side with Gloria and Zack. He wanted to tell her that up until a few days ago, Rufus had been flat broke, but he bit his tongue. He had never liked hustlers, yet hanging around Rufus, his sense of fair play had become curiously elastic.

"He's got the magic touch," he said.

Rufus joined them and smiled at Gloria. "I owe you, Ms. Curtis," he said.

"You do?" she asked.

"Moon balls."

"How about an interview?" she asked.

"You know me," Rufus said. "I love to talk."

They walked out of the casino and across the lobby to the entrance of Celebrity's poker room. A leader board had been erected by the front doors. Skip DeMarco was still in a commanding position, with everyone else far behind. Rufus read the board, then made a disparaging noise that originated deep in his throat.

Gloria's cameraman did a sound check, then held his hand up in the air.

"Five . . . four . . . three . . . two . . . one. We're rolling."

"This is Gloria Curtis, coming to you from the World Poker Showdown in Las Vegas," Gloria said into her mike. "Standing beside me is legendary gambler Rufus Steele, who just beat a former world champion Ping-Pong champion in a winner-take-all match for half a million dollars. Rufus, you've beaten a race horse in the hundred-yard dash, and now you've beaten a world champion athlete. What's next?"

"Once this tournament is over, Skip DeMarco and I are going to sit down and play poker for two million dollars, winner-take-all," Rufus said.

"DeMarco is the tournament's chip leader, and considers himself the best poker player in the world," Gloria said. "How do you rate your chances against him?"

"Being the chip leader doesn't mean much," Rufus said. "Neither does playing in a tournament. People who play in tournaments for a living are what gamblers call fun players. When they're not playing, they're singing in the church choir or playing volleyball at the YMCA."

"Are you saying that DeMarco is *not* the best player in the world?"

A smile spread across Rufus's leathery face. "I don't mean to be disrespectful, but every time that boy gets on television and says he's the best, a few dozen guys around the country jump out of their chairs and run to the toilet before they ruin the rug."

"How would you rate him?"

"I wouldn't."

"But he's the tournament chip leader. Surely that means something."

Rufus's smile spread. "Afraid not."

"Could you explain?"

"A tournament is several days long, and luck plays a big part in determining the winner. When DeMarco and I play, luck won't have anything to do with the outcome."

"If DeMarco does win the tournament, will that change your opinion of him?"

The friendly expression vanished from Rufus's face and he scowled at the camera. "Giving DeMarco a trophy and calling him the best player in the world is like putting whip cream on a hot dog. No, it wouldn't change my opinion of him one bit."

Beating Takarama at Ping-Pong had gotten Rufus's competitive juices flowing, and once again he denounced DeMarco, as though the sheer volume of his

angry words would expose the younger man as a fraud.
It gave Valentine an idea, and he slipped inside the poker
room.

The World Poker Showdown had started with over
five thousand players, and probably just as many dreams.
Less than a hundred remained, and they sat at a dozen
felt tables in the room's center, bathed in bright TV
lights and surrounded by fans. At the feature table was
DeMarco with seven other players.

Standing on his tiptoes, Valentine watched DeMarco
play. He was a handsome kid, and seemed to be enjoying himself. Tournament poker was different from your
friendly neighborhood game because of the elimination
process. If you played a couple of bad hands in tournament poker, you were gone. As a result, most people
played tight, and bet only when they had good cards.

But DeMarco didn't play this way. Because of his
blindness, he held his two cards up to his face, then
placed them on the table, and did not look at them
again. Instead, he focused his attention on his opponents' bets and calls. When the bet came to him, he in-
evitably made the right decision, and either threw away
a losing hand—which he flashed to the table—or stayed
in with winning cards. The crowd was in his corner, and
each decision was met with thunderous applause.

Backing away from the table, Valentine shook his
head. The whole thing smelled like three-day-old fish.
DeMarco wasn't playing cards—he was *acting* like
someone playing cards. Had he any common sense, he
would have purposely lost a hand, just to keep things
looking normal. Only he liked to showboat.

Valentine's eyes scanned the room. DeMarco didn't

go anywhere without his handlers, and George Scalzo and his bodyguard stood by the bar, watching their boy. Nevada did not let mobsters into its casinos, and Valentine still did not understand how Scalzo had managed to be at the tournament and not get arrested. A cocktail waitress walked by, and he touched her arm.

"I need a favor," Valentine said.

"I'm busy," she said curtly.

He dug out his wallet and stuffed a twenty into the tip glass on her tray.

"Name it," she said.

He borrowed her pen and a frilly cocktail napkin. On the napkin he wrote:

HEY GEORGIE, YOUR BOY IS GETTING TRASHED IN THE LOBBY

He handed it back to her. "See the guy that looks like Don Corleone?" He pointed across the room at Scalzo. "I want you to give him this."

The waitress walked away with a bemused look on her face that made him think of his son's crack about him playing cops and robbers. She delivered the note. Scalzo read it, then crumbled the napkin into a ball. He motioned to his bodyguard, and they marched out of the poker room.

It was the opportunity Valentine had been waiting for. He edged up to the feature table, and pushed his way through the crowd until he was in front. A new hand was about to begin, and he stared intently at the table. The tournament had gotten nailed several days ago for employing dealers with criminal records, and he watched the dealer at the table shuffle the cards. The shuffle looked fair, as did the cut that followed it, but something about the dealer's body language wasn't right. The dealer, who had a walrus moustache and a square jaw, looked apprehensive. It could have been the presence of the TV cameras, but Valentine's gut told him otherwise.

Each player got two face-down cards, and the dealer sailed them around the table in a slow, deliberate manner. It was slower than any deal Valentine had ever seen, and he found himself staring at the dealer's hands. The dealer's right hand, his dealing hand, was completely stiff. That wasn't normal.

Finished, the dealer placed the deck on the table. Dealers who used sleight-of-hand to cheat were always conscious of their manipulations. No matter how good they were, they knew that a trained observer could nail them. As a result, there was always a moment of truth after the cheating was done.

The dealer looked up. There was hesitation in his eyes. He glanced into the crowd of spectators and saw Valentine. He swallowed hard.

Gotcha, Valentine thought.

Valentine had always liked movies when the cavalry showed up to save the day, and felt an adrenaline rush seeing Pete Longo and three uniformed cops come barging into the poker room. They were moving fast, the uniforms having unsnapped the harness on their revolvers. He wondered if they were going to nail DeMarco, or the dealer, or both of them. It was about time.

The crowd was slow to get out of their way, and Longo flashed his silver detective's badge to hurry them along. Valentine stared at the dealer, and saw a look of panic distorting his face.

Longo came up to the tournament director, and the two men had a talk. Part of the director's job was to act as an MC, and announce when players had won hands. To do this, he used a hand-held microphone, which he now raised to his face. "Ladies and gentlemen, we're going to have a five-minute recess. Dealers, please stop your games and reshuffle. Thank you."

Longo and the three uniforms had broken away from the tournament director, and were coming around the table. The dealer had pushed his chair back and placed both his hands palms down on the felt, a sure sign that he'd been arrested before. Longo walked past the dealer and directly toward Valentine while barking an order to the uniforms. Reaching into his jacket, Longo removed a pair of handcuffs from the clip on his belt.

"Tony, you're under arrest," Longo said.

"For what?" Valentine said incredulously.

"Two counts of second-degree murder."

"You're making a mistake," Valentine said.

"Like hell I am. Lift your arms into the air."

The crowd was giving the police plenty of room now, and Valentine felt their hostile stares. He'd arrested hundreds of people in his life, and had always wondered what it felt like. Now, he was going to find out.

He lifted his arms into the air, and a uniform frisked him. Then his wrists were handcuffed behind his back. He hadn't done anything wrong, but that didn't matter;

he *felt* like he'd done something wrong, and his face was burning.

As Longo led him out of the poker room and into the lobby, Gloria and Rufus stood off to the side, watching with horrified faces. Valentine wanted to tell them that he was innocent, but instead stared down at the ugly carpet as he walked past.

23

Skip DeMarco sat frozen in his chair. There were cops in the room—he could feel the tension in the air—but he couldn't hear what was being said. Had they figured out the scam, and were they about to arrest him? He tried to act nonchalant, and shuffled a stack of chips with one hand. What was his uncle's expression? Never run if you're not being chased. The chips fell out of his hand and spilled across the table. He felt himself shudder uncontrollably.

"Here you go," the dealer said, pushing the chips back.

"What's going on?"

"The cops just arrested some guy in the crowd," the dealer said.

The dealer's voice was strained, like he was afraid of something. Although his uncle had not explained how the scam worked, DeMarco knew someone in the room was reading his opponents' cards and signaling them to him. He'd ruled out the dealer, simply because the dealer had a job to do. But now he sensed the dealer was involved. DeMarco felt a hand on his shoulder, and nearly jumped out of his chair.

"Sorry to startle you," the tournament director said. "We're taking a break. You're free to get up."

DeMarco rose from the table. He waited for Guido and his uncle to appear. When they didn't, he grew nervous. Where had they gone? And why hadn't they told him they were leaving? The guy sitting next to him announced he was going to the bathroom. His name was Bruce Ballas, and when he wasn't playing cards, he was strumming a guitar in a band. DeMarco asked if he could walk with him.

"Sure," Ballas said.

They walked together to the lavatory. The joke of the tournament was that the men's lavatory had a dozen stalls, the women's only three. Ballas led DeMarco to an empty stall at the end of the row, and he locked himself in.

Sitting, he buried his face in his hands. When his uncle had come to him with a way to scam the World Poker Showdown, he hadn't hesitated to say yes. The scam would let him cheat the people who'd cheated him, and claim what was rightfully his. But he'd never considered that he might get caught. How stupid was that?

His chest was heaving up and down. He took several deep breaths, and told himself to calm down.

Ballas was waiting when DeMarco came out a minute later. "There's a woman wants to talk to you," Ballas said. "Said she was a big fan, wanted to say hi."

"Nice looking?" DeMarco asked.

"A major league speed bump," Ballas said.

DeMarco had promised his uncle not to talk to strangers. Only he'd heard the other players talking about the women they'd seen hanging around the tournament. Women beautiful beyond compare. He'd gone to bed thinking about them every night.

"Lead the way," he said.

Ballas led him to a table in the corner of the room. DeMarco heard the woman rise from a chair, felt her hand clasp his. Her perfume was strong and lilac scented. He envisioned a long-legged, dark-haired beauty, and waited to hear what she had to say.

"Hello, Skipper," she said. "Do you remember me?"

He felt something catch in his throat. Her voice was vaguely familiar, but he could not place from where. "I don't know if I remember you or not," he said.

"You were little. It was a long time ago."

"How long?"

"Twenty years. You were a child."

"You worked for my uncle as a nanny, right?"

"No, I was before your uncle," she said.

The tournament director's voice came over the public address system. Play would resume in one minute, and players needed to return to their seats. Ballas touched DeMarco's sleeve, said he was going back to the game.

"I'll get back on my own," DeMarco said.

"You sure?" Ballas asked.

DeMarco said yes. Ballas walked away, and DeMarco asked, "What do you mean, before my uncle?"

"You had a life before you went to live with George Scalzo," she said. "I was a part of it."

"What are you talking about?"

"I used to make you raisin cookies and sing you

songs. On your birthday, I bought you a Roy Rogers costume, and you went to your party as a cowboy."

DeMarco heard a series of rapid clicks in his earpiece. Play had resumed, the dealer sailing the cards around the table. The clicks were in Morse code, the dots and dashes telling him what cards his opponents held. He listened intently. His opponents had ace–king, a pair of deuces, 2–9, a pair of fours, 7–8 of clubs, and a k–9, also known as a Canine. He didn't like missing the hand, but wanted to hear the woman out.

"You didn't work for my uncle?" he asked.

"No."

"Then who are you?"

The woman grabbed his wrist and tried to stuff something into his hand. It was stiff, and felt like a photograph. When he wouldn't take it, she shoved it into the breast pocket of his shirt.

"What did you just give me?" he asked.

"A gift. I saw you on the television, and flew here from Philadelphia to see you."

"Please let go of my wrist," he said.

She released him and he stepped back. He wanted to tell this woman to stuff her head in a toilet. The only person in his life before Uncle George was his mother, and she was lying dead in a cemetery in New Jersey. Uncle George had taken him to her grave.

"I tried to contact you many times," she said, "but your uncle wouldn't let me near you. I even once tried to visit you at school. Do you remember that?"

"No," he said.

"You were in the third grade. I came to the school, and the teacher pulled you from the class."

"I don't know what you're talking about, lady. I need to go."

"Your uncle sent his bodyguard to my house in Philadelphia," she said. "He threatened me. Said he'd hurt my family if I tried to contact you. So I stayed away."

"Good," he said.

"You don't care?" she said.

"Not in the least."

She stifled a tiny sob. He'd wounded her, and heard her hurry away. *So this is what it feels like to be a celebrity,* he thought.

DeMarco let the noise of the poker room guide him back to the table. Before he reached his chair, his uncle was by his side, holding his arm and breathing on his neck. "Skipper, where the hell you been?" his uncle asked.

"Some woman grabbed me, started chewing my ear off," DeMarco said.

"I don't want you talking to strangers," his uncle said.

"So tell the strangers that."

DeMarco returned to his seat. The hand was still going on, with two players playing for a huge pot. It pissed him off to know he'd missed out, and in anger removed the photograph the woman had given him from his pocket, ready to tear it up. Ballas, who'd dropped out of the hand, spoke up.

"Man, you haven't changed a bit."

"What do you mean?" DeMarco said.

"The photograph."

"What about it?"

"You haven't changed since you were a kid. It looks just like you."

DeMarco stiffened, then raised the photograph to his face, and stared at the little boy dressed in shorts and bright red suspenders staring back at him.

24

"**S**o what?" Valentine asked.

"What do you mean, 'so what?' " Longo said.

"A chambermaid found my bloody shirt in the trash in my bathroom. So what?"

They sat in Longo's cluttered office at Metro Las Vegas Police Department headquarters, a few blocks from Glitter Gulch. The door was open, and in the other detectives' offices they could hear suspects lying their fool heads off. *Their* conversation felt normal, only Valentine was handcuffed to the arm of a chair. Lying on the messy desk was a tagged evidence bag containing his bloody shirt.

"It's a solid piece of evidence—" Longo said.

"That I had a bloody nose."

"—to you murdering those two guys."

"You're making a big leap, Pete."

"I'm too old for that," Longo said.

"What are you, fifty? That's not old."

Longo pushed himself back from his desk. He'd dropped a lot of weight in the past six months, and his face looked like a refugee's. "Tell me what happened again."

"Two guys barged into our room and attacked us," Valentine said. "My nose got busted during the scuffle, and I bled all over myself."

"Are you saying our forensics team won't find any of those guys' blood on this shirt?"

"I kneed one of them in the face. He may have bled on me. That's not evidence to hold me for suspicion of murder, and you know it."

"No one's arguing that an altercation occurred in your suite," Longo said. "But the fact is, you and Rufus Steele are still walking around, and those two guys are growing cold in the morgue. I have to treat this as evidence."

"How long will it take your forensic people to examine the shirt?

"A day or two."

Valentine tried to raise his hand to his face, and heard the handcuff's chain rattle. The tournament would be over by then. Had someone set him up, just to take him out of the picture? There was a cold cup of coffee on the desk. He raised it to his lips with his free hand and took a slurp. Longo glanced up from his paperwork.

"Someone from the hotel called you and told you about the shirt, didn't they?" Valentine asked.

"That's right," Longo said.

"They also told you I was in Celebrity's poker room."

"Right again."

The cup was empty, and Valentine stared at grains. Before he'd taken the job, the hotel's general manager, a stuffed suit named Mark Perrier, had threatened him with a lawsuit if Celebrity's reputation was smeared by Jack Donovan's murder investigation.

"Was it Mark Perrier, the general manager?"

Longo put his pencil down, trying not to act surprised. "Who told you that?"

"Believe it or not, I figured it out by myself," Valentine said.

"You have a history with this guy?"

"He threatened me a week ago. Didn't want me investigating his tournament. This was before Bill Higgins hired me."

Longo gave him a thoughtful look. "You're saying Perrier set you up."

"I'm investigating a cheating scandal inside *his* hotel. Of course he set me up. Last night, I had you paraffin me for gunshot residue. I may have changed my shirt, but I hadn't showered. Do you think I would have told you to give me the test if I'd shot those guys?"

Most cops didn't like the kind of backward logic he was throwing at Longo. It made them go outside their comfort zones. Longo looked at the bagged shirt.

"I need to wait for the blood test," he said.

"You mean you're going to hold me," Valentine said, exasperated.

"Afraid so."

A woman's voice came out of the black squawk box on the desk. Longo pressed a button on the box. "Hey Lydia, what's up?"

"Bill Higgins, director of the Nevada Gaming—"

"I know who Higgins is," he snapped. "Is he on the line? Tell him I'm busy and will call him back."

"He's standing next to my desk," she said.

Longo clenched his teeth. "Send him in," he said, and took his finger off the button.

Like most people who worked in law enforcement, Bill had a tough side. When he got angry, he tended to throw his considerable weight around. He was doing that now, and Longo was shrinking in his chair.

"How dare you arrest Tony without first calling me," Bill said, leaning on Longo's desk like he was going to do a push-up. "I got authorization from the goddamn governor to keep Tony on this job. You're screwing with my investigation. If you don't let Tony go right now, I'll burn your ass so badly you won't be able to sit down."

The lowlifes and miscreants in the other detectives' offices had stopped talking, the only sound coming from the overhead air-conditioning. Longo pointed at the bagged shirt lying on the desk. "What about this?"

"So what?" Bill said, mimicking Valentine perfectly.

"It's evidence," Longo protested.

"It corroborates Tony's story, but it doesn't corroborate *your* story," Bill said. "Why don't you ask the hotel to show you the surveillance tapes from the stairwell, if you want to know who shot those two scumbags? There's your evidence, Pete."

"I already asked the hotel," Longo said.

"And?"

"They said there isn't a surveillance camera in the stairwell," Longo said. "It's optional under state law to have cameras in stairwells, and they didn't do it."

"Who told you that?" Bill asked.

Longo swallowed a rising lump in his throat. "Mark Perrier."

"Perrier fed you that line of bullshit?"

"How do you know it's bullshit?" Longo asked.

"Because any door leading off the main lobby of a casino, or its hotel, must have a working surveillance camera according to Nevada state law," Bill said. "The stairwell where those two scumbags got plugged was right off the lobby. Celebrity couldn't have gotten a license to operate its casino if there wasn't a camera in there."

"But why would Perrier lie?" Longo asked.

Bill finally did his push-up. He worked out religiously, and looked like he could do a hundred of them. "I don't know, Pete, why don't you ask him?"

Rubbing his wrist, Valentine walked out of Longo's office and followed Bill past a warren of detective's offices to the main reception area. In one office, a black pimp was getting processed by the detective who'd arrested him. The pimp wore flashy clothes and enough gold jewelry to open a pawn shop. Seeing Bill, he threw up his arms.

"I need you, man," the pimp said.

Bill stopped in the open doorway. "What did you say to me?"

"I said I need you. You know, your services."

Both of the pimp's wrists were cuffed to his chair, a sure sign he was a threat. On the desk were his personal belongings, which included an enormous wad of cash and a handful of hundred-dollar black casino chips.

"What the hell are you talking about?" Bill asked.

The pimp glanced sideways at the detective who'd busted him, then looked at Bill. "I heard you chewing out that mother down the hall. You sound like you know your stuff. What's your going rate?"

"You think I'm a lawyer?"

The pimp acted startled. "You're not?"

Bill marched into the office. Grabbing the chips off the desk, he began peeling back the paper logo on each one. Valentine guessed Bill was looking for the microchip that casinos were required to put in chips over twenty dollars in value. The pimp's chips didn't have the microchips, and Bill shoved them into the arresting detective's face.

"These are counterfeits," Bill said. "Nail this asshole."

Part III

Deadman's Hand

25

Lou Preston had struck gold.

The director of surveillance for Bally's Atlantic City casino had contacted the island's eleven other casinos, and persuaded them to search their digital databases for any blackjack players who'd recently beaten them and who'd been wearing New York Yankees baseball caps. The search had turned up forty-eight players, all of whom were between the ages of forty and sixty and of Italian descent. Casinos kept records on players who won a thousand dollars or more, and each of these players fell into that category.

As the casinos e-mailed pictures of the players to Preston, Lou projected them onto the wall of video monitors in Bally's surveillance control room. Gerry, Eddie Davis, and Joey Marconi stood in front of the wall, drinking coffee the color of transmission fluid while watching a montage of sleaze take shape before them.

"These guys give Italians a bad name," Marconi said.

Gerry sipped his drink, his eyes floating from face to face. The Mafia's great strength was also its great weakness. The mob didn't let in outsiders, and consequently there were no women, Asians, blacks, or Hispanics in their ranks. It was all mean-faced, middle-aged Italians with fifties haircuts who tended to stick out like sore thumbs.

He tossed his coffee cup into the trash. His father was always saying that people got what was coming to them. He'd never believed that, especially when it came to crime, but now had a feeling his father was right. George Scalzo was about to get what was coming to him.

He went to the master console where Preston sat. Lou had gotten the directors of surveillance of the other casinos to send him any notes they had on the men whose faces were on the monitors. Surveillance technicians kept copious notes during their shifts, and wrote down anything that was deemed unusual.

"Anything interesting?" Gerry asked.

"All of these guys refused Player's Cards when they were offered to them," Preston said. "That's not normal."

It was standard practice for casinos to offer gamblers Player's Cards. The card entitled the person to receive complimentary meals and show tickets and even rooms if their business was strong enough.

"Guess they didn't want to hand over their identification," Gerry said.

"My thoughts exactly," Preston said. "Forty-eight players, all refusing comps. What do you think the odds of that are?"

"Pretty astronomical," Gerry said.

Preston picked up the gaffed Yankees cap lying on the console. There was a can of soda beside it, which he also picked up. "It's one more piece of evidence that these players are part of a massive conspiracy to defraud Atlantic City's casinos."

"So let's find out who they are, and arrest them."

"I wish it was that easy."

"What do you mean?"

Preston killed the can and wiped his mouth on his sleeve. "The police don't have a digital database like we do. It would take hundreds of hours for them to figure out who these guys are, maybe more."

"Won't they do that?"

Preston rubbed his face tiredly. "They would if they had the manpower. The island's high crime rate isn't going down anytime soon. The police won't pull officers off the street to do photo matches."

Gerry felt his spirits sink. Ruining Scalzo's Atlantic City operation was the sweetest payback he could think of. He stared at a montage of faces on the video wall.

"I can find out who they are," Gerry said.

Preston sat up straight in his chair. "You can?"

"Yeah. Ever heard of a guy named Vinny Fountain?"

"Vinny 'the Sleazy Weasel' Fountain? Sure."

"I know him. Vinny's rubbed elbows with mob guys his entire life. I'll get their names from Vinny, and the police can find out where they live. My father told me that once the police know where a cheater lives, he's history."

"That's true," Preston said. "The cops will stake out the cheater's house. When the cheater goes to a casino, the cops alert the casino, and the casino follows him around with surveillance cameras. Once he makes his move, they pounce."

"So we'll screw Scalzo's gang that way," Gerry said.

"Are you sure Vinny will help you?" Preston asked. "Generally speaking, hoods won't rat out other hoods."

Gerry and Vinny Fountain had nearly died in a warehouse on the outskirts of Las Vegas. Gerry's father had rescued them, and Vinny owed Gerry's father his life. Gerry had no problem calling in that marker.

"He'll help," Gerry said.

Harold's House of Pancakes was an Atlantic City institution. Of the two hundred restaurants that had once flourished on the island's north end, Harold's was one of the last standing. It served greasy breakfast food all day, its signature egg dish called "the whore's special" by locals. Marconi pulled into the parking lot, and grabbed a spot by the front door. Davis, who rode shotgun, turned to look at Gerry in back.

"I don't like you going in there alone," Davis said.

"You want to check the place out first?" Gerry asked. "Be my guest."

Davis climbed out and went inside. The way he was moving, you wouldn't know he'd gotten his back sliced open while dodging a bullet a few hours ago. It was the one characteristic about cops that Gerry had always admired. Davis reappeared moments later. "Your friend's in a booth in the back."

Gerry got out of the car, wondering how Davis had made Vinny. The answer became obvious as he entered the restaurant. The girls were out in force, and Vinny was the only male in the place. Prostitution was a part of Atlantic City's culture, and had only gotten worse with the casinos. He slid into Vinny's booth.

"That cop with you?" Vinny asked.

"My bodyguard, courtesy of my father," Gerry said.

"Your old man still watches out for you, doesn't he?"
Gerry nodded.

"That's nice. My old man hardly talks to me anymore. You said over the phone you wanted me to look
at some photographs."

Gerry removed an envelope from his jacket pocket,
slid it across the table. "Some mobsters are running a
blackjack scam in town. They're working for our friend,
George Scalzo. I was hoping you'd look at these photos,
and see if you know any of them."

Vinny took a cigarette out of the ashtray, and blew a
monster cloud of smoke in the air. You weren't supposed to smoke in Harold's, but people did anyway.
Two hookers at the next table started hacking their
lungs out. Vinny ignored them.

"You trying to take Scalzo down?"

"I'm working on it," Gerry said.

"You going to pay him back for what he did to us in
Vegas?"

"Yeah, and for killing Jack Donovan."

Vinny flashed a crooked smile. He was a skinny guy,
with pocked skin and bad teeth. What set him apart was
his ability to talk. Opening the envelope up, he said,
"Walk up to the cash register, and see if it doesn't send
you down memory lane."

"What am I looking for?"

Vinny laughed through a mouthful of smoke. "Our
first scam together," he said.

*   *   *

Gerry slid out of the booth and went up to the register. He kept his eyes to the floor, avoiding the working girls' sideways glances. The first pretty girl he'd ever seen was a hooker trolling the Atlantic City Boardwalk. He'd been eight, and his mother had told him this was not the type of girl he wanted to know.

The cashier was a wizened old man with half-dead eyes. He had a tic in his neck that didn't quit. It was the only way you could tell he was alive.

"Need something?" the cashier asked.

Gerry spotted the ultraviolet light sitting next to the register and nearly burst into laughter. He'd done a lot of dumb things as a teenager, and selling ultraviolet lights to every store owner on the island had been one of them.

"I need a menu," Gerry said.

Gerry returned to the booth with a menu and a smile on his face.

"Pretty funny, huh?" Vinny said.

"We should tell the guy," Gerry said.

"No, we shouldn't," Vinny said.

Back during their senior year in high school, Vinny had purchased several boxes of ultraviolet lights from a merchant on Canal Street in New York. Then he and Gerry had pooled their money together, which had amounted to eight hundred bucks, and Vinny had gone to the bank and exchanged it for eight new hundred-dollar bills.

Vinny had painted the hundred-dollar bills with ultraviolet paint, which when dry was invisible to the naked eye. Gerry's job had been to go to different restaurants on the island, and spend the hundred-dollar bill on a meal. A few hours later, Vinny would come in, posing as a salesman. He'd tell the owner that a lot of counterfeit hundreds were floating around, and that the special light he was selling could detect them. He always offered to give a demonstration.

The owner would take the hundred-dollar bills from his register, and run them beneath the light. The doctored bill would light up like it was radioactive. Vinny would tell the owner that by federal law, he had to confiscate the counterfeit and turn it over to the FBI. He'd pretend to feel bad for the owner's situation, and offer to sell him the ultraviolet light at cost, which he claimed was fifty bucks. The owner always said yes.

"That was some summer," Gerry said.

"I bought a car," Vinny said, pouring through the photographs.

"So did I."

"Mine was nicer."

A waitress took Gerry's order. He asked for the whore's special. She raised a disapproving eyebrow while tapping her pencil on her pad.

"You some kind of comedian?" she asked.

"He's a native," Vinny said.

"One whore's special it is," she said.

Vinny continued poring over the photographs. Like Gerry, he'd flunked out of college, but had plenty of street smarts and a good memory. Shaking his head, he slipped the photographs back into the envelope. "Don't know them. They must be from off island. What's the deal with the baseball caps?"

Gerry lowered his voice. "There's a receiver and three LEDs sewn into the rim of the cap. The cards at the table are nail-nicked. A member of the gang reads the nicks, and knows what the dealer is holding. He electronically transmits the information to the guy wearing the cap."

"Wow," Vinny said. "You got the cap?"

Gerry hesitated. Vinny was, and always would be, a scammer. He didn't want to be giving him any ideas, especially when it involved a case he was working on.

"It's outside in the car," Gerry said.

"Get it," Vinny said.

"I can't."

"Why not?"

"The detectives working the case are in the car."

"So what? I'm trying to help you bury Scalzo, aren't I?"

Gerry's food arrived. Three eggs sunny-side up, a gristly piece of ham, and a mound of hash fries swimming in bubbling grease. The cook hadn't lost his touch.

"How can you help me bury Scalzo if you can't identify these guys?" Gerry asked.

Vinny lit a cigarette off the one he was smoking. He blew another cloud at the girls at the next table and got them coughing. "Easy. I'll find out who made the cap."

26

It doesn't get any better than this, Karl Jasper thought.

Jasper stood at the rear of the crowd in Celebrity's poker room, chewing an unlit cigar. The scene was absolutely beautiful. Skip DeMarco was beating the pants off the competition and the spectators were cheering his every move. The kid was going to be known in every home in America by the tournament's end. *Every home.*

Jasper watched the action while trying to calculate how much money DeMarco would make in endorsements. He'd cut his teeth working for a Madison Avenue ad agency, and could not look at success without equating it with a dollar figure.

Only trying to figure out DeMarco's worth was tricky. The kid was an overnight sensation, and advertisers tended to be wary of those. But DeMarco appealed to that all-important demographic—males eighteen to forty-nine—which meant he could endorse anything from condoms to cars, and be a hit.

Finally Jasper hit on a number. Twenty million in endorsements the first year, not including any deals from

Europe, and that was being conservative. He would have to talk to Scalzo about managing the kid.

The crowd had grown quiet, and Jasper stood on his tiptoes to watch. A monster pot was building, with three players in the hunt. Fred Rea, an amateur player from Vero Beach, Florida, "Skins" Turner, a seasoned pro from Houston, and DeMarco.

Rea was the short stack at the table with four million in chips. It sounded like a lot, only his opponents had more. By declaring himself "all in," Rea was putting his tournament life at stake.

Skins called him, and shoved four million in chips into the pot as well.

DeMarco immediately called Rea and Skins. The kid had a special savoir faire that Jasper loved. The five community cards had already been dealt and were lying face up on the table. Each player was allowed to use his two cards plus the community cards to make the best possible hand.

Rea turned over his two cards. He had two pair, fours and sevens.

DeMarco turned over his cards. He also had two pair, kings and sevens. He'd beaten Rea, and the crowd broke into wild applause. Jasper clapped along with them.

When the applause died, Skins Turner cleared his throat. "Afraid I've got you beat, son." Skins turned over his cards. He had three kings, or what gamblers called "a set." He raked in the pot while laughing under his breath.

The crowd let out a collective groan, and so did Jasper. Even though he didn't know how Scalzo's scam worked, he knew that DeMarco couldn't lose. Yet somehow, DeMarco *had* lost. Jasper stared at the electronic leader board hanging over the feature table. DeMarco was now in third place.

Jasper's cell phone was vibrating in his pocket. He pulled the phone out, and stared at the face. Mark Perrier, the hotel's general manager, had sent him a text message: COME TO MY OFFICE! Jasper punched in Perrier's number, heard Perrier pick up on the first ring.

"What's going on?" Jasper asked.

"I'm going to close down your fucking tournament," Perrier informed him.

"I'll be right up," Jasper said.

Perrier's office was on the hotel's top floor, not big, but with a breathtaking view. Jasper took the private elevator up while staring at the bad carpeting job. The hotel was a big white elephant, and once the newness wore off, its bad location was going to catch up with it. Perrier knew this, so he'd agreed to host the World Poker Showdown.

Perrier was standing by the window when Jasper walked in.

"Have a chair," the general manager said.

Perrier was a drop of water in an Armani suit, and not the kind of guy Jasper took orders from. He joined him by the window.

"Great view. What's the problem?"

Perrier's eyes bore into Jasper's face with an animal-like intensity. "Were you aware that I sicced the police on Valentine?"

"No, but it was a good idea," Jasper said.

"Do you know why I did that?"

"You wanted him out of the way?"

"I wanted to buy time," Perrier said.

"To do what?"

"Sit down, and I'll show you," Perrier said.

The sitting area in Perrier's office was dwarfed by his desk, and Jasper wedged himself into the stiff-backed chair that sat in front of it. Perrier went to the DVD player that was part of an entertainment unit, and fiddled with the remote. A flat-screen plasma-TV flickered to life.

"Nice picture," Jasper said. "That high definition?"

Perrier remained standing, his arms crossed in front of his chest. "When you came to me with this tournament, I knew it wasn't clean, and that I'd probably have to cover your tracks. That's why I've put up with that mobster Scalzo in my hotel, and why I didn't say anything when I heard you were using dealers with criminal records. I kept my mouth shut, and cleaned up your mess as best I could. But we've got a new mess, a real big one, Karl, and I'm not going to clean it up for you."

"What are you talking about?" Jasper asked.

Perrier jerked his thumb at the TV screen. "Take a look."

Jasper squinted at the flickering images on the screen. The picture was grainy black-and-white, and taken from above. "What am I looking at?"

"A surveillance tape."

Jasper took out his glasses, fitted them on, and squinted at the screen. The tape showed two men standing at the bottom of a stairwell, one black, the other white, the camera's angle revealing the worried looks on their faces. Jasper stared at the bottom right-hand corner of the tape. It contained the date and time the tape had been recorded, which was at a few minutes past midnight. He felt himself growing restless. "Come on, Mark, what am I looking at?"

Perrier continued looking at the screen. "Here we go."

On the tape, the door to the stairwell burst open, and a silver-haired man rushed in wielding a handgun. He shot each man in the forehead, then ran out of the picture. It was over in a matter of seconds.

Jasper heard himself exhale. On the tape, the two guys lay dead, blood pooling around their heads. He knew who they were. Hitmen, hired to kill Valentine. Scalzo had said that Valentine had shot them in the stairwell, only now Jasper knew otherwise. It was Scalzo who'd shot them. Jasper rose from his chair.

"Give me a drink," he said.

Perrier poured Jasper a Scotch on the rocks at the bar. The drink was strong and made Jasper's mouth burn. They stood by the window, staring into the distance.

"The police asked me about the surveillance camera in the stairwell," Perrier said, sipping water. "I lied, and told them it didn't exist."

"Good move," Jasper said.

"Maybe. I could tell them I was wrong, and turn the tape over to them. Or, I could destroy the tape. What I do depends on you."

Jasper stared at Perrier's reflection in the glass. "How so?"

"The tournament is a winner, and everyone wants it

to continue. But there's a hitch. We have a mobster running around killing people in the hotel. I want you to make the mobster go away."

"I can't do that," Jasper said.

"No?"

"He's my partner. He put up the cash."

"Make him go away, anyway."

"How? You saw what kind of person he is."

"That's your problem. All I'm doing is giving you an out," Perrier said. "If I turn over the tape to the police, you and Scalzo will go to jail, and the World Poker Showdown will go up in flames. Your career and everything you've worked for will be ruined. You don't want that, do you?"

Jasper took a gulp of his drink. His stomach was empty and the booze went down hard. It made him nauseous, and he felt cold beads of sweat march down his neck. He'd always wondered what his day of reckoning would feel like, and now he knew.

"No," Jasper heard himself say.

"The tournament is a huge success. Get rid of the mobster."

Jasper nodded stiffly. The tournament was making money, so he was being given another chance. It was better than the alternative, he supposed.

"Okay," Jasper said.

27

Leaving police headquarters, Bill Higgins drove Valentine back to Celebrity. The freeway was jammed with traffic, and Valentine sat in the passenger seat with his window cracked, staring at a cloudless sky and leaden sun.

"There's one part of this case that I can't figure out," Valentine said.

"What's that?" Bill asked.

"Why haven't you run George Scalzo out of Las Vegas? Nevada has spent twenty-five years cleaning up its image of being controlled by the mob, yet this guy runs around town like he's Teflon-coated. I don't get it."

Eyes glued to the car in front of him, Bill emitted an exasperated breath. "I've tried to run him out."

"Did someone stop you?"

Bill nodded his head almost imperceptibly.

"Mind telling me who?"

"Call them the powers that be," Bill said.

Valentine knew that the rules were different in Vegas. There were only a handful of ways to make money in the desert, and right and wrong sometimes got a little fuzzy.

"But the guy's a crook," Valentine argued.

"Scalzo is a *reputed* crook," Bill said. Traffic was moving, and he inched the car ahead. "The fact is, he's never spent a day in jail, never been convicted of a crime, has paid his income taxes every year, and enjoys all the freedoms and protections of every other law-abiding citizen. He's just as entitled to come here as you are."

"But he's helping his nephew scam the tournament," Valentine said.

"Trust me, Tony, I've told everyone who'll listen that I think Scalzo and Skip DeMarco are up to no good."

"And?"

"Everyone asks me what the scam is. I say I don't know, and they change the subject."

"But you and I both *know* that they're cheating. Together, we've got over fifty years' experience catching cheaters. Doesn't that count for something?"

Traffic again halted and Bill slammed on his brakes. Moments later, a motorcyclist driving on the white line in the highway sped past, mocking them. Bill watched the motorcyclist with a disgusted look on his face, then faced his friend.

"When it comes to Scalzo and DeMarco, it doesn't mean shit," Bill said.

"How's your blood pressure?" Bill asked as they climbed the stairs to Celebrity's surveillance control room on the third floor.

"A little high," Valentine admitted.

"So's mine. My doctor wants me to monitor my blood pressure regularly. I bought one of those machines from CVS. You should think about doing the same thing."

"You think so?"

"Yeah. It's a silent killer."

They had reached the third floor and Valentine was puffing. He walked two miles a day, and kept in good shape. Maybe he *was* stressed out. Perhaps it had something to do with George Scalzo and his nephew robbing the joint blind. Or perhaps it was that this was his fifth day in Vegas, and the town had become transparent. They marched down the hallway to the steel door at the end where the surveillance control room was housed. A security camera was perched above the door, and Bill knocked loudly, then peered up into its lenses.

"So what are we doing here, anyway?" his friend asked.

"I had an epiphany during the drive over," Valentine said. "Somebody I spoke with the other day lied to me, and I want to talk to him with you present."

Bill's face hardened. "Someone working in Celebrity's surveillance department?"

"Yes."

"Am I going to have to arrest him?"

"You might."

The door opened and a lanky shift supervisor greeted them.

"We need to talk to one of your people," Bill said.

The shift supervisor blinked. "Is there something wrong?"

"That's what we're here to find out."

"Who do you want to talk to?" the shift supervisor asked.

Bill looked at Valentine.

"Sammy Mann," Valentine said.

The shift supervisor led them through the surveillance control room to the offices that lined the back wall. He knocked on a door, then cracked it open. "You've got visitors," he announced.

The shift supervisor left, and Bill and Valentine entered. The office was hardly big enough for them to squeeze in, and Valentine sucked in his breath as he shut the door. Sammy Mann sat behind the desk, staring at computer screen containing a live feed from a surveillance camera on the casino floor. Seeing them, he smiled. Sammy was a man of sartorial splendor, and wore a silk sports jackets with mother-of-pearl buttons, a baby blue shirt with French cuffs, and a gold tie with a perfect Windsor knot. He was the classiest cheater Valentine had ever known. Now retired, he hired himself out to Las Vegas casinos as a consultant.

"Good morning, gentlemen," Sammy said pleasantly. "Welcome to my humble abode. Make yourselves at home."

"I've got a bone to pick with you," Valentine said.

The smile left Sammy's face. "You're here on business?"

"That's right," Bill said.

"What's wrong?" Sammy asked.

Valentine dug out of his pocket the Silly Putty and paper clip that Rufus had found in Celebrity's poker room, and placed them on the desk. He deliberately shoved the paper clip into the putty, and saw Sammy wince.

"We've got a mucker cheating the World Poker Showdown, and I think you might know who it is," Valentine said.

Smart crooks never lied; they just kept their mouths shut. Sammy's lips closed and he continued to stare at the bug. Sammy's speciality had been switching decks of cards at casino blackjack tables. Because of him and his well-trained gangs, every casino in the world now chained their dealing shoes to their tables.

"Start talking," Bill said.

Sammy wore a perpetual tan, and it was unsettling to see the color drain from his cheeks. "Are you going to arrest me?" he asked.

"I might if you don't give us some straight answers," Bill said.

"On what grounds?"

"Collusion," Bill said.

"With who?"

"You know every mucker in the country," Valentine jumped in. "Hell, you trained most of them. The question is, did you see one working the tournament?"

Sammy reached into the pocket of his sports jacket and removed a medicine bottle. He spilled a few dozen tiny pills onto the table, then stuck one on the tip of his tongue. He washed it down with a glass of water sitting on the desk.

"For my heart," he said, taking a deep breath.

They waited him out. Las Vegas's casinos liked to boast that they didn't use ex-cheaters in surveillance, but it wasn't true. Nearly every casino used them, and for good reason. There was no other way to learn how grifters worked.

"To answer your question," Sammy finally said, "no, I have not seen anyone I know from the past scamming the poker tournament."

Valentine slammed his hand on the desk, making Sammy jump.

"That wasn't the question."

"It wasn't?" Sammy asked meekly.

"No. I asked you if you'd spotted any muckers you know, not if you saw them switching cards. My guess is, if you recognized someone, you *wouldn't* watch them, just so you couldn't be pinned down later."

Sammy was breathing hard. Not reporting a scam was a felony, punishable by up to three years in state prison. Sammy had visited the crossbar motel before, and knew how harsh prison life was for cheaters.

"If you're asking me if I spotted anyone in the tournament who I know from the past, the answer is yes," Sammy said. "There are many guys playing here who cheated at one time or another. But that doesn't mean they're cheating here."

"Did you *watch* them to make sure they weren't cheating?" Valentine asked.

A sweat moustache appeared above Sammy's upper lip.

"No," he said.

"You're in serious trouble," Bill informed him.

The best thing a cop could do to a crook was make him sweat. Leaving Sammy in the office, they went into the surveillance control room to have a little chat.

"What a crummy prick," Bill said. "He's sitting there collecting a paycheck to catch cheaters, yet isn't reporting cheaters he knows are playing in the tournament. When I'm finished with him, he won't be able to get another job in town."

"Actually, I was hoping you'd let him skate," Valentine said.

Bill's mouth opened a few centimeters. "You were?"

"Yes. I want him working for us."

"You sound like you've got a soft spot for the guy."

Bill wasn't far off the mark. Sammy had class. Like Rufus, he could charm the pants off a person while stealing their money. "I wanted to scare him, and we have," Valentine said. "If you give Sammy another chance, I feel certain he'll lead us to the mucker. When he does, you can call the governor, and tell him you want to raid the tournament. That way, we'll kill two birds with one stone."

"We will?"

"Yes. I watched DeMarco play earlier, and I'd be willing to bet dollars to doughnuts that the dealer at his table is involved in the scam."

"Which dealer are you talking about?"

"Heavyset guy with a walrus moustache. He's doing something fishy when he deals. His movements are too slow."

"Is he reading the cards and somehow signaling DeMarco?"

The air-conditioning never stopped blowing in a surveillance control room, and Valentine shivered and said, "No. The dealer hardly looked at the deck when he dealt. But I'm certain he's involved."

"So the mucker is an excuse to raid the game," Bill said.

Valentine nodded. He had been studying DeMarco's scam for a week, and was no closer to the solution than the day he'd started. The proverbial sand was slipping from the hourglass. If he didn't solve this puzzle soon, DeMarco would be crowned the champion, and he and Bill would look like chumps.

"Sounds like a plan to me," Bill said.

28

Mabel was on the computer when she heard the front door slam. Not long ago a man had entered the house under false pretenses, and held her hostage. She'd learned a valuable lesson from the experience, and reaching across the desk, she grabbed a copy of *Crime and Punishment* nestled between a pair of bookends, and removed a loaded Sig Sauer that Tony kept in the hollowed-out interior. She rose from her chair.

"I'm armed," she called out.

"Don't shoot," a familiar woman's voice called back.

"Yolanda, is that you?"

"Yes."

"How did you get here so fast?"

"I flew Southwest."

Mabel returned the gun to its hiding place and went to the foyer. Tony and his late wife had bought the house to retire to, and it was a charming relic that represented the way Florida houses used to be made, with hardwood floors, crown molding, and jalousie windows. Yolanda stood by the front door, the baby cradled in her arms.

"I've missed you," Mabel said, hugging her.

"I missed you, too," Yolanda said. "The baby's diaper needs changing. Talk to me in the kitchen."

The kitchen was in the back of the house, and faced a postage-stamp-size backyard. Yolanda put the baby on the kitchen table and said, "So tell me why Tony and Gerry are in trouble."

"Right before we spoke, I got a phone call from Special Agent Romero of the FBI," Mabel explained. "He told me that Tony and Gerry have gotten on the wrong side of a notorious mobster, and are in danger."

"So they *could* end up dead, like in my dream," Yolanda said.

"Yes."

Yolanda tickled the baby's stomach and made her giggle. The baby was named Lois, and resembled Tony's late wife, whom she'd been named after. As a result, Yolanda had Tony and Gerry wrapped around her little finger, yet rarely took advantage of it. Lifting the baby to her shoulder, she said, "I suppose I should call them, and ask them to come home, but somehow I have a feeling that they'd both tell me they're okay, and not to worry. Am I right?"

Mabel sunk down into a chair. Yolanda was right. Tony and Gerry weren't going to be forced out of a case by anyone.

"Besides, think of the long-term consequences if I ask them to come home," Yolanda said, patting the baby's behind.

"What long-term consequences?"

"I'd be drawing a line in the sand," Yolanda said, "and telling Tony and Gerry that I'm not willing to let them work under certain situations. If I did that, they might as well close Grift Sense, and go into some other line of work."

Mabel swallowed hard. She hadn't thought of it that way. "I see your point."

"Good. I suggest we take another tack."

"Which is?"

"Maybe we can help them solve this case, " Yolanda said.

"How are we going to do that? We don't know anything about it."

Yolanda handed her the baby, then dug a piece of folded paper from her pocket. Yolanda was big on writing things down, and unfolded a page filled with notes.

"Oh yes, we do," the younger woman said.

They went into Tony's office with Mabel still holding the baby. She'd raised two children of her own, and looked back fondly at the experience, even though she hardly heard from either of them now. One day, they'd have children of their own, and start calling her more regularly. It was how it had worked with her mother.

"I spoke with Gerry last night," Yolanda said, laying her notes on the desk. "He told me the key to solving this scam was at the Atlantic City Medical Center. His friend Jack Donovan stole something from there that's being used to invisibly mark cards, and Gerry is trying to find out what it is. Well, I think we can help him."

"How?" Mabel asked.

"The first thing Gerry has to realize is that things get stolen from hospitals, and never get reported to the police."

"Why's that?"

"Hospitals are no different than anywhere else," Yolanda said. "Stuff disappears, including narcotics and prescription drugs, and the police never hear about it. People internally know about it, but that's where it stops."

The baby was starting to squirm. Mabel put her on the floor, and watched her crawl away.

"Bad for business?" Mabel asked.

"Worse than bad," Yolanda said. "If the state medical board hears that a hospital is losing drugs to thieves, they might pull the hospital's license. As a result, thefts routinely get hushed up. Gerry can't rely on anyone working at the Atlantic City Medical Center to be truthful in regards to what Jack Donovan might have stolen from them."

"So the hospital is a dead end," Mabel said.

"Not necessarily. Oh, better grab the baby."

Lois had crawled across the floor and was drooling on the newest addition to Tony's collection of cheating equipment. It was a crooked roulette wheel, courtesy of the famed London Club, that'd hired Tony to determine why they were losing on the wheel. Using a computer software program, Tony had analyzed a week's worth of winning numbers, and determined that half were coming up too often. He'd gotten the casino to take the wheel apart, and remove all the screws holding the metal separators between the winning numbers, called frets. It was discovered that the threads of these screws were thinner than normal, and offered less resistance when hit by the spinning ball. The casino had arrested the roulette repairman, who'd immediately confessed to the ingenious crime.

Mabel scooped the baby up. "Why not necessarily?"

"If the hospital *is* confronted by the police about a theft, they'll help in the investigation, for the same reasons I just explained. The hard part is getting enough evidence for the police to feel comfortable doing that." Yolanda glanced at her notes on the desk. "Right now, we know the following: Jack Donovan stole something from the hospital, which he hid inside a metal strongbox under his bed. The strongbox was missing after Jack was murdered, leaving everyone to assume that the murderer stole it. Now, here's the interesting part. Gerry saw the murderer coming down a stairwell in the hospital, right?"

"Correct," Mabel said.

"But the murderer wasn't carrying a strongbox, a duffel bag, or anything at all," Yolanda said. "Gerry said his hands were empty."

"Maybe the murderer took the secret out of the strongbox, and put it in his pocket."

"I don't think so. We know the secret is dangerous, which is why it was kept inside the strongbox in a duffel bag. I have another theory as to what happened to Jack's secret."

Mabel rocked the baby against her chest. She sensed that Yolanda had found something that everyone else had missed. Something hiding in plain sight, to use one of Tony's favorite expressions.

"Tell me," she said.

"I think George Scalzo stole it," Yolanda said.

Mabel blinked. She knew a lot about Scalzo, courtesy of Special Agent Romero. Scalzo had murdered Skip DeMarco's mother, a prostitute, in order to get custody of DeMarco when he was a little boy. Scalzo would stop at nothing to get what he wanted.

"If that's true, then Scalzo was in the hospital during the murder," Mabel said.

"I think so," Yolanda said.

"You don't think he would have sent one of his men?"

"Scalzo wants his nephew to win the World Poker Showdown," Yolanda said. "Do you think he would have trusted one of his men to steal the scam from Jack's room?"

Mabel considered it, then shook her head. "No, he would have done it himself."

"So my theory makes sense," Yolanda said.

"It makes perfect sense," Mabel said. "If we can put Scalzo in that hospital, he's an accomplice to Jack Donovan's murder."

"Most hospitals require visitors to sign in at a reception area," Yolanda said. "There might be a record of Scalzo being there."

Mabel handed Yolanda the baby. Yolanda didn't know enough about crooks to know that most of them never used their real names. But that didn't mean they couldn't prove her theory. Special Agent Romero had said that the FBI was watching Scalzo twenty-four hours a day. The FBI would know if Scalzo was at the hospital that night.

Romero's number was written on a slip of paper on the desk. Mabel punched the number into the phone, then looked appreciatively at Yolanda.

"I'm so glad you're home," Mabel said.

29

"**W**hat fucking happened?" Scalzo whispered.

"I don't know," DeMarco whispered back.

"You don't know?"

"No, Uncle George. I don't know what happened."

"I'll tell you what happened," his uncle whispered, his breath hot on his nephew's neck. "A guy named Skins Turner just beat you out of a monster pot, and took a third of your chips away from you. You're no longer in first place."

"I know, Uncle George."

"So tell me how Skins did it," his uncle said.

"I told you, I don't know," DeMarco replied.

DeMarco and his uncle and Guido were standing on the far end of the poker room, next to the wall and away from the other players and mob of spectators. The tournament took a fifteen-minute bathroom break every two hours, and the players ran like lemmings to the johns. DeMarco had instead gone over to be with his uncle, whose voice hinted that he was on the verge of losing control.

"But Skins had three of a kind," his uncle said, his

voice rising. "You bet into a better hand, and lost. Why the fuck did you do that, Skipper? Tell me why you did that."

DeMarco leaned against the wall, which was icy cool against his skin. Everything he touched inside the casino was cold and unfriendly, and he found himself wanting to return to Newark and the safety of his house. "It just happened."

"But you knew Skins was holding a pair of kings before the flop," his uncle shot back. "You knew what his cards were. You're not supposed to lose monster pots, Skipper. You could get knocked out of the tournament."

"I know, Uncle George."

"You know?"

"Yes."

"That's not good enough, Skipper."

"It's not?"

"No. You gotta do better."

DeMarco could hear the implied threat in his uncle's voice, and wondered if his uncle thought he'd lost the hand on purpose, and was trying to sabotage his own chances of winning the tournament. That was the strange thing about his uncle George; his uncle loved him, but sometimes didn't trust him.

DeMarco realized his chest was heaving. He took several deep breaths, trying to calm down. The truth was, Skins hadn't started the hand with two kings. According to the clicks DeMarco had heard in his earpiece, Skins's cards were a king and a three. Somehow, they became a pair of kings, and DeMarco had lost the biggest pot of the tournament. Either the receiver in his earpiece had malfunctioned, or Skins was cheating.

His uncle stood a few feet away, speaking in hushed tones to Guido. DeMarco wanted to ask his uncle what he was supposed to do. Should he ask the tournament director to stop play, so they could fix his earpiece? Or should he tell the tournament director that Skins was cheating because DeMarco had known Skins's cards, and they weren't a pair of kings? Those were his only two options, and either one would get him tossed from the tournament, and probably arrested.

DeMarco found the strength to laugh. He was stuck between a rock and a hard place, and there wasn't a damn thing he could do about it.

"What's so funny?" his uncle asked, drawing close.

"This is another fine mess you've gotten me into, Uncle George," DeMarco said.

"What's that supposed to mean?"

"It's a joke, Uncle George. Lighten up."

"Don't talk to me like that," his uncle snapped.

DeMarco pushed himself away from the wall. He could vividly remember the day his uncle had come to him with his scheme about scamming the World Poker Showdown. Winning would be child's play, his uncle had said, and would make DeMarco the most famous poker player in the world. Only it wasn't turning out that way, and DeMarco sensed they were about to get beaten at their own game.

"Where you going?" his uncle asked.

"To take a leak," DeMarco said.

"Have Guido walk with you."

"Whatever you want, Uncle George."

DeMarco felt his uncle's hand on his wrist.

"You sure you're okay, Skipper?" his uncle asked.

"I'm great, Uncle George. Just great."

For as long as he could remember, DeMarco had hated to lose. It didn't matter what the game was, or the stakes: if he didn't end up on the winning end, he lost his temper, and sulked for days. He *had* to win, just as some guys had to be the best at a particular sport. As he'd gotten older, he'd wondered if it had something to do with being blind, as if winning put him on a level playing field with everyone else.

Only today had been different. He'd lost a monster pot, and it hadn't fazed him. The *surprise* of losing had been upsetting, but the actual loss hadn't affected him the way it normally did. He couldn't put his finger on why, and as he and Guido walked to the lavatory, he thought about the snapshot he'd been given. He'd studied it between hands, and decided the little boy in the photograph was indeed him, the woman holding his hand, his mother. Everything else was a mystery, and he hoped the woman who'd given him the photograph hadn't been driven away by his obnoxious behavior.

Guido stopped. "We're here. Want me to go inside with you?"

"No, Guido. Go watch my uncle. He's acting strange."

"I can't just leave you here," the bodyguard said.

"It's okay. I'll get one of the players to walk me back."

"You sure, Skipper?"

There was real concern in Guido's voice. As nannies went, Guido had always been there for him. "Yeah, Guido. I'm sure. Thanks. I'll see you in a few."

The bodyguard walked away, and DeMarco went into the lavatory. When he emerged a minute later, he smelled lilac-scented perfume, and offered a smile when he felt a woman's hand on his arm. "I need to talk to you," a familiar voice said.

"Sure," DeMarco said.

The woman led him to a corner table and they both sat down. She positioned her chair so their knees were touching. "Did you look at the photograph I gave you?" she asked.

"Yes. It's of me and my mother, isn't it?" DeMarco said.

She placed her hand on his wrist, her grip strong and firm. "That's right."

"Where did you get it?"

"Your mother gave it to me."

"Who are you?"

"I'm your mother's younger sister, your aunt."

And where have you been for the past twenty years? he nearly asked.

"What's your name?" he asked instead.

"Marie DeMarco."

It felt like a scene out of a daytime soap opera, and DeMarco guessed he'd be dealing with plenty of people like her, now that he was famous. Out of curiosity, he leaned forward and brought his eyes a few inches from the woman's face. The resemblance to his late mother was slight. He leaned back.

"Why did you come here?" he asked.

"I wanted to see you," she said. "Your father also wanted to come. He lives in Philadelphia, not far from where I live."

"My *father*?"

"That's right."

DeMarco removed her hand from his wrist. His father had abandoned him and his mother a long time ago. His uncle had told him so, and he'd accepted the explanation, simply because he'd never heard from his father. "I don't know what your angle is, but I'm not giving you any money. You've got a lot of nerve coming here, and pulling this shit."

He heard her sharp intake of breath, then her dress going *swoosh!* as she rose from her chair. "I don't want your money, Skipper. I came here to check up on you. I saw a piece on television that said you'd cheated the tournament, and was afraid you might be in trouble. So I came to make sure you were okay."

The first day of the tournament, his uncle had arranged for a bunch of players to fold to him, giving DeMarco a huge stack of chips to play with. It was a ploy used by many top-flight players to ensure they survived the early rounds of tournaments, only DeMarco had the bad fortune to knock out Rufus Steele, who'd gone on national television and told the world what he'd done.

"Your father was going to come with me, but he's in court, trying a case," she went on. "He's a criminal defense attorney."

"Where's he been all my life?"

"He didn't know that you existed until I contacted him a few years ago. Once he found out he had a son, he tried to contact you, just like I tried. Only your uncle stopped us. Your uncle's bodyguard threatened to kill us if we didn't stay away."

"That's bullshit. My uncle wouldn't do that."

She abruptly sat back down. This time when she took his wrist, her fingernails dug into his flesh, and when she spoke, her voice was as sharp as a knife.

"Do you really want to know the truth?" she asked.

"Of course I want to know."

"Are you sure, Skipper?"

DeMarco took a deep breath. He'd caught his uncle in enough lies over the years to realize that there was a lot about his past he didn't know. Was this woman finally going to reveal it to him?

"Yes," he said.

"It's like this. Your mother got hooked on drugs when she was a teenager, and became a prostitute to support her habit. We tried to help her clean herself up. Myself, her mother, her friends, we all tried. She went into rehab, and for a while she was clean. That was when your mother met your father, who was in law school. She hid her past from him, and they fell in love. Then she got pregnant, and ran away.

"She had you without any of us knowing. Then went back to drugs and the street. We didn't hear from her for several years. I finally tracked her down and persuaded her to come home. She lived with me for a while, and so did you. She wanted to contact your father, but never did. I think she was afraid of telling him the truth about herself.

"Your mother couldn't stay off the drugs. One day I came home and she was gone. She called a month later from Atlantic City, said she was living there. The next call came from the police, saying she was dead. You were put into a foster home. I tried to get you back, but George Scalzo paid off a judge and adopted you."

DeMarco shut his eyes. He tried to speak and heard his voice crack. He forced out the words anyway. "My mother was a hooker?"

The woman put her fingers to DeMarco's lips, and gently closed them. "Your mother was a beautiful woman who loved you more than anything in the whole world. Never forget that, Skipper."

The air trapped in DeMarco's lungs had escaped, and he felt empty and hollow and lost. He heard her rise from her chair, and rose as well.

"I need to fly home to Philadelphia this afternoon," she said. "I have a husband and family waiting for me."

"Can I ask you something?"

"Of course."

"Why did you come here?"

"I wanted you to know that you have a family besides your uncle," she said. "Your father and I care about you. We both wanted you to know that. That's why I came."

He heard her open her purse, then felt a stiff piece of cardboard being put into his hand. He lifted it to his face and stared. It was a business card for Christopher Charles Russo, an attorney in Philadelphia. He felt her lips brush against his cheek.

"Good-bye, Skipper," she said.

30

"**Y**ou've never gambled, have you?" Bill Higgins asked.

"Never," Valentine replied.

"Ever tempted?"

"No. I got the cure."

"What happened?"

They were sitting in Celebrity's sports bar, waiting for their hamburgers. Bill had given Sammy Mann another chance, and they'd left him in the control room to come downstairs for lunch. All around them sat guys who'd been knocked out of the tournament and relegated to watching the action on the giant-screen TV behind the bar. DeMarco had lost a twelve-million-dollar pot, and the room was buzzing.

"Two things," Valentine said. "The first was because my old man was a gambler, and I saw what it did to my mother. The second happened when I was eighteen. I lent three hundred bucks to a friend of mine who *thought* he was a gambler. That cured me."

"Did your friend blow the money?"

"Yeah."

Lunch came, and they dug in. Once upon a time, food in Las Vegas was a real bargain. Then the corporations had taken over. Now, a burger cost ten bucks, and the french fries could be counted on the fingers of two hands.

"What happened?" Bill asked.

"It was the summer of my eighteenth birthday," Valentine said, "and I was caddying at the Atlantic City Country Club. The pay was fifty bucks a week, and I'd saved three hundred bucks and was planning to buy a used car. There was another caddy named Kenny Keane. Kenny was a degenerate gambler and would bet on anything. One day, he begged me to lend him three hundred dollars, said he needed to see a doctor. I was pretty naive, so I lent it to him.

"Kenny immediately marched into the clubhouse and challenged the club champ to a match. Kenny was an eight-handicap, and the champ was a scratch golfer. They went out and started playing. Luckily, the champ played tight when there was money on the line, and on the last hole, Kenny sank a miracle thirty-foot putt, and won by a stroke. As we were walking back to the clubhouse, Kenny said, 'I told you I could beat that guy!'

"I told Kenny I wanted my money. I was dreaming about owning that car. Kenny said sure, and we went to take a shower. When I got out, I found Kenny in a poker game in the locker room. I looked at his hand. He had absolutely nothing. A stone cold bluff. I begged him for my money. He said, 'I can beat these guys.' And he did. They folded, and Kenny won two grand.

"We went into the clubhouse, and Kenny headed for the casino in the back room. Gambling was illegal in Atlantic City then, but that didn't stop anyone. I told Kenny to give me my money or I'd never speak to him again. He said, 'Can't you see I'm on a roll? I'm going to make us famous tonight.'

"I watched Kenny play blackjack and double our money. Then he played craps, and doubled it again. The guy was absolutely on fire. Then he went to the roulette table, and put everything on the black. The ball rolled and I remember saying a prayer when it dropped. It landed on the red.

"Kenny didn't stop yelling for ten minutes. I remember wanting to cry, only there were too many people around. As we were leaving, another caddy came up and asked Kenny how much money he'd lost. Kenny said, 'Just three hundred bucks that I borrowed from this dope.' "

Bill's cell phone was lying on the bar, and began to crawl between their plates. It was on vibrate mode, and Bill picked it up and stared at its face.

"I need to take this," he said.

Bill retreated to a less noisy area of the bar, and Valentine continued eating while watching the TV behind the bar. The players had taken a break, and the network was showing a replay of the monster pot DeMarco had lost. Valentine hadn't paid much attention to it the first time—everyone lost when they gambled—but watching it a second time, he felt the hairs on his neck stand up. The player who'd beaten DeMarco was a scruffy Houston gambler named Skins Turner, a lanky guy with a hooked nose, a prominent Adam's apple, and a vagrant wisp of hair on his head. But his arresting feature was his hands. They were large and delicate, with long tapering fingers and manicured fingernails. They could have belonged to a surgeon, or a concert pianist, but in the world of gambling, they belonged to another animal. They were a mucker's hands.

The camera shifted to DeMarco, who'd lost a third of his chips to Skins. DeMarco was shaking his head, and Valentine sensed that the kid knew he'd been cheated.

Bill was still on the other side of the bar, talking on his cell phone. Valentine borrowed a pen from the bartender and scribbled on a cocktail napkin that he was going upstairs to the surveillance control room. He tucked the note beneath Bill's plate then threw down money for their meals and left the bar.

Entering Celebrity's surveillance control room, Valentine went to the office where Sammy Mann was holed up. To his surprise, the old hustler had cleared out. He found a technician and asked him where Sammy had gone.

"He went home ten minutes ago," the tech said.

Valentine talked the tech into pulling up the tape of the twelve-million-dollar pot, then he pulled up a chair to watch the action. The tech had a boyish face and didn't look old enough to be driving a car. Sensing that something was brewing, the tech put down the Slurpie he was drinking, and stared intently at the video monitor.

They watched the dealer shuffle the cards then sail them around the table, with each player getting two. In Texas Hold 'Em, the player's starting cards were critical, with the best hand being two aces, followed by two kings. As Skins got his two cards, his hands covered their backs, and he lifted up their corners to peek at their values.

"See that?" Valentine asked.

"No," the tech said. "What happened?"

"Play it again, and I'll explain."

The tech rewound the tape. He hit play, and they watched the dealer sail the cards around the table.

"Freeze it," Valentine said.

The tech froze the tape, and Valentine pointed at Skins. "See his hands? He's got a king palmed in his right hand. It was stuck in a bug beneath the table."

The tech brought his face so close to the picture that his breath fogged the screen.

"Well, I'll be. But where did he get the king from?"

"He mucked it out earlier," Valentine said. "Hustlers call it doing 'the chop.' When he tossed his cards to the dealer, he only tossed one."

"The dealer didn't notice?"

Valentine shook his head. The technique of stealing a single card during play had been developed by blackjack cheaters, and it flew by most dealers. Stealing a card was even easier in poker, since no one paid attention to a player when he dropped out of a hand. Valentine made the tech restart the tape.

"Now watch the switch," he said.

The tape continued, and they watched Skins cover his cards with his hands. The tech slapped his knees. "Holy cow. He peeked at his cards without letting the hidden camera in the table see them," the tech said. "That's on purpose, isn't it?"

Valentine nodded. The kid caught on fast.

"Okay," the tech said. "Now he's doing the switch, even though I can't see the move."

"Cameras can't see through hands," Valentine said.

"No, but I can tell when someone's got a card palmed, and this guy does." The tech pointed at Skins's right hand, which rested on the table edge. "He's got the card he just switched hidden in his palm, doesn't he?"

"Correct."

"What will he do? Destroy it later on?"

"No," Valentine said. "He'll add it to his cards, and toss it into the muck. That way the deck won't be short. Hustlers call it 'cleaning up.'"

On the monitor, they saw Skins drop his guilty hand into his lap and stick the switched card into the bug. If a problem arose during the game, Skins would simply toss the card beneath the table.

"So let's arrest this guy," the tech said. "We've got enough evidence."

It was the sanest thing Valentine had heard anyone say since he'd started investigating the tournament. He felt a hand on his shoulder and looked up. Bill Higgins was standing behind him with a grim look on his face. Valentine got up, and they went to a corner where no one could hear them.

"I just got some bad news from the FBI's Las Vegas office," Bill said. "Guess who escaped from Ely prison this morning."

"Someone I know?"

"Al 'Little Hands' Scarpi. The FBI thinks Scalzo was behind it."

Valentine clenched his teeth. Every holiday, postcards from Ely State Penitentiary appeared in his mailbox, the name *U.R. Dead* scribbled in the return address box. Of all the twisted souls he'd put away, Al Scarpi was the one he still had nightmares about.

"Look, Tony, I won't be mad if you say you want to leave town," Bill said. "This is getting awfully hairy."

Valentine shook his head. He would leave Las Vegas after he busted Scalzo. It was that simple.

"I'm not going anywhere," he said.

31

"I've never ridden in a helicopter before," Little Hands shouted, gazing down at the flat, unforgiving landscape of northern Nevada. The pilot, an athletic blonde wearing aviator shades with mirrored lenses, flashed a toothy grin. He'd picked Little Hands up on a dusty field outside the Ely Conservation Camp ninety minutes ago, tossed a bag lunch into Little Hands's lap, then pointed his chopper toward Las Vegas.

"Where do you pee in this thing, anyway?" Little Hands asked.

The pilot continued grinning. It was a long trip, over 250 miles, and Little Hands had wished like hell he'd taken a leak before departing.

"You got a radio to listen to?" Little Hands asked.

The pilot continued to grin. Then Little Hands got the picture. The pilot couldn't hear him over the roar of the helicopter's blades. Little Hands felt like a fool and folded his hands in his lap. In prison, he'd gone to the library every day and tried to educate himself. If he'd learned anything from the books he'd read, it was that the best thing a dumb person could do was keep their mouth shut and say nothing at all.

Rows of identical tract houses littered the landscape, the roofs dotted with satellite-TV dishes. Past them, a giant steel structure shaped like a needle pierced the sky. Little Hands realized it was the Stratosphere, the tallest casino in Las Vegas.

The pilot tapped him on the arm, then pointed at a sprawling industrial park down below. Behind the park was a concrete helipad with a car parked beside it. Little Hands sucked in his breath as the helicopter descended.

Once the helicopter's blades stopped whirring, Little Hands climbed out and stretched his legs. It was hard to believe that less than five hours ago he'd been pumping iron in the prison weight room. The pilot pulled a duffle bag out of the helicopter, and dropped it on the ground. "This is yours, buddy," he said.

Little Hands unzipped the duffle bag and pulled out its contents. New clothes to replace his prison work outfit, a set of car keys for the vehicle parked beside the helipad, and an envelope stuffed with twenty-dollar bills. The envelope also contained a typed sheet with the hotel and room number where Tony Valentine was staying. Taking the money out, he quickly counted it.

One thousand bucks.

He ran over to the helicopter. The pilot had restarted the engine and was about to take off. Little Hands tapped on the pilot's window, and he pulled it back.

"Where's the rest of my money? I get five grand for a job."

"You'll get the rest when the job is done," the pilot said.

"Fuck that shit. I want it now."

"Do the job, then call the number on the back of the instructions. They'll meet you, and give you the rest."

"I want it now."

"I don't have it," the pilot said.

"You're saying they didn't pay you, either?" Little Hands shouted.

"What they paid me is none of your business. You should be happy you're out of jail," the pilot said.

Little Hands stuck his hand through the open window and got his fingers around the pilot's throat. Before he could squeeze the life out of him, the pilot drew a gun from the console between the seats and stuck it in Little Hands's face.

"Want to die, asshole?"

Little Hands let go of the pilot and withdrew his arm.

"You're a dumb son-of-a-bitch, you know that?" the pilot said. "Now, stand back."

Little Hands retreated a few steps. The helicopter rose uncertainly, like a bird testing its wings. When it was at face height, Little Hands leaped forward and wrapped his arms around the landing gear, called skids. He twisted and pulled the skids as the helicopter continued to rise. He wasn't going to let the pilot call him dumb.

When the helicopter was higher than a house, Little Hands let go, and fell back to earth. He landed on the grass and rolled onto his back. He waited for the pain in his legs to subside while staring into the sky. The helicopter was spinning crazily, the skids twisting. The pilot wouldn't be able to land without crashing.

Little Hands saw the pilot shaking his fist and cursing him. He laughed.

He drove into Las Vegas thinking about the money. A thousand stinking bucks. He'd never taken a job without getting paid up front. Either his employer didn't know the rules, or wanted to keep him on a short leash. *It's like I'm still a prisoner,* he thought.

He came into town on the north side, where the Riviera, Frontier, and Sahara were still struggling to survive, and parked beneath the Frontier's mammoth marquee, its giant letters proclaiming BIKINI BULL RIDE, COLD BEER, DIRTY GIRLS.

Across the street from the Frontier was the Peppermill restaurant and lounge. The local cops didn't like the prices, and as a result criminals often used the cocktail lounge for meetings. He needed time and a place to think, and decided it was as good a spot as any.

The lounge was behind the restaurant, a mirrored room with a sunken fire pit and plenty of intimate seating. The place was dead, and he took a seat at the bar and ordered a draft from the cute bartender, who seemed happy for the company. She set a tall one in front of him. "You look familiar," she said.

It was his first beer since going to the joint. He savored it, saying nothing.

"Now I remember," the bartender said. "You came in here awhile back, and stuck your hand in the fire pit."

The fire pit was the lounge's gimmick, the bright orange flames erupting from a bubbling pool of green water. Little Hands had stuck his hand into the flames on a dare and burned himself real good. "That was a long time ago," he said.

She smiled like he'd made a joke, then tapped the screen of the video poker machine in front of him. Every seat at the bar had a video poker machine. It was how the lounge made money.

"Make sure you play Joker's Wild," she said.

"Why's that?" he asked.

"It's paying off real good."

He drank some more beer. She played this game with every customer who came in. She sold them on the idea of winning, even though no one ever did. He needed to figure out how he was going to kill Valentine, and fished a twenty out of his pocket.

"Thanks," he said.

The beer went straight to his head, and he could hardly sit upright in his chair. *This was how guys who broke out of jail got caught,* he thought. The bartender came back. "How you doing?" she asked.

He looked at the video poker screen. "Shitty."

She watched him play a hand. On the screen five cards appeared. He had a pair of jacks. He discarded the other three cards by pressing on them with his finger. The machine dealt him three more cards. They didn't help his hand, and he won a dollar. She reached over the bar and touched his wrist.

"Can I give you some advice?"

"Sure."

"Play the maximum amount of coins each time. That way, if you get a good hand, you'll win big."

He'd been betting a quarter a hand, thinking it would

let him play longer, which would increase his chances of winning. Only, she was saying that it was a bad strategy, and would deny him the chance to really win. He pushed the button on the screen that said PLAY MAXIMUM AMOUNT.

"There you go," she said.

Five new cards appeared on the screen. The ace of hearts, king of hearts, three of clubs, nine of hearts, and ten of hearts. He started to discard all the cards but the ace and saw her eyebrows go up.

"Discard the three and nine," she said. "That way, you might make a royal flush."

A royal flush was the best hand of all. According to the payout chart on the screen, he'd get two grand for a royal flush.

"Nobody gets those," he said.

"That's because they don't try," she said.

The day had been filled with surprises. He discarded the three and the nine. Two new cards appeared on the screen, a queen of hearts and a joker. She let out a war whoop. "You won! You won!"

He stared at the screen. "No, I didn't. That ain't a royal flush."

"Yes, it is. Jokers are wild. That's why they call it Joker's Wild."

He realized the screen was flashing. It didn't feel real, and he touched the PAYOUT button with his finger. A slip of paper spit out of the machine saying he'd won $2,000. He handed it to her, and she went into the restaurant to get the money from the manager.

He sucked down the beer left in his glass. Living in Vegas, he'd heard countless stories about people winning big in casinos, and how it had changed their lives. He'd always assumed the stories were bullshit.

The bartender returned holding a thick stack of bills. She counted the money onto the bar then pushed it toward him. Lifting her eyes, she looked into his face expectantly.

He hesitated picking up the stack, wondering how many customers heard her spiel each day. Fifty? A hundred? Giving suckers hope was how she made her living. He knew that, yet it didn't change how she'd made him feel.

He put three hundred on the bar and walked out.

32

Valentine was ready to make a bust.

He'd shown Bill Higgins the surveillance tape of Skins Turner mucking a card. Bill had seen his share of muckers, and he whistled through his teeth when Skins did his switch in plain view of everyone else at the table.

"Guy's got balls," Bill said.

"He's also got tremendous misdirection," Valentine said.

"How so?"

"Everyone's watching DeMarco."

Taking out his cell phone, Bill had put into motion the necessary steps to go into Celebrity's casino, and arrest Skins Turner. For starters, he alerted the casino's head of security and explained exactly what Skins was doing. Then he gave a detailed description of what Skins looked like and where he was sitting in the game. More than one cheater had gotten away when a security guard had, in his haste to make a bust, nabbed the wrong person.

Then Bill called the Metro Las Vegas Police Department and went through the same drill with a sheriff.

Skins would eventually end up in the Metro LVPD clink, and Bill didn't want some judge letting him out on a hundred-dollar bail because the arresting officer hadn't understood the seriousness of the charge.

The next thing Bill did was invite the other techs in the room to look at the tape of Skins and confirm that cheating was taking place. Juries in Nevada hated the casinos and would not convict a cheater without clear and compelling videotape evidence. A cop's word simply wasn't good enough.

Once the techs had agreed Skins was cheating, Bill did a background check on Skins. Nothing could be more helpful to prosecuting Skins than him having a prior conviction for cheating. Bill got Skins's name and address from the hotel's reservation department, and then called it in to the police, and his own people. If Skins had ever been arrested, either Metro or the Gaming Control Board would have a record of it.

Ten minutes later, both Metro and the GCB called Bill back.

"Damn," Bill said, hanging up the phone.

"He's clean?"

"Got a couple of speeding tickets down in Houston, but that's it. Where the hell is Sammy Mann, anyway? Maybe he knows this guy from the past."

"Sammy flew the coop," Valentine said. "He ran right after we grilled him."

Bill clenched his jaw. "That lousy prick. I gave him a second chance, and this is how he repays us." He asked the tech to replay the tape of Skins, and they both watched it again. Bill cursed under his breath. "This isn't good enough to convict."

"It isn't?"

"No." Bill pointed at Skins's right hand. It hung over the edge of the table and beneath his other arm, hiding the palmed card from his opponents but not entirely from the camera's eye. A tiny sliver of card showed between Skins's third and fourth fingers. Cheaters called this "leaking."

"Our illustrious mayor, who used to be a high-priced defense attorney, was able to get specific laws put on the books in regards to how close a mucker's hands had to be to the table for a crime to have actually been committed," Bill said. "Skins's hands aren't close enough."

"But we saw him switch cards," Valentine protested.

"We saw him cover the cards with his hands," Bill corrected him. "We didn't see the actual switch. The only evidence we have of foul play is him leaking the card, and since his hand is off the table, that isn't technically cheating. I know it sounds stupid, Tony, but it's the law."

Valentine felt himself getting angry, and took a walk around the room. Old-time gamblers had a special name for conversations like this. They called them "Who shot John?" They were so ridiculous, there was absolutely nothing to compare them to.

When he came back, Bill was still standing there.

"So what do we do?" Valentine asked.

"We wait, and get another tape of Skins cheating," Bill replied.

"You're going to let Skins play some more?"

"I don't have a choice."

"But that's crazy. It's an elimination tournament.

Every time Skins cheats, some poor guy is getting knocked out."

"I want the evidence to stand up in court," Bill said. "Look, you want to bust DeMarco at the same time, right? Grab the dealer and the equipment and figure out once and for all what the kid's doing. Well, if we arrest Skins, and it doesn't hold up, then neither will a case against DeMarco if we find evidence of him cheating. His attorney will be able to say we seized his client under false pretenses."

"Hey," the tech who'd originally replayed the tape for Valentine called out. "They're back playing poker."

Valentine and Bill went over to the tech's monitor and stared at the screen.

Within ten minutes of play resuming, Skins chopped a card from his hand, stuck it beneath the table, and on the next hand, mucked the card in, and won the pot. DeMarco had folded and sat at the other end of the table, wearing a disgusted look on his face. *He knows something's wrong,* Valentine thought.

The tech replayed Skins doing the switch on a monitor. Bill cursed.

"Let me guess," Valentine said. "The video isn't good enough."

"You don't see the switch actually taking place," Bill said. "It won't fly in court."

Valentine felt like kicking something. Nothing made him angrier than a cheater ripping off innocent people. He supposed it had something to do with the crime itself. The cheater wasn't just stealing money. He was betraying a trust as well.

The tech spoke up. "Maybe I can help."

"How?" Bill asked.

"There's another surveillance camera on the table. The angle's from the side."

"Let's see it," Bill said.

The tech played the tape from the second surveillance camera. On this tape, the palmed card in Skins's hand was visible while it rested on the table. Bill slapped the tech on the back.

"Let me know if you ever want to come work for the GCB," Bill said.

"Thanks, Mr. Higgins."

"Is that enough to nail him?" Valentine asked.

"Yes," Bill said. "Now, how do I handle this, so we can expose DeMarco?"

Valentine pointed at the dealer on the monitor. "The dealer needs to be grabbed, plus whatever he brought to the table with him. Either he's wearing transmitting equipment, or it's hidden somewhere nearby."

"How's he sending the signals?"

"It happens when he deals the cards," Valentine said.

"How's DeMarco reading the signals?"

"Either he's wearing an inner-canal earpiece, or a thumper strapped to his leg, or they're coming through a cell phone on vibrate mode in his pocket."

"You figured this all out just now?"

Valentine nodded, annoyed he hadn't seen it sooner. The only way to effectively transmit information to a blind person was through sound. That was the secret to DeMarco's scam. Now, Valentine just had to find out how the cards were being read, and the case could be put to bed.

Bill put his hand appreciatively on Valentine's shoulder. "Good going," his friend said.

Picking up the phone on the tech's desk, Bill called downstairs to Celebrity's head of security and informed him that they were coming downstairs to "freeze" the table where Skins and DeMarco were playing. The GCB's greatest power was its ability to enter any casino, stop a game, and cart away the equipment for examination in their labs. Bill hung up the phone and looked at his watch. "Head of security needs five minutes to get his troops together."

"You need to tell him to be prepared to grab Scalzo and his bodyguard as well," Valentine said. "They might get violent when we expose what's going on."

"Good idea." Bill reached for the phone when it began to ring. The tech answered it, then turned as white as a sheet. He meekly handed the receiver to Bill.

"It's for you, Mr. Higgins. It's the governor."

Bill brought the receiver to his mouth. He identified himself, then listened to what the governor had to say. After a few moments, the puzzled look on Bill's face turned to anger. He said good-bye and dropped the receiver loudly into its cradle on the desk.

"What's wrong?" Valentine asked.

"The governor has ordered me not to disrupt the tournament."

"*What?*"

"He doesn't want the bust being filmed and shown on national television."

"*How the hell did he know?*"

"Someone on the floor called him. He told me to arrest Skins after play ended for the day."

Valentine stared at the live feed from the tournament on the tech's monitor. The action at the feature table was heavy, with Skins involved in another monster pot. He felt something inside of him snap and headed for the door.

"Where are you going?" Bill called out.

"To put a stop to this," Valentine said.

33

Valentine took the stairs two at a time down to Celebrity's main floor. He was mad as hell, and his feet had a real bounce in them. Entering the poker room, he headed straight for the feature table.

He was going to take Skins out of the picture. Letting Skins continue to scam the tournament reminded him of drug stings he'd heard about that let dealers continue to sell narcotics while the cops built up evidence. The purpose was to get the guy at the top, but in Valentine's view, that was wrong. Cops were supposed to protect the innocent, which meant stopping the crime the moment you saw it happening.

The feature table was aglow in the TV cameras' bright lights. Eight players were at the table. Skins, DeMarco, and six other guys who were probably decent players but didn't have a chance with two cheaters working them over.

Valentine came up behind Skins. There were two ways to deal with a cheater. You could arrest him, or scare him. Scaring a cheater had its benefits. The cheater never came back, and he'd tell his friends about the experience. The casino would get a reputation, which wasn't a bad thing.

A security guard materialized in front of him. Blond, late twenties, and built like a small gorilla. "Please keep away from the table while play is going on," the guard said.

"Isn't this the no limit, sixty-and-over tournament?"

A smile appeared on the guard's face. "No, sir. You must be lost."

Valentine crossed the room to the cash bar. Taking out his wallet, he tossed a handful of cash in front of the bartender then picked up a tray sitting on the bar and balanced it on his upturned palm. "Six beers," he said.

"Where are you taking my tray?" the bartender asked.

"I'm playing a joke on my friends. I'll bring it back. Scout's honor."

The bartender pulled six beers from a cooler and put them on the tray. Valentine raised the tray to his face and approached the feature table with no one paying attention to him. A player at the table raised his arm and caught Valentine's eye.

"Over here," the player said.

Valentine served the guy a beer. The guy pulled a monster wad out of his pocket and dropped a twenty on the tray. "Keep the change."

Valentine stuffed the money into his pocket, then circled the table so he was behind the dealer. He spied a silver cigarette lighter to the dealer's right. The lighter had Celebrity's logo stamped on its side. Several dealers in the tournament had the same lighter, and he'd assumed they were a promotional gimmick. Now, he wasn't so sure.

He kept moving and came around to where Skins was sitting. He served Skins a beer, and Skins shot him a puzzled look.

"Compliments of the lady at the bar," Valentine said.

"Thanks," Skins said.

He sensed motion in the crowd and looked up. The guard he'd spoken with was standing nearby with four other guards. A posse. If he did something stupid, they'd pummel him. At the same time, he couldn't let this nonsense with Skins continue.

Then he had an idea.

He placed his thumb below Skin's shoulder and drew an imaginary line down the cheater's back. It was called the brush off, and used by casinos to tell undesirables to hit the road. Skins sat up in his chair like he'd been shocked with a live wire.

"You've been made," Valentine said under his breath.

"Excuse me?" Skins said.

Skins was an old-timer, with tobacco-stained teeth and a crooked nose, and he was not willing to give up a big score so easily.

"They have it on tape," Valentine said.

"I don't know what you're talking about."

"The surveillance camera caught you mucking. You need to practice some more. The card palmed in your hand leaked."

Skins swallowed hard. Play had resumed, and Valentine walked away from the table and into the waiting arms of the casino's security guards.

*   *   *

The guards took the tray away from Valentine and hustled him into the lobby. They were big and mean and didn't mind shoving him around. He tried to tell them he was doing a job for the Gaming Control Board, but they wouldn't listen. One of the guards started to read him the riot act when Valentine heard a familiar voice.

"Tony? What's going on?"

It was Gloria Curtis coming out of the hotel restaurant. She was trailed by Zack, his camera slung over his shoulder. Valentine caught her eye and silently mouthed the word *Help!* She instantly understood and stepped up to the guards.

"Excuse me, but what's going on here?" she demanded.

"Ma'am, please stand back," a guard said.

"I will do no such thing," she replied matter-of-factly. "I'm Gloria Curtis with WSPN news, and this gentleman is Tony Valentine, president of Grift Sense, a consulting firm hired by the Nevada Gaming Control Board to investigate a cheating scandal at the World Poker Showdown. Who are you?"

"I work for casino security," the guard said.

"Do you have a name?" she asked.

The guard didn't answer. Gloria snapped her fingers, and Zack handed her a mike, then started to film. She shoved the mike in the guard's face. "I'm sure our viewing audience would be interested in hearing why Celebrity, which is hosting the tournament, would choose to pull an investigator off the floor. Care to respond?"

The guard released his grip on Valentine's sleeve. Then he whipped a cell phone from his pocket and made a call. He explained the situation to whoever was in charge. Satisfied, he folded his phone.

"Our mistake," the guard said. "Sorry to bother you, Mr. Valentine."

Without another word, the guard and his posse marched back inside the poker room.

"What in God's name was that all about?" Gloria asked.

The lobby was crowded with people, and Valentine pulled Gloria over to a large birdcage filled with exotic parrots, the birds flapping their wings and eyeing them suspiciously. "Bill Higgins and I caught a player named Skins Turner on videotape switching cards," he explained. "Bill was going to arrest him but got ordered by the governor to wait until play had stopped for the day."

"Let me guess," she said. "The governor's afraid of the bad publicity."

"That's all he seems to be afraid of."

"What do you mean?"

"Skins was cheating, just like DeMarco's cheating. But the governor is more interested in protecting the town's interests than he is in protecting the integrity of his games."

"Are you in trouble?"

There was always follow-up when a customer got escorted out of a casino, and it was usually negative. "Probably," he said.

"That's terrible, Tony. Has that ever happened to you on a job before?"

Valentine shook his head. He'd been in the consulting racket for two years and never been treated like this before. It was a real low point. Gloria took his hand and gave it a squeeze. She was the one good thing that had come out of this job, and he supposed he could live with whatever happened.

Zack appeared. He'd slipped into the poker room and announced that Skins had lost over five million in chips to DeMarco on a bluff. On the very next hand, Skins had gone "all in," shoved his remaining chips into the pot, and lost. He was now out of the tournament.

"Thanks for the update," Gloria said.

They watched Zack walk away. Gloria squeezed his hand again. "See?" she asked.

"See what?" Valentine said.

"Every once in a while, the good guys *do* win."

Valentine wasn't so sure. Skins's loss had put DeMarco back in the leader's spot. DeMarco was going to win the tournament and the damage would be done. He felt his cell phone vibrate and pulled it from his pocket. It was Bill.

"How much trouble am I in?" Valentine asked his friend.

It was rare for Bill to be at a loss for words. His friend coughed into the phone.

"I just got off the phone with the governor," Bill said. "He heard about what you just pulled with Skins Turner."

"Was he angry?"

"Just a little. You've been barred from the tournament."

34

"**T**his had better be good," Detective Joey Marconi said, driving south on Atlantic Avenue.

"Yeah," Detective Eddie Davis said, sitting beside his partner. "You keep us waiting in the parking lot for an hour, this had better be *real* good."

Gerry Valentine sat in the backseat of Marconi's car. He'd started reminiscing with Vinny Fountain inside Harold's House of Pancakes and not only forgotten the time, but also the two detectives outside, neither of whom had slept in the past two days.

Marconi followed Vinny Fountain's car on Atlantic Avenue. Vinny drove a souped-up Pontiac Firebird with racing stripes down both sides. Vinny had told Gerry that he could find out who'd made the gaffed Yankees cap found in Bally's casino. Gerry had told Davis and Marconi, and the detectives had agreed to follow Vinny, but not without letting him know how pissed off they were.

"You have a good breakfast?" Davis asked.

"Just some coffee," Gerry lied.

"How did you get that jelly stain on your chin?" Marconi wanted to know.

Gerry appraised his reflection in the window. The stain was on the point of his chin. *Busted,* he thought.

"It's a birthmark," Gerry said.

"You're something else," Marconi told him.

They drove to Margate City on the southernmost tip of the island. At Huntington Avenue, Vinny hung a left. Marconi followed him, and when Vinny parked on the street, Marconi pulled his vehicle directly behind him. It was a residential neighborhood of two-story shingled houses and small, well-kept yards. Across the street, a dog strained against its chain, barking at them.

"Any idea where we are?" Davis asked.

"This is where Vinny's father lives," Gerry said, checking the numbers on the doors. He'd known Vinny since junior high school and had come over here many times. The house looked smaller than he remembered, but so did most things on the island.

"Would you gentlemen mind staying here?" Gerry asked.

Davis and Marconi turned around and shot him wicked stares.

"Better not keep us waiting," Marconi said, his lips hardly moving.

"Wouldn't dream of it," Gerry said.

Vinny's father, Angelo Fountain, was a professional tailor and ran his business out of the living room of his house, his customers getting fitted in front of a display case filled with black-and-white wedding pictures of

Angelo and his late wife, Marie. In the case was also a sign: CHEAP CLOTHES ARE MADE, GARMENTS ARE BUILT.

The TV set was on when they came in, Jerry Springer reading off a card. Angelo was a small, delicate man, and balanced himself on the edge of the couch, a yellow tape measure hanging around his neck. He looked up in surprise.

"Get the hell out of my house," he said.

Vinny stood in the foyer, unbuttoning his jacket. Gerry hung behind him.

"Didn't you hear what I just told you?" his father asked.

"I've got a visitor with me," his son said.

"Like that makes a difference? Who did you bring this time, John Gotti?"

"He's dead, Pop."

"Then I'm sure it's someone just like him," his father retorted. "Every time I turn around, the police are wanting to talk to me about you, or something you've done. My son, the professional crook."

Gerry glanced at Vinny's profile, wondering what effect this old man's words were having on him. If the verbal assault bothered Vinny, he didn't show it. Tugging his jacket off, Vinny tossed it on a chair and entered the living room.

"I brought an old friend with me," Vinny said. "You remember Gerry Valentine, don't you, Pop?"

Angelo Fountain had come to the United States on a boat from Italy, and had brought with him manners and class. He killed the TV with a remote, stood up, and graciously stuck out his hand. "Of course I remember. Tony Valentine's boy."

Gerry shook his hand. "It's good to see you, sir."

"And you as well. Are you still running an illegal bookmaking operation?" Angelo Fountain asked.

There was an edge to his voice that made Gerry hesitate. He took out a business card, and handed it to the older man. "I gave up the rackets, Mr. Fountain. I'm working with my father now."

Angelo Fountain removed his bifocals to study the card. In his late seventies, he wore a navy blue suit overlaid with a faint windowpane check. His spread-collar shirt was light blue, his necktie a soft red, as was his matching pocket foulard. He'd always dressed like a head of state, even though he rarely left the neighborhood.

"I thought your father retired," Angelo said.

"He did," Gerry said. "My mom passed away, and he went back to work as a consultant."

"How long you work for him?"

"It's going on six months."

The older man's face softened. "You like it?"

That was a loaded question if Gerry had ever heard one. His father could be a bear, and sometimes drove Gerry nuts. But it was an honest business, and he could tuck his daughter in at night knowing he wasn't doing things she might someday be ashamed of.

"Love it," Gerry said.

Angelo Fountain brewed a fresh pot of coffee and served his guests. Gerry had the foresight to ask him to make two extra cups, and took them outside to the two detectives parked by the curb.

"Service's improving," Marconi said.

Gerry grabbed the Yankees cap off the backseat. He

hadn't wanted to bring the cap into the house and just stick it under Mr. Fountain's nose. Going back inside, he found Vinny and his father practically at blows.

"You're a bum," his father said.

"Says who?" Vinny replied.

"Every single person on this island."

"I've never been convicted of a single crime," his son protested.

"You and O.J. Simpson," his father said.

Gerry made Vinny squinch over and sat down between father and son on the couch. They stopped arguing, with Angelo glaring at his son.

"Mr. Fountain, I need your help," Gerry said, handing him the cap. "This baseball cap turned up during a case. Vinny thinks you might be able to tell me who stitched it."

Angelo Fountain examined the receiver and LEDs sewn into the cap's rim. His hands were small and fine-boned, the skin almost translucent. A minute passed. He was taking too long, and Gerry guessed it was someone he knew and didn't want to snitch on. The locals were famous for closing ranks when it came to protecting one another.

"I wouldn't have come here, and put this imposition on you, if there wasn't a good reason," Gerry said.

Angelo Fountain looked into his visitor's face. "And what might that be?"

"The man who had this cap made has a contract on my father's life."

"Ahh," Angelo Fountain said.

Another minute went by. The older man put his hand on Gerry's knee, gave it a friendly squeeze. "I like your father. He's a good man. I'll help you out."

"Thank you, Mr. Fountain."

"A tailor on the island made this baseball cap. I recognize the stitching," Angelo Fountain said. "This tailor was in prison, made friends with some bad people. When he got out of prison, he started taking jobs from these people."

"What kind of jobs?" Gerry asked.

"Tailoring jobs. To help them steal from the casinos."

"Steal how?"

"I'll show you." Angelo Fountain went to the other side of the living room, pulled open a drawer on a cabinet, and returned holding a paper bag that he dropped on Gerry's lap. "This tailor gets a lot of work from these people. Sometimes, he asks me to help out. I always say no, but he still comes by."

Gerry removed the bag's contents. There were several cloth bags made of dark material, and a metal contraption tied up with wire that looked like a kid's toy. Gerry untied the wire, and realized he was holding a Kepplinger holdout, a device used by card cheaters to invisibly switch cards during a game. The Kepplinger was worn beneath a sports jacket, and secretly delivered cards into a cheater's hand through his sleeve, the mechanism powered by a wire stretched between the cheater's knees. In order for the Kepplinger to work properly, it had to be fitted to the jacket, and Gerry remembered his father saying that only a handful of people in the country knew how to do this.

Gerry examined the cloth bags. They were subs, a device used by crooked employees to steal chips. The mouth of each sub had a flexible steel blade sewn into it, with an elastic strap attached to both ends. The sub was worn in the pants, between the underwear and belt line. The crooked employee would palm a chip off the table, and by sucking in his gut, drop the chip into the mouth of the sub. The move took a second, and was invisible if done properly.

Gerry put the Kepplinger and the subs back into the paper bag. Angelo Fountain had just told him something important. This tailor had so much work, he couldn't handle it all. A one-man factory.

"The police would like to talk to this tailor," Gerry said.

"They going to send him back to prison?" Angelo Fountain asked.

Gerry shook his head. "Making cheating equipment isn't against the law. They just want to ask him who ordered the baseball cap."

"That's all?"

"That's all, Mr. Fountain. They just want the name."

Angelo Fountain got a pad of paper and a pencil from the kitchen. He wrote the tailor's name and address on the pad, his handwriting painstakingly slow. Then he tore off the slip and gave it to Gerry. They shook hands in the foyer.

"Tell your father I said hello," Angelo Fountain said.

Gerry and Vinny stood on the front porch buttoning their jackets, the wind blowing hard and cold off the nearby ocean. Davis and Marconi were at the curb, the car's windows steamed up. Gerry guessed they would drive straight to the tailor's address, and pressure him. That would put them one step closer to stopping George

Scalzo's operation in Atlantic City, and putting a bunch of hoodlums in prison.

"You need to take your father away for a while," Gerry said.

"Why?"

"Just to be safe."

Vinny looked back at the house and shuddered from something besides the cold. "My father and I don't happen to get along, in case you didn't notice."

"He still talks to you, doesn't he?"

"Meaning what? You and your father didn't talk?"

"Not for a long time," Gerry admitted.

Vinny lit up a cigarette, blew a cloud that hung over their heads. "So what changed?"

That was a good question. Up until six months ago, his relationship with his father had been no better than Vinny's and his father's. But it had done a one-eighty since he'd gone to work with his father. Now they talked in civil tones and ate meals together and even shared a few laughs. It wasn't perfect, but if he'd learned anything in his thirty-six years on this earth, few things in life ever were.

"Me," Gerry said. "I changed."

35

Valentine folded his cell phone and dropped it in his pocket. He'd been barred from the tournament. It didn't seem possible, and he tried to guess how many millions of dollars he'd saved Nevada's casinos since becoming a consultant. Fifty million, and that was a low estimate. And this was how they repaid him. The leper treatment.

"The news wasn't good, was it?" Gloria asked.

"You're a mind reader," he said.

They were still standing beside the cage of noisy parrots in the lobby. Gloria put her hand on his wrist. She was a toucher, something he'd always found attractive in a woman. The lobby noise made it hard to talk, but she tried anyway.

"I hope it wasn't about your son," she said.

"No, Gerry's fine. At least the last time I checked."

"He's sort of unpredictable, isn't he?"

"That's a nice way to put it."

"Was it about the job?"

"Yes. The governor has barred me from stepping foot

inside Celebrity's poker room while the tournament is taking place. I've also been nicely told to leave town."

"That's wrong. I hope you aren't going to comply."

There was something in Gloria's voice that hadn't been there a few days ago, and he guessed the feeling-out process was over. "I really don't have much choice."

"But you haven't nailed DeMarco."

"I'm not sure they want me to," he said.

"You need to stall them."

"I do?"

"Yes. So you can have more time to solve the case."

He didn't have to talk to Gloria very long to be reminded that she was in the entertainment business and liked happy endings. "That's not a bad idea. How would you suggest I stall them?"

She bit her lower lip, thinking, then snapped her fingers. "Got it. You're here on a job for the Nevada Gaming Control Board, right?"

"Correct."

"Make them pay you before you leave. Cash."

It wasn't a bad idea, and he could see Bill agreeing to it, knowing exactly what he was up to. He pulled out his cell phone. Moments later, he had Bill on the line and he made his request. His friend chuckled softly into the phone.

"I'll come by in the morning with your money," Bill said.

"Not too early," Valentine said. "You know how I like my beauty rest."

"Look, Tony, there's only so far I can push this," Bill said. "I'll meet you in the lobby at noon with your cash. I'd suggest you leave town after that."

Valentine glanced at his watch. It was easy to lose track of time in Las Vegas, and he was surprised to see it was four o'clock in the afternoon. Bill was giving him another twenty hours to crack the case.

"Noon is beautiful," Valentine said.

He tucked his cell phone into his pocket then took out his wallet and removed the valet stub for his rental car. Gloria shot him a concerned look. "You off again?"

"Yes. You're coming, too."

Coins of crimson appeared on each of her cheeks. "I am?"

"I need you to help me crack this case."

"You do?"

"Yes. There's something wrong with this picture, and I can't seem to figure out what it is. My old sergeant used to make his detectives share cases, in the hopes that another pair of eyes might see something that the first detective missed."

"I'm game. Where are we going?"

"To see an old crook," Valentine said.

Ten minutes later, they were in Valentine's rental cruising down the strip. Vegas looked different during the day, like a whore without her makeup. Hindsight being 20/20, he now knew that he should have chased Sammy Mann down the moment he'd heard Sammy had run out on them. Sammy was scared, and not because he hadn't reported the other cheaters he knew to be playing in the tournament. Sammy knew they were close to solving the case, and hadn't wanted to be around when it happened.

Las Vegas was the fastest-growing city in the country, and pricey condo buildings were starting to sprout up on the strip. Sammy lived on the tenth floor of a building called the Veneto in a nice corner apartment. Valentine had visited him back when Sammy was fighting cancer, and he'd been impressed by the expensive furnishings. Most crooks died penniless. Sammy had saved up for a rainy day.

"Who are we here to see?" Gloria asked as they parked in the condo's lot. "Or is that a surprise?"

"Sorry," Valentine said. "His name is Sammy Mann. He's a retired cheater."

"How do you know he's home?"

Valentine glanced up at the towering glass structure. He *didn't* know for sure. Sammy might have left town, but that seemed unlikely. Most older people felt safest in their homes. They entered the building's lobby, and Valentine found Sammy's name on the intercom address book and pushed the button for Sammy's apartment. Sammy answered with a hoarse "Yes?"

"It's Tony Valentine. I'm here with a friend. Let us up."

"I'm sick," the old cheater replied.

"You're going to be a lot sicker if you don't talk to me," Valentine said.

The front door buzzed open.

Gloria laughed. "You're something else," she said.

Sammy answered the door in a threadbare bathrobe and leather slippers. No greetings were exchanged; he simply opened the door, and they followed him into a living room with a leather couch that faced a picture window looking down on the strip. He motioned and they sat. From a pitcher he poured three glasses of ice water and set them on a coffee table. Then he sat in a chair and showed them his profile.

"Let me guess," Valentine said. "You have a sore throat."

"Very sore," Sammy said.

"Probably prevents you from talking."

Sammy nodded solemnly. Valentine glanced around the room, seeing a lot of upgrades since his last visit, but nothing that would tell you what Sammy did for a living. You had to know him to know what he was.

"You want to hear a funny story?" Valentine asked.

"I love a good laugh," Sammy said.

"You don't sound like you have a sore throat."

Sammy coughed into his hand.

"That's better. Okay, here it is. I'm a rookie cop in Atlantic City, and as green as they come. One day, I'm walking my beat with my partner, and he tells me that the crooks in Atlantic City are more violent than the crooks in New York. He tells me that in New York, if one crook is trying to steal a truck of furs, and another crook steals the truck first, the first crook won't take it personally. Not so in Atlantic City. If a crook catches another crook trying to steal the truck away from him, he'll kill him.

"That didn't make any sense to me. Why would the crooks in Atlantic City, which has twenty thousand residents, be more violent than crooks in New York, which has six million residents? I was obviously missing something, and finally my partner explained it to me. There were less things to steal in Atlantic City. A lot less. In New York, a crook could go steal something else. But in

Atlantic City, big scores were few and far between. That was the piece I was missing.

"So here's the thing, Sammy. I'm missing something that's right in front of my face, and it's bothering the hell out of me. I *have* to know, you know?"

Sammy lifted his arms off the armrests of his chair. Let them hang in the air for a few seconds, then shrugged and dropped them. "You know the answer," he said.

"I do?"

Sammy nodded. "You just told it to me. Atlantic City is different than New York. Well, Las Vegas is different, too."

Gloria slipped off the couch and came up beside Sammy's chair. She knelt down and put her hand onto Sammy's arm, all the while looking into the old cheater's eyes, which were dark and unflinching. "How is it different?" she asked.

Sammy laughed under his breath and looked at Valentine. "How long you been a team?"

"You're our first victim," Valentine said.

"You'd never know it," the old cheater said.

Rising, Sammy went to an entertainment center on the opposite side of the room, pulled open a drawer, and rummaged through a collection of videotapes, taking out two. He powered up the TV, then popped a tape into the VCR. Returning to his chair, he picked up a glass of water and took a sip.

"Just watch," he said.

The tape was of a heavyweight boxing match, the grainy color showing its age. George Foreman fighting a game German kid named Axel Schultz. Valentine followed boxing and had a vague memory of the fight. Mid-nineties, Las Vegas, with Foreman getting slapped around for twelve unspectacular rounds, yet somehow winning the decision. Schultz had gone back to Germany, never to be heard from again.

Sammy shut the tape off after the decision was read, and Foreman announced the winner. Poor George hadn't looked like the winner, his face more damaged than Freddy Kruger's in the *Halloween* movies. Sammy stuck the second tape into the VCR, fast-forwarded it to a spot near the end, then returned to his chair. The tape was of a college football game and looked more recent.

"I recognize this tape," Gloria said, still kneeling beside Sammy's chair. "This is a game between the Wisconsin Badgers and the Las Vegas Rebels played here in Vegas a few years ago, isn't it?"

"That's right," Sammy said. "You like college football?"

"I've covered it for years," she said. "This game was a big upset. The Rebels were heavy favorites, but the Badgers ran them all over the field and won by twenty points. If I remember correctly, something odd happened at the very end of the game."

Sammy raised his eyebrows expectantly. "Yes?"

"The lights in the stadium went out, and the game was awarded to the Badgers," Gloria said. "I don't think that's ever happened in a college football game before."

"First time it ever happened," Sammy said. He pointed at the screen. "Watch."

On the screen, a team of guys in red jerseys were playing a team of guys in white. The white team was getting the worst of it and looked ready for the showers. A healthy-sized crowd was cheering the red team on. Suddenly the stadium lights flickered, then went out altogether, throwing both teams into darkness. The action on the football field stopped, with no one knowing what to do.

The tape ended and the screen went dark. Sammy shifted his gaze to the window, his eyes fixed on the casinos lining the strip. "People think this is a gambling town, but it's not," he said. "Las Vegas does not gamble. Never has, and never will. Take the Foreman fight. This city hosts a hundred boxing matches a year. Nobody cares who wins, or loses. Except if there's a lot of money on the fight. Then *everyone* cares.

"Axel Schultz beat George Foreman silly that night. Every journalist and sports writer who was there said so. But the judges gave the fight to Big George. Why do you think they did that?"

"Because a lot of German tourists came to the fight, and bet heavily on their boy to win," Valentine said.

"That was one reason," Sammy said. "There's another."

"I know," Gloria said. "George Foreman was a huge draw, and Axel Schultz wasn't. If the judges gave the fight to Schultz, he'd take the belt home to Germany, and Las Vegas would lose out."

Sammy nodded. "Very good. By denying Schultz the title, Las Vegas didn't lose any big fights."

"What about the football game," Valentine said. "What happened there?"

"Seventeen thousand Wisconsin fans were in town for

that game, and bet heavily on the Badgers to beat the Rebels," Sammy said.

"But the Badgers *did* beat the Rebels," Gloria said.

"Yes, but the Wisconsin fans didn't collect," Sammy said. "Las Vegas's sports books have an unusual rule. If a football game is stopped with more than four minutes left to play, the game is considered no contest, and everyone's money is returned. When the stadium lights went out, there were more than four minutes left on the clock."

"So the lights were turned out on purpose," Gloria said.

Sammy nodded.

"That's unethical," Gloria said.

"No one out here saw it that way," Sammy said. "Just smart business. You're probably asking yourself, what does this have to do with the World Poker Showdown? The answer is simple. Every casino boss in town knows DeMarco's cheating. But if he's exposed, it will hurt their business. So the town is going to let it slide until the tournament is over. After that, it will get cleaned up."

"But what about the other players in the tournament? Or the fans?" Gloria asked, unable to hide the indignation in her voice. "Don't they matter?"

Sammy shook his head sadly. Valentine pushed himself off the couch. *Las Vegas doesn't gamble.* It was another way of saying that Las Vegas wasn't in the business of losing. He supposed someone had to pay for all those fancy casinos and flashing neon signs. He shook Sammy's hand and thanked him for his time, then escorted Gloria out of the apartment.

36

Gerry Valentine was surprised. He'd expected Detectives Eddie Davis and Joey Marconi to drive to the address of the tailor who Angelo Fountain had fingered and grill him. But the detectives had instead driven to the municipal courthouse on Atlantic Avenue and gone upstairs to the second floor to see a judge in his chambers.

Marconi and Davis had an interesting theory that they'd presented to Gerry during the drive. The detectives had originally thought that the baseball caps were being manufactured on an assembly line. But while sitting outside Angelo Fountain's house, they'd had a change of opinion.

If a tailor was making the caps, then the caps were custom jobs. If that was true, then George Scalzo's blackjack cheating gang were coming to the tailor's place of business, getting fitted, then returning when the cap was done. That meant the tailor probably had records containing the gang's names and phone numbers. It would be enough evidence to show that the gang was conspiring to cheat the island's casinos, and land them in jail.

"A slam dunk, " Davis had said in the car.

Gerry hadn't seen it that way. The tailor wasn't going to rat out the mob.

"*If* the tailor has records," Gerry had replied.

"Every good tailor keeps records," Marconi said, handling the wheel. "It's part of the business. The only thing we need is a warrant to search the tailor's premises. That's where you come in."

"Me?" Gerry said.

"Yes. We'll need to have you explain the scams to the judge. You're the expert."

Gerry had shifted uncomfortably in his seat. "Whatever you say."

The judge they went to see was named Alva Dopking. Dopking was a lanky, cleft-chinned former prosecutor who'd been making criminals' lives miserable in Atlantic City for thirty years. Gerry had come up before him in juvenile court and had not enjoyed the experience. Sitting in Dopking's book-lined chambers, he kept his eyes glued to the floor while Davis and Marconi stood in front of Dopking's desk, and argued their case.

Dopking listened while sucking on an unlit cigar. His wavy dark hair had turned snow white; otherwise, he looked the same as Gerry remembered. He was a tough nut, and he didn't like it when his directions weren't followed.

"I'm just not buying your argument," Dopking said, tossing his cigar into an ashtray on the desk. "First of all, the tailor who gave you the information—Angelo Fountain—how do you know he doesn't have a gripe with this other tailor, Bruno Traffatore, and isn't out to make the man's life miserable?

"Second, I'm not comfortable with your theory that these gaffed baseball caps are being custom-made by Traffatore. I've had cheating cases brought before me in the past, and the equipment came from magic shops or companies that mass-produce this stuff."

Davis stepped forward. "Your Honor, we have an expert who's been helping us with this case. The consulting firm he works for specializes in catching casino cheaters. He'll confirm everything we've said to you this afternoon."

Dopking looked Gerry's way. "Him?"

"Yes, Your Honor."

Dopking shot Gerry an unfriendly look, and Gerry felt himself squirm. Dopking had a reputation for unflinching honesty, and as a result, commanded more respect than all the island's politicians rolled together.

"What is this expert's name?" Dopking asked.

"Gerry Valentine," Davis replied.

The hint of a smile played on Dopking's lips. "I'd like to hear what Mr. Gerry Valentine has to say," he said.

Davis turned around, and motioned for Gerry to come forward. Gerry wedged himself between the two detectives and identified himself.

"Tony Valentine's son?" Dopking asked, as if wanting to be sure.

"That's right. I mean, yes, Your Honor."

Dopking's smile vanished. "I thought you were a bookie."

Gerry opened his mouth but nothing came out. The judge leaned forward.

"I do keep track of the people who step before me, you know," Dopking said.

Gerry found his voice. "Yes, Your Honor. I gave up the rackets and now work in my father's consulting business. I'm here to ask you to grant the detectives' request, and give them a warrant to search Bruno Traffatore's place of business. I will personally vouch for the integrity of Angelo Fountain, the informant who gave us the name. He offered up the name only after I pressured him."

"So he has no gripe with this other tailor?"

"No, Your Honor."

Dopking studied him. "I'm still doubtful of the detectives' claim that Traffatore is custom-making cheating equipment. Aren't these things mass-produced?"

"The items that are mass-produced are junk. The real work is made by pros."

The gaffed baseball cap was sitting on the desk. "Give me an example besides this baseball cap," Dopking said.

Gerry removed a five-dollar casino chip from his pocket and handed it to the judge. The chip was actually a shell with a hollowed-out interior. Dopking examined it, then said, "Explain how this works."

"It's a dealer/agent scam, Your Honor. Let's say a blackjack dealer wants to rip off his own game. His agent plays at his table, and bets the shell. Every time the agent loses, the dealer picks up the shell and places it over another player's losing bet. The shell is put in the dealer's tray, and the agent buys the shell back. What he gets in return is the shell, and whatever denomination chip the dealer just stole off the table."

Dopking tossed the shell back to him. "And these shells are custom-made?"

"Yes, Your Honor. They have to be."

"Why is that?"

"Because of the extremes casinos take to ensure their chips aren't counterfeited, Your Honor. A shell must be made from one of the casino's own chips."

"Do you know this from experience?" the judge asked.

Gerry flushed. He'd thought a lot about the file Marconi had shown him that linked his name to numerous scams on the island. He guessed there were a lot of law enforcement people who had a bad opinion of him as a result of that file. "No, Your Honor. I've never used that scam, nor have I ever scammed a casino. My father explained it to me."

Dopking leaned forward. "That was inappropriate of me to ask. Please accept my apologies."

"Of course, Your Honor."

"Tell me something. You did well as a bookie, didn't you?"

Gerry didn't know what to say. Part of the success of being a bookie was his ability to hide the success of his operation. From the law, the Internal Revenue Service, and his father. Telling a judge how well he'd done didn't seem like a good idea.

"My uncle was a bookie, used to work out of the Marlborough-Blenheim Hotel," Dopking went on. "He did well, so I'm assuming you also did well."

"It wasn't a bad way to make a living," Gerry conceded.

"I'd like to know why you left that and joined your father's business."

The hardest part of going straight was having to tell the truth. Gerry didn't like it—the truth made you vulnerable—but in this case, he saw no other choice.

Taking out his wallet, he showed Dopking a recent snapshot of his wife and daughter.

"I'd say you made a smart choice," the judge said. "Is there anything else you wish to add?"

Gerry couldn't tell which way Dopking was leaning, and didn't want to leave his chambers empty-handed. "Yes, Your Honor. Bruno Traffatore has made other items used to scam Atlantic City's casinos. If Detectives Davis and Marconi search the tailor's business, I believe they'll find the records of these other scammers."

"So we're talking about more than one crime, here?"

"Many crimes, Your Honor."

"Would you be willing to sign a sworn affidavit supporting the need for a search warrant? You can do it anonymously, with the detectives attesting to your honesty."

Gerry hesitated. He was about to take a bunch of crooks down, and had a feeling that some people he knew were going to get burned as a result. He felt bad about it, but wasn't going to let that stop him. "Yes, Your Honor, I would."

Without further discussion Dopking issued the warrant to the detectives. As they started to leave, the judge said, "I heard about your mother's passing. How's your father holding up?"

"He's back to his old tricks," Gerry replied.

Dopking picked up his cigar and sucked on it. "Good. Tell him I miss him."

Bruno Traffatore lived on the east side of the island in a depressing neighborhood of 1950s shotgun-style houses. Gerry remained in Marconi's car while the detectives went inside the house and searched the premises. After ten minutes, a black Cadillac Eldorado pulled up in front of the house and parked in front of Marconi's vehicle. The big Italian guy who climbed out was the epitome of a goombah, and carried a crumpled paper bag. Seeing Gerry, he sauntered over.

"Yo," the goombah said.

Gerry rolled his window down. "Hey."

The goombah scratched his stomach. "You waiting to see Mr. Traffatore?"

Another customer, Gerry thought. "Yeah," he said.

"Let me go ahead of you," the goombah said, removing a Yankees cap from the paper bag. "I'm in a rush, you know?"

Gerry hid the smile forming on his lips. They'd hooked a live one. "Sure," he said.

The goombah stuck his meaty paw through Gerry's open window and they shook hands. Gerry guessed his age to be about thirty, his rank in Scalzo's organization no higher than a soldier. He watched the goombah walk up the brick path to Traffatore's house and punch the bell. Moments later, Davis opened the front door. From the car, Gerry pointed at the goombah while mouthing the words *Arrest him*. Davis flashed him the okay sign, then ushered the goombah inside.

Fifteen minutes later Davis emerged from the house, the look of exhaustion on his face having been replaced by one of glee. He knelt down next to Gerry's open window. "Looks like we hit the mother lode. Traffatore keeps records of all his clients in a shoe box. We've got the names, phone numbers, and addresses of every member of Scalzo's gang."

"What about the goombah?" Gerry asked. "Did you arrest him?"

"Yeah. Name's Albert Roselli. He's screaming for a lawyer."

"Screaming?"

"Yeah. I've never seen anything like it. Marconi told him to shut his yap or we'd tape it shut. Guy's sweating, too."

Gerry stared at the Eldorado parked in front of him. *I'm in a rush.* Was Albert going to work, and needed to get his baseball cap fixed? He relayed his suspicion to Davis, and saw the detective's face light up.

"Wait here," Davis said.

Roselli's vehicle was unlocked and Davis gave it a thorough search. When he finished, he came back to Marconi's car and tossed Gerry a black address book.

"The hits just keep coming," Davis said.

Gerry thumbed through the address book, his eyes scanning the pages. It was Scalzo's play book, and it contained the names of the island's casinos and the dates and times they were to be ripped off by his gang.

"Beautiful," Gerry said.

It took Davis two hours to marshal the necessary manpower to start making the busts. Over half of Scalzo's gang were working that afternoon, and over a hundred police and casino security forces were needed to arrest them.

Gerry stayed with Davis and Marconi as they went from casino to casino and systematically apprehended

Scalzo's gang. The baseball caps made the gang members easy to locate and allowed the detectives to march up to the tables, speak to the gang members by name, and arrest them. As Gerry watched the gang members being led away to vans waiting outside, he was surprised the gang hadn't retired the scam after the incident at Bally's the night before. His father said that what usually brought cheaters down was the greed factor. Once a cheater started stealing, it was often hard for him to stop.

The final arrests were made at Resorts International, the island's oldest casino. By now it was dark, and Gerry stood outside on the Boardwalk, sipping a double espresso to stay awake. He'd scored a big victory, but it felt hollow. He still didn't know how Scalzo was ripping off the World Poker Showdown, and suspected that none of the people who'd been arrested knew, either. Davis came out through the double doors and gave him a whack on the arm. "I owe you dinner, man."

Gerry forced a smile. The busts were going to make Davis and Marconi into heroes. That was worth celebrating, even if he wasn't in the mood.

"You're on," he said.

37

It was quitting time, and Mabel was heading out the door when the phone on Tony's desk rang. Glancing at the Caller ID, she saw that it was Special Agent Romero of the FBI.

"It's about time," she said aloud.

She'd called Romero earlier, gotten an impersonal voice mail, and left a message saying she urgently needed to speak with him about George Scalzo. She'd expected a prompt call back, having done Romero a huge favor a few days ago. The fact that he'd taken over half a day to respond was annoying to say the least.

"Grift Sense," she answered.

"Hello, Ms. Struck," Romero said. "I apologize for not getting back to you sooner, but I had to testify in court today, and they don't permit cell phones at the federal courthouse."

Mabel smiled into the receiver. An immediate apology, and a believable one to boot. "Thanks for calling back. I need your help."

"I'll do what I can," Romero said.

She settled into her chair. "I'm assisting my boss with

a case which involves a murder I believe George Scalzo was involved with."

"A recent murder?"

"Yes. It took place two weeks ago at the Atlantic City Medical Center. I'm trying to determine Scalzo's whereabouts during the time of the murder. When we spoke a few days ago, you told me that the FBI watches Scalzo, which I assume means you follow him whenever he goes out in public."

Romero cleared his throat. "That would be a logical assumption."

"Good. I realize that this is all hush-hush, but figured since we're both trying to accomplish the same thing—"

"Which is?"

She hated when men turned dense, and she let her tongue slip. "To put the murderous bastard in jail."

Romero laughed softly. "Yes. That's the FBI's goal as well. Please continue."

"I was hoping that you could look at your records and see if Scalzo visited the Atlantic City Medical Center the night of the murder. It would be a tremendous help in putting another piece into this puzzle we're wrestling with. Of course, it would remain strictly confidential."

There was silence as Romero weighed her request. Mabel picked up a pair of misspotted dice lying on Tony's desk and rolled them across the blotter. The dice had the numbers 2, 4, 6 printed on both sides. Because the human eye could see only three sides of a square, the duplication went unnoticed, allowing the cheater to win 90 percent of the time that he used them in a game of craps.

"I will need to speak with the agent in charge of monitoring Scalzo," Romero said. "It will be his decision whether or not to release the information you're asking for."

"Of course," Mabel said. "Should I give you the date?"

"Please."

Mabel gave Romero the date and time of Jack Donovan's murder.

"I'll see what I can do," Romero said. "Good-bye, Ms. Struck."

"When should I expect to hear back from you?" Mabel asked.

There was another silence on the line. Then Romero said, "Is this an emergency, Ms. Struck?"

Tony and Gerry were tangling with a man who wanted them both dead. If that wasn't an emergency, she didn't know what was. "It most certainly is."

He exhaled into the phone. "How about twenty minutes?"

"Twenty minutes would be perfect," she said.

Mabel had once bought a pamphlet off the Internet that detailed all the free stuff you could get from the government. It included the obvious health care benefits and food stamps, and the not-so-obvious government grants. What the pamphlet didn't mention was free help from the FBI, which to Mabel's way of thinking wasn't as outlandish as it sounded. The FBI were civil servants, no different from the working folks who picked up the trash and worked at the post office. They needed to be reminded of that every now and then.

She heard the front door slam. "Yolanda, is that you?"

"Yes," Yolanda replied from the front of the house. "I was out taking a walk and saw the light was on."

"Come on back, I could use the company," Mabel said.

Yolanda appeared, holding her sleeping baby. The office was small, and she settled on the floor, sitting in a lotus position. She wore cut-offs and a T-shirt, no makeup, her hair topknotted carelessly. Mabel thought she'd never known a woman as comfortable in her own skin.

"Any luck with the FBI?" Yolanda asked.

"Matter of fact, that's who I'm waiting to hear from," Mabel said. "I spoke with Special Agent Romero and explained your theory about George Scalzo being involved with Jack Donovan's murder."

"Our theory," Yolanda corrected her.

"Our theory. He promised to look into it and get right back to me."

"Are you hungry?"

"Starving."

"Me too. Stay put, and I'll whip something up. Do you mind holding the baby?"

"Of course not."

Yolanda put the child on Mabel's lap and headed for the kitchen. Lois was fast asleep, yet Mabel felt compelled to sing to her. Six months old and the picture of innocence. *It was hard to believe we all started out this way.*

"Does Tony have stock in Subway?" Yolanda asked a few minutes later. Finding several Subway sandwiches in Tony's refrigerator, she'd cut them up and put them on paper plates. She returned to the floor and took the baby. They started to eat.

"I've tried to convince Tony to cook for himself, but it's a lost cause," Mabel said. The phone rang and she snatched it up. "Grift Sense."

"Ms. Struck, I think I've got something for you," Special Agent Romero said.

Mabel scribbled on a legal pad while Romero talked. When he was done, she had over a page of notes. He reminded her that the information was confidential.

"Of course," she said. "Thank you for going to all this trouble."

"No problem. Good evening, Ms. Struck," he said.

Mabel hung up feeling goose bumps on her arms. Yolanda put down her sandwich and wiped her mouth with a paper napkin. "Something good?"

"Yes." Mabel squinted at her own handwriting. "On the night of Jack Donovan's murder, Scalzo's bodyguard drove Scalzo from his home in Newark to Atlantic City Medical Center. While the bodyguard stayed in the car, Scalzo went into the hospital and stayed for thirty minutes. The FBI agent who was tailing Scalzo went into the hospital and talked to the receptionist at the main greeting area. According to the receptionist, Scalzo said he was seeing a sick friend."

"So our theory is correct," Yolanda said. "Scalzo met up with the killer at the hospital, and took Jack Donovan's secret out with him."

"It certainly appears that way. Now, here's the odd part. According to Special Agent Romero, Scalzo also visited the hospital the following morning carrying a bouquet of flowers. The FBI agent thought it was odd and this time followed him inside.

"Scalzo went to the cancer ward and talked to a nurse on duty. The nurse went on break, and they both went downstairs to the cafeteria. He bought her breakfast and gave her the flowers. They talked for about fifteen minutes, then Scalzo left."

"Did the agent get the nurse's name?"

"Yes. Susan Gladwell. She's a senior nurse, worked at the hospital for ten years. The agent checked her out, said her record was clean."

"Until now," Yolanda said.

Mabel looked up from her notes. "What do you mean?"

"Don't you see? Nurse Gladwell is in cahoots with George Scalzo. That's how Scalzo was able to sneak Jack Donovan's secret out of the hospital without being spotted. She covered it up."

"That would make her an accessory to Jack Donovan's murder," Mabel said.

"It most certainly would."

Mabel chewed reflectively on the eraser end of her pencil. It was a good theory, only it wasn't logical. Why would a veteran nurse risk her career to help a mobster? And the flowers. Why had Scalzo brought those? There was something else going on here, a thread running beneath the surface that neither of them were seeing.

"You don't agree?" Yolanda asked.

Mabel shook her head. "I think we're both missing something."

"What?"

"The connection between Scalzo and this nurse."

Yolanda bit her lip. "What should we do?"

"I think I'll call Gerry and tell him what we've found," Mabel said. "Maybe he can make sense of it."

38

"**G**od, I must be the most naive person in the world," Gloria said.

"Second most naive," Valentine said.

"Who's the first?"

"Me."

They sat at a table in Celebrity's noisy sports bar, Gloria nursing a ten-dollar glass of chardonnay, Valentine a Diet Coke. They'd driven back from Sammy Mann's condo in a funk, with neither of them uttering more than a few words. Las Vegas had not been built on winners, but Sammy's explanation of the skullduggery taking place at the World Poker Showdown took that philosophy to a whole new level.

"I'm sorry things turned out this way," she said.

"I'm not."

"No? Why is that?"

He'd busted more hustlers than he could remember, and the ones that got away were particularly grating, but he'd never let his work overshadow the things in life that really mattered. He leaned across the table and kissed Gloria on the lips.

"Because I got to meet you," he said, pulling away.

She lowered her eyes and blushed. It was the first time he'd seen her look the least bit vulnerable. She had a wonderful exterior, but beneath it there was something equally wonderful. He hadn't done well with the opposite sex since his wife had died, but this relationship was one he wasn't going to let go. Out of the corner of his eye, he spotted Rufus Steele lurching past the bar, his Stetson tilted rakishly on his head, a glass of whiskey clutched in his hand like a grenade. Seeing them, Rufus staggered over.

"Just the person I was looking for," Rufus said, putting his glass on the table. "There's this rumor floating around that you got banned from the tournament this afternoon."

"Afraid so," Valentine said.

"That's horseshit. You're one of the good guys."

"Sometimes good guys finish last," Valentine said.

"Well, I hope you plan to stick around," Rufus said. "Once the tournament is over, I'm going to play DeMarco for two million bucks, winner-take-all, and I want you there to make sure he doesn't cheat me."

Valentine sat up straight in his chair. He'd forgotten about Rufus's challenge to DeMarco and now realized it would be the ideal opportunity to figure out what DeMarco was doing and expose him without it affecting the tournament.

"I'll be there," he said.

"Good," Rufus said. "In the meantime, I was hoping I might ask you a favor."

Rufus suddenly stopped looking drunk, and Valentine realized he was putting on an act, and probably had a sucker he was trying to reel in. Valentine's eyes canvassed the bar, and saw the Greek sitting on the other side of the crowded room.

"What's that?" Valentine asked.

"The Greek has been running around the hotel saying I cheated him with my Ping-Pong bet. He's claiming the reason he didn't challenge me was because of you."

"Me?"

"Yessir. The Greek says I hired you to protect me, and that you were an ex-cop with a bad reputation. He's also saying you're a suspect in a double homicide, and he was afraid you'd put a bullet in him if he squawked about me using the iron skillets as paddles in the game."

"Is that so?"

"Yessir. I've been fixing to make the Greek eat his words, and figured you might enjoy helping me."

Valentine considered Rufus's request. He'd already helped Rufus scam the Greek several times, and each time told himself no more. Scamming people wasn't right, even if they deserved to be taught a lesson. Then he reminded himself that the Greek had been part of a team that had cheated Rufus in a card game in an effort to make the old cowboy leave town. The Greek was a crook, and crooks needed to be punished. He glanced sideways at Gloria and placed his hand atop her wrist. "Do you mind if I help Rufus?"

"Only if you let me watch," she said.

"Hot damn," Rufus said.

The Greek was waiting as they approached his table. He'd finally taken a shower and combed his hair, and no longer resembled a clump of seaweed washed up on the beach. Sitting beside him was a red-haired poker player named Marcy Baldwin, whose departure from the tournament had included loud cursing and flipping the bird to the TV cameras. Marcy believed every male player was out to get her, yet she still competed in men's events. On her lap was a designer handbag containing a sleeping Persian cat.

"Hey, Marcy, you calmed down yet?" Rufus asked, back to his drunk act.

"Fuck you," she said.

"Sore head." He turned to her companion. "So, Greek, any truth to the fact that you want to challenge me again?"

The Greek eyed him suspiciously. "What do you have in mind?"

"I hear you're good at golf," Rufus said, sipping his whiskey. "Someone said you were runner-up at the National Amateur Championship once. That true?"

"That's right," the Greek said.

"You still play?"

"Now and then."

"What's your handicap?"

"I don't have one," the Greek said.

"Except that lovely lady sitting beside you."

"Fuck you," Marcy said.

"Mine's about ten," Rufus went on. "Want to play?"

The Greek was still simmering from the losses he'd suffered at Rufus's hands. If a gambler had anything in abundance, it was ego, and the Greek's had taken a beating.

"For how much?" the Greek asked.

"Same as before," Rufus said. "Half a million bucks,

winner-take-all. I'll even give you an edge, since I know you don't trust me, and figure I'm going to cheat you."

"What kind of edge?" the Greek asked suspiciously.

"On every hole, I'll let you take three drives. You can pick which drive you want to use, and that will be your ball. Sound fair?"

Valentine couldn't believe what Rufus was suggesting. He'd tried golf a couple of times, and knew it was a game in which you beat yourself. Giving a scratch golfer three drives a hole was the same as throwing the match.

"Do I get to pick the course?" the Greek asked.

"Sure," Rufus said.

The Greek looked at Marcy, their eyes communicating silently. She was an attractive woman, save for the harshness her chosen lifestyle had produced.

"Go for it," she said. "I'll call my mother."

"You sure she'll lend it to you?" the Greek asked.

"Sure," Marcy said. "She's loaded."

"You're on," the Greek said to Rufus. "When do you want to play?"

"How about crack of dawn, tomorrow?" Rufus said.

"Okay," the Greek said.

They shook hands on it. Rufus pretended to notice Marcy's cat for the first time. With his finger he pulled her handbag farther open. The cat cracked an eye, but did not stir.

"Nice cat," Rufus said. "What's its name?"

"Medusa," Marcy said.

"Is she friendly?"

"No."

"Just like her owner," Rufus said.

"Fuck you, and the horse you rode in on," Marcy hissed.

Rufus downed the rest of his whiskey, wiped his mouth on his sleeve. As if adding an exclamation mark to the picture, he belched into his hand. "I used to train house cats down on my ranch. They can do just about anything, once you teach them. You train this one, Marcy?"

"You're drunk," Marcy said. "Cats can't be trained."

"Says who?"

"Says me. I've owned cats my entire life."

"I can train *any* cat. Including yours."

"Train them to do what?"

"Circus tricks, real clever stuff."

"That's bullshit, and you know it."

"Wanna bet?"

"Sure," Marcy said. "I'll bet you."

Rufus went to the bar, returned with an unopened sixteen-ounce bottle of Coca-Cola. He dropped it on the table with a loud *plunk!* "Five thousand bucks says I can train Medusa to pick up that bottle, cross the room, and drop it on a table of your choice."

Marcy did not hesitate. She turned to the Greek. "Put up the money," she said.

The Greek pulled back in his chair. "But . . ."

"No buts, unless you don't want to see mine anymore," she said. "Put it up. There's no way on God's green earth that this broken-down cowboy is getting my cat to do *that*." She looked at Rufus. "You're not going to hurt her, are you?"

"I'll handle your kitty with kid gloves," Rufus said.

"Take the bet," Marcy told the Greek.

"But . . ."

"Do it!"

The Greek put up the five thousand.

Rufus reached into his pockets and removed a pair of tan gloves. Slipping them on, he reached into Marcy's handbag and removed the comatose kitty, putting her elastic body on the table. He grabbed the animal by the base of the tail and lifted her into the air. The cat opened its eyes and emitted a scream horrible enough to wake the dead.

"You said you wouldn't hurt her!" Marcy screeched.

"I said I'd use kid gloves," Rufus corrected her. "These are kid gloves I'm wearing."

"Do something!" Marcy told the Greek.

The Greek had crossed his arms in front of his chest, and seemed resigned to his fate. "Go ahead," he told Rufus.

Holding Medusa by the base of the tail, Rufus lifted her clean into the air. The cat twisted its body and tried to scratch him, but couldn't get through the gloves with its claws. In desperation, Medusa stuck its paws out, and attempted to latch onto the table. Rufus positioned her paws directly over the Coca-Cola bottle, and the cat grabbed the bottle by the cap and lifted it clean into the air. It was truly something to see: a drunk cowboy holding a screaming kitty holding a bottle of pop.

"Which table?" Rufus inquired.

"Make him stop!" Marcy cried.

"That one," the Greek said, pointing across the room.

"God damn you!" Marcy exclaimed.

Rufus crossed the bar while holding the screaming cat

at arm's length. It was a great way to clear a path, and someone snapped a picture of him. Rufus came to the specified table and stopped. A handsome young guy was sitting there, chatting up a pretty young girl. Introducing himself, Rufus asked the guy to hold out his hands. The guy obliged him, and Rufus loosened his grip on Medusa's tail. The cat dropped the bottle into the guy's hands, then slipped out of Rufus's grasp and ran away.

The guy handed the bottle to his girlfriend.

"Thanks, mister," the guy said.

Rufus returned to the Greek's table. Medusa had run to Marcy's handbag and was shivering in fear. Marcy had turned her back on the Greek and acted like she was never going to speak to him again. The Greek wiped a crocodile-size tear from his eye.

"I win," Rufus declared.

Part IV

Showdown

39

"**Y**ou busy?" Gerry Valentine asked.

Nurse Susan Gladwell lifted her eyes from the hospital report she was filling out. It was a few minutes past midnight, and she'd just come on her shift at the cancer ward of Atlantic City Medical Center, which was as quiet as a church.

"Yes, I am," she said.

"Do you know who I am?"

"Yes, you're Gerry Valentine, Jack Donovan's friend," she replied, putting her pencil down. "We spoke yesterday about the poker scam you were investigating. I was going to look into the hospital records to see if anything was stolen from our medicine department while Jack was here. Which I actually did, believe it or not." Reaching across the cluttered desk, she plucked a blue folder from a stack. "Here's the report."

Gerry was standing at the nurse's station where Gladwell worked. He'd brought a cup of steaming hot coffee for himself, and one for her. He made no attempt to take the file. "Let me guess," he said, "there was nothing stolen."

She held the file motionless in the air. "That's right. How did you know?"

"Because most hospitals don't report theft of medicines to the police. I learned that from my wife. She's a doctor."

Gladwell dropped the file on the desk, made an annoyed face. "If you knew that, then why did you have me go to the trouble of pulling up the records?"

"I didn't know it when I asked you," Gerry explained. "But I know now, along with a bunch of other stuff. You and I need to talk."

"Is that what the coffee is about?"

"Yes."

"Not interested. Maybe some other time."

Her eyes dropped to the form, giving him the ice maiden treatment. He cleared his throat. "See that black dude standing in the hallway behind me?"

"I said I'm not interested," she said.

"He's a cop."

Her head came up very slowly. "I see him. Is he with you?"

"Yes," Gerry said. "He's an undercover detective named Eddie Davis. If you don't talk to me, he's going to haul you down to the police station and grill you about a conversation you had with George Scalzo the morning after Jack Donovan was murdered. He's going to want to know why Scalzo brought you flowers and bought you a meal."

She stiffened. "How did you know about that?"

"Does it matter?"

She stared at Eddie Davis standing in the hallway. She wore little makeup, her face pleasantly plain, with tiny freckles on her nose, and soft amber eyes. Something in her face melted, and suddenly she looked scared. Rising from her chair, she took the steaming cup from Gerry's outstretched hand.

"I'll talk, but not here."

"How about the cafeteria?" Gerry suggested.

"Just so long as no one is around," she said.

The cafeteria was fairly quiet, with a maintenance man mopping the floor. They took a table in the back of the room, and Gladwell waited for a couple of doctors at the next table to leave, then spoke while staring at the reflection in her drink. "I really liked Jack Donovan. He was fun to be around, even when he was getting chemo. Nurses and doctors aren't supposed to get involved with patients, but it happens. Take off the white coats, and we're no different than anyone else."

Gerry glanced at the rings on her third finger, let out a deep breath.

"I saw Jack on the sly for three months," she went on. "He confided in me, told me about scams he pulled on the casinos. There was one I'll never forget. He had a tiny mirror glued to the bottom of a beer can. He could hold the can on a blackjack table, and see the face of the cards as they were dealt out of the plastic shoe. He'd know what the dealer had before the dealer did. Jack said he only had to see the dealer's hand once an hour to clean up. I never figured out what he meant."

"Jack was a card counter," Gerry said. "He played with an edge to begin with. By cheating once an hour, the edge increased, and guaranteed him a winning night."

"Did you show him that scam? Jack said he learned a lot from you when you were growing up."

Gerry thought back, smiled. "Come to mention it, I did show that to him."

"I thought so." She gulped her coffee, grimaced. "Jack also told me about the poker scam. At first, he wouldn't explain how it worked, just said that a player could know his opponents' cards and never lose.

"Jack told me he was going to sell the scam to a mobster named George Scalzo, and that Scalzo was going to give Jack's mother a hundred thousand dollars for it. I'd met Jack's mom, knew she was living on federal assistance, so I didn't say anything."

"Would you have otherwise?"

Her head snapped, eyes flaming. "Just because I loved Jack doesn't mean I approved of what he did. I normally don't hang out with people like you and Jack."

Gerry's face reddened. "Sorry."

"One afternoon at Jack's apartment, he sat down at the kitchen table and showed me the poker scam," she said. "First he gave me an earpiece, which he said was a modified children's hearing aid, and made me put it in my ear. Then he gave me a deck of cards and had me shuffle them. He took the cards, dealt us a hand. Each time one of the cards came off the deck, I heard a series of clicks. The clicks were in Morse code. Jack had a Morse code chart, and he let me read it while listening to the clicks. The clicks were always right.

"It was pretty amazing. Jack let me examine the cards. I couldn't find anything wrong with them. The clicks just seemed to come out of thin air."

Ever since Jack had died, Gerry had wondered how

the poker scam worked, and he put his elbows on the table and knocked his drink over. Gladwell grabbed the cup before too much of the liquid spilled out and righted it.

"Down, boy," she said.

She wiped up the spill with a paper napkin. Gerry could see her and Jack hitting it off. Jack had liked strong women.

"Did he show you the secret?"

"I eventually pried it out of him," she said, smiling at the memory. "There was a cigarette lighter sitting on the table. The lighter had a dosimeter hidden inside that Jack had stolen from the hospital."

"What's a dosimeter?"

"It's a device used to detect X-rays or radiation. You see them in dentists' offices. When Jack passed the cards over the lighter, the dosimeter picked up a signal from the card and sent it to a computer strapped around his waist. The computer read the signal then told me the card's value in Morse code. Jack said he'd borrowed the technology from some Japanese company that used it in kids' toys."

A group of female nurses came up to the table and spoke to Gladwell while checking out Gerry. Gerry rose, and introduced himself as Gladwell's old high school friend. The nurses chatted for another minute and left.

"You didn't have to do that, but thanks anyway," Gladwell said.

Gerry returned to his chair. "You're leaving out the important part. How was the dosimeter reading the cards?"

Gladwell's eyes fell to the dull tabletop. She seemed to

be wrestling with her conscience, and a long moment passed before she spoke again. "That was the secret that Jack sold to George Scalzo. You could examine the cards, but nothing would show up. Jack made me promise not to tell. And so did Scalzo."

Gerry thought back to what Yolanda had said over the phone earlier. The FBI had tailed Scalzo coming to the hospital. They'd seen him bring flowers to Gladwell, then go to the cafeteria with her and have breakfast together. As if reading his mind, Gladwell said, "I wasn't on duty the night Jack died, and didn't hear the news until the next day when I came in. Then Scalzo shows up with flowers, tells me how sorry he is that Jack's dead. He *knew* I'd been having an affair with Jack, and over breakfast told me I needed to keep quiet, if I knew what was good for me."

"So Scalzo threatened you."

"He didn't have to. If word got out about my affair with Jack, I'd lose my job, my nurse's license, and probably my marriage. I had a sword hanging over my head, and Scalzo knew it." She lifted her eyes. "There's your friend again."

Gerry glanced over his shoulder. Eddie Davis was sitting on the other side of the room, peeling the plastic off a cafeteria sandwich. Gerry looked back at Gladwell.

"You're scared, aren't you?"

"I think the word is *petrified,*" she said.

"I can make this nightmare go away."

"Right."

"I'm being serious."

"How can you make it go away?"

Gerry leaned forward, this time making sure no

drinks were in striking range. "Tell me Jack's secret, and you'll never hear from me, the police, or George Scalzo again. That's a promise."

"How do I know you'll keep this promise?"

His eyes scanned the cafeteria, and when he was certain no one was watching, he reached across the table and put his hand on her wrist. She did not resist his touch. "You and I share one thing in common. We both loved Jack. So when I tell you that on my friend's grave I can fix this situation, you've got to believe me."

Gladwell shuddered from an unseen chill. She drank what was left in her cup, grimacing again.

"All right," she said.

40

Four o'clock in the morning, and Skip DeMarco lay awake in his king-sized hotel bed, his sightless eyes gazing at the ceiling. On the other side of the room, his laptop made a gurgling sound. Its screen saver was an underwater scene, complete with coral, bright tropical fish, and sound effects. Hours ago, he'd gone onto the Internet and found the Web site of the law firm where Christopher Charles Russo, the man claiming to be his father, worked. The site had a section with photographs of the firm's lawyers. His laptop's screen was sharp, and he'd planned to enter the section, click on Russo's picture, then raise the laptop to his face, and take a look at the guy.

It hadn't happened.

He'd gotten cold feet and slipped back into bed. He was twenty-six years old and had lived with his Uncle George for twenty-one of those years. But he still remembered the first five. The memory of his mother was particularly strong.

But he had no memories of his father. Not one. Maybe Russo wasn't his father, and the story the woman had told him was a lie. Maybe Russo was a scammer, or a crackpot, or someone he'd beaten at cards looking to pay him back in the cruelest possible way.

DeMarco had spent hours lying in bed, weighing the possibilities. Finally he'd come to a decision. The only way he was going to know for sure was to look at the guy's picture, and try to find a resemblance. That wasn't so hard.

Only he couldn't do it.

He was comfortable living with his Uncle George. The house they shared was huge, the third floor practically his. He had his own bedroom, private gym, music room, study, and a maid and cook downstairs willing to do his bidding. And his uncle was easy. DeMarco had brought girls up to his room and smoked dope and his uncle had never said a word. It was a sheltered existence, his uncle having convinced him that the real world was not for him. In the real world, he was a victim. At home, he was a king.

He shut his eyes and tried to sleep. He imagined he was at home, listening to music with the headphones on. It didn't work, and in frustration he kicked off the sheets and sent them to the floor.

At four thirty, he climbed out of bed and shuffled across the room. Sitting down at his laptop, he made the screen saver disappear. He needed to be a man about this. He'd take a look at Russo's picture, then decide what his next step should be. Simple as that.

He went to the law firm's Web site, found the photo section, and scrolled through the players. It was a big firm, and according to the home page, specialized in legal representation for white-collar fraud. Big bucks, he guessed.

He stopped scrolling on Russo's picture. It was small, and had a short biography beneath it. He dragged the mouse over Russo's picture and clicked on it. The picture enlarged, filling the screen. DeMarco picked up the laptop with both hands. Holding the screen a few inches from his face, he stared hard. Russo looked to be in his late forties, with a heavy face, blunt nose, connected eyebrows, and an engaging smile. There was no family resemblance at all. None.

DeMarco felt something drop in his stomach, and he placed the laptop back on the desk. Russo was a fake, and so was the woman claiming to be his aunt. They were scammers, out to make a score.

"Go to hell," he said to the screen.

He shrunk Russo's picture back to its original size, then felt the tension trapped in his body escape. He'd stayed up half the night for nothing.

His eyelids suddenly felt heavy. He needed to get some sleep. The tournament was down to twenty-six players, and by tomorrow night, he expected to be sipping champagne with Uncle George, the title of world's best poker player firmly his.

As he stared to turn off the laptop, he noticed Russo's biography on the screen and lowered his face to have a look. Maybe when he got back home, he'd take Guido along with him and pay Russo a visit.

Christopher Charles Russo (nickname Skip)
Christopher Russo is a partner in Hamilton Pepper Russo LLP, resident in the Philadelphia office. He con-

centrates his practice in defending companies against frivolous class-action lawsuits. Most recently he had a $100 million lawsuit against the Acme Styrofoam Cup Company of Philadelphia overturned. The lawsuit had been brought by a hundred plaintiffs whose fingers were singed by hot coffee served in the company's cups.

Russo earned his Bachelor of Arts, magna cum laude, from St. Joseph, and his law degree, cum laude, from Villanova University School of Law. He is admitted to practice law in both Pennsylvania and New Jersey.

Russo is an avid poker player, and put himself through school playing cards. In 2002, he was named by *Philadelphia Magazine* as one of the city's most eligible bachelors. His other hobbies include listening to music and exercising.

DeMarco felt light-headed, and leaned back in his chair. It was all there, like a genetic fingerprint. Poker, music, working out. All the things Christopher Charles Russo loved were the things *he* loved. Even their nicknames were the same. *That* couldn't be a coincidence.

He dragged the cursor on his computer across the screen, and returned to Hamilton Pepper Russo's home page. At the top was the firm's address and main phone number. He memorized the number, then shut down his computer.

Crossing the room, he retrieved the sheets from the floor, and climbed into bed. He lay absolutely still and felt something swell up in his chest. It was three hours later back east, and he imagined Russo at his desk right now, the tireless defender. He took the phone off the night table, placed it on his chest, and punched in zero.

"How can I help you, Mr. DeMarco?" a hotel operator said brightly.

"I'd like to make a long distance call."

"My pleasure, Mr. DeMarco."

He recited Hamilton Pepper Russo's telephone number to the operator, and she made the call for him. The room had turned chilly, and as the call went through, he felt the receiver's icy plastic against his chin.

"Hamilton Pepper Russo LLC, can I help you?" a male receptionist answered.

"Is Christopher Russo in?"

"I believe he is," the receptionist said.

"Put me through to him."

The receptionist forwarded his call.

"Christopher Russo's office," a female secretary answered.

DeMarco hesitated. As far back as he could remember, he'd imagined that one day he'd track his father down, and have a talk with him. Now the moment had come, and he didn't have the slightest idea what to say.

"Hello, is anyone there?" the secretary asked.

"I'd like to speak with Christopher Russo."

"Mr. Russo is in court this week, and cannot be disturbed. If you'd like to give me a message, I'd be happy to relay it to him."

"Disturb him, would you?"

"Excuse me? Who is this?"

That was dumb, DeMarco thought. "I'm sorry. This is an old friend. We knew each other back when he was in college. I wanted the call to be a surprise."

"In college?" the secretary asked suspiciously.

"When he was at St. Joseph."

"Please hold for a moment."

The secretary put him on hold. DeMarco lay motionless, no longer sleepy. One of the things he'd wondered about was his father's voice. Would it be strong or soft, deep or high-pitched? The secretary came back on.

"Still there?" she asked.

"I'm here."

"I'm sorry, but Mr. Russo does not take calls from anonymous callers. If you'd care to leave a message, I'm sure—"

"Tell him it's Skip," DeMarco said.

"Skip?"

"That's right. Skip."

"Skip who?"

"He'll know who it is."

"Sir, I'm sorry, but Mr. Russo won't talk to you now. If you'll leave a message, Mr. Russo will get back to you once his trial is finished."

She sounded ready to hang up on him. DeMarco couldn't let that happen. He had to hear Russo's voice, and connect to the man that, until now, he'd only dreamed about.

"Tell him it's his son," he said.

41

Little Hands sat in his car in Celebrity's parking lot, the rising sun searing his eyes. It was seven o'clock in the morning, and he'd driven to Celebrity prepared to kill Tony Valentine. He'd killed several dozen men in Las Vegas, and it usually went like this: He went to their hotel room early in the morning, kicked the door down, ran in, and strangled them with his bare hands. Usually the victim was sleeping and didn't put up a fight, or he was in the john, which made it harder; one guy had sliced him with a razor before Little Hands broke his neck. But, whatever the situation, the result was always the same. He caught his victims with their guards down and ended their miserable lives. Tony Valentine would be no different.

As the sun crested over the distant mountains, Celebrity's neon sign went off, and he smothered a yawn. After leaving the Peppermill, he'd gotten involved in a craps game at a joint called Lots of Slots across the street. The craps table was on the sidewalk in front of the casino, the action hot. He'd gotten on a roll, and had turned five hundred bucks into a thousand, then two, and finally built his winnings up to seven grand. The process had taken him well into the night, and by the time he'd gotten into his car, his heart had been pounding so hard he couldn't have slept if he'd wanted to.

His money sat in a paper bag on the seat beside him. It contained seventeen hundred from the video poker game at the Peppermill, seven grand from the craps game at Lots of Slots, and the thousand down payment for whacking Valentine. It was enough to go to Mexico, and start his life over.

He stared up at Celebrity's top floors, and envisioned Valentine fast asleep in one of the rooms. The last time they'd tangoed, Valentine had tricked him and broken Little Hands's nose. A dirty movie had been playing in the motel room they were fighting in, and Little Hands had seen the movie and given up. He'd always had a thing about dirty movies. According to the prison psychiatrist at Ely, it was his mother's fault. He'd seen her having rough sex when he was a kid, and never gotten over it.

The clock in the dashboard said 7:05. He picked up the paper bag from the passenger seat and looked at the money. It was *more* than enough to start his life over. So what the hell was he doing here, risking everything?

"Screw this," he said aloud.

He pulled the car out of the lot and drove down a winding road that took him past Celebrity's front entrance. Celebrity hadn't existed the last time he'd been in Las Vegas, and he slowed down, craning his neck to look at the array of colorful parrots trapped in giant cages by the front door.

Satisfied, he started to speed up, then spotted Valen-

tine walking out the front door with a nice-looking
blonde on his arm. With them was a lanky cowboy carrying a golf bag filled with clubs. Little Hands had
thought about Valentine every day since going to prison,
and fantasized about paying him back. Pulling up along-
side the curb, he threw his vehicle into park.

Valentine and the woman were holding hands and
sharing meaningful glances. Another car pulled up to
the curb; a valet jumped out. Valentine tipped the valet
while the cowboy put his clubs into the trunk. The cowboy got into the back, the blonde into the passenger
seat, and Valentine slipped behind the wheel. The car
pulled away from the curb.

Little Hands decided to follow them.

Soon he was on a narrow road heading toward
Celebrity's golf course. His window was open, and the
wind rustled the paper bag on the passenger seat. The
mouth of the bag was open, and he glanced at the money
and imagined all it would buy down in Mexico. He
didn't need to kill Valentine. His life was set.

He continued to follow Valentine's car anyway.

Valentine had always been a fan of the Marx Broth-
ers, his favorite film being *A Night at the Opera*. In the
film, Chico Marx plays an unusual piano solo. Beginning on the lower keys, he performs a lightning-fast run
until his fingers run off the piano and continue to play
furiously in midair.

Whenever Rufus Steele tried to persuade suckers to
bet against him, Valentine was reminded of that magical
piano solo. Like Chico Marx, Rufus always went well

past the end, his language as outlandish as music produced in thin air.

"Come on, boys, what do you say? Money talks, nobody walks. It's time to put up or shut up." Rufus smiled at the group of suckers who'd come to Celebrity's golf course to watch him play the Greek. "This is one you can't lose, what my daddy called a mortal cinch. No tricks, no deception, just a friendly game of golf. My opponent was a runner-up in the National Amateur Championship and is a scratch golfer. Isn't that so, Greek?"

The Greek and Marcy Baldwin sat stoically in a golf cart. Lying in Marcy's lap was Medusa, who'd emitted a horrified shriek upon seeing Rufus.

"That's right," the Greek replied.

"What's *your* handicap?" a sucker asked Rufus suspiciously. He was a squirrel-like guy with a sprout of hair on his chin that resembled a dirty paintbrush.

"Besides my shining personality?" Rufus said. "It's a ten. If you don't believe me, call the pro at Caesars' golf shop. I've been playing his course for twenty years."

"Did you check that out?" the sucker asked the Greek.

"Yes," the Greek said. "His handicap is ten."

"What is Rufus trying to pull?" Gloria whispered in Valentine's ear. "He's going to lose if he's not careful."

Valentine felt the same way. He and Gloria stood by the practice tees, a small but dedicated rooting section. Golf was a game where you beat yourself, not your opponent. He couldn't see Rufus overcoming ten strokes no matter how well he played.

"Explain the rules again," the sucker said.

"Be happy to," Rufus said. "The Greek and I are

going to play eighteen holes of golf. Because many of you expect me to pull a fast one, I've given the Greek an edge. He gets to hit three drives on every hole, then pick the best ball to play with."

"How many drives do you get?" the sucker asked.

"Just one," Rufus replied.

"What kind of odds are you offering?"

"Even money. The Greek is betting me half a million dollars. I'd be happy to take your action or anyone else's, if you're so inclined."

The suckers went into a huddle. Gloria nudged Valentine with her elbow, and he reluctantly went over to where Rufus stood. "How you feeling?" Valentine asked.

"Never better," the old cowboy replied.

"You don't think this is a mistake?"

"Only suckers make mistakes," Rufus said.

The suckers ponied up another thirty grand, which Valentine agreed to hold for safekeeping. Rufus went to where their caddies stood by the bags. The Greek joined him and said, "I've got one stipulation before we start."

"What's that?" Rufus asked.

"I want our caddies to take off their shoes," the Greek said.

"You got a shoe fetish or something?"

"No, I just want to look at them."

Rufus turned to the caddies. "Boys, what do you say?"

The caddies removed their spiked golf shoes and handed them over. The Greek examined each shoe, pulling forcefully at the sole.

"What are you doing?" Marcy Baldwin called from the golf cart.

"I'm making sure the soles don't come off," the Greek said. "I had a guy trick me one time. His caddy's shoes had removable soles. Every time his ball went into the rough, his caddy picked up the ball with his toes, and dropped it in a favorable lie."

"Ha!" Marcy Baldwin said.

" 'Ha' is right," the Greek said. Finished, he handed the shoes back to the caddies. "Don't let me catch you pulling any fast stuff, hear me?"

"Yes, sir," they both said.

The Greek went to his bag and pulled out his driver, then removed three brand-new golf balls from the bag's side pocket. He walked over to the first hole, teed up a ball, and drove it 250 yards down the fairway, then teed up two more balls, and drove them equally as far. His swing was clean and pure, and Valentine and Gloria craned their necks, watching the balls fly gracefully through the air.

"I'll use the third ball," the Greek said.

"Third ball, it is," Rufus said.

Rufus teed up, and drove his ball 150 yards down the fairway. His swing was awkward and ugly, its only saving grace that it made the ball go straight.

The Greek burst out laughing. His ball was a hundred yards closer to the pin than Rufus's. He hopped into the golf cart and Marcy gave him a kiss.

"Good going, honey," she said.

By the ninth hole, the Greek was ahead by eleven shots, and insulting Rufus at every opportunity. The

Greek had finally found a game he could win, and was doing victory dances on the greens each time he sank a putt.

"This is insulting," Gloria said, sitting in a golf cart with Valentine. "Go sock him in the nose, will you?"

Valentine was at the wheel. She knew him too well, and he said, "I would, but there are witnesses."

"I'll lift my blouse and distract them," she said.

He tried not to laugh too loudly and glanced at Rufus standing on the edge of the green, trading one-liners with his caddy. He'd helped Rufus win a lot of money in the past few days, and Rufus had given him his share that morning. Valentine had already decided that he wasn't going to keep it, and now had an idea where it should go.

"Do you know anything about wiring money?" he asked Gloria.

"I've done it a few times. Why?"

"There's a woman in Atlantic City I want to send the money Rufus gave me."

"Is this woman someone I should know about?"

He nearly said yes. The case had started with Jack Donovan trying to sell his poker scam so he could give his poor mother in Atlantic City money to live on. That had been Jack's dying wish, and now he was going to fulfill it.

"Just trying to help someone out," he said.

Gloria's arm encircled his waist. She pulled close to him and kissed him on the lips. "Why doesn't that surprise me?" she said.

*   *   *

By the time they reached the thirteenth hole, the Greek appeared to be a sure winner. His victory dances had gotten longer, with him snapping his fingers and puffing out his chest like Tevye from *Fiddler on the Roof*. Then a strange thing happened.

The Greek teed up his first ball and hit his drive. Instead of flying straight and true, the ball shanked left and flew over a stand of trees, landing on the fairway of the third hole, which ran parallel to the thirteenth. Cursing, he teed up his second ball, and again shanked it left. In disgust he teed up his third ball and smacked it. The result was exactly the same.

"Those balls are out of bounds. That's a two-stroke penalty," Rufus said.

"I know the rules," the Greek said testily.

The Greek pulled three more balls from his bag, teed up the first, and drove it. The ball again shanked left. Moments later, they heard a golfer on the third hole let out an angry yell.

"Sounds like you hit someone," Rufus said.

The Greek shanked his second ball left, and his third. The yelling from the third hole became a bellowing rage.

"That's another two-stroke penalty," Rufus said.

"Shut up!" the Greek roared.

"He's playing like he couldn't hit the side of a barn," Gloria said under her breath.

Valentine leaned back in his seat, seeing the trick that Rufus had played on the Greek. Driving a golf ball required a lot of arm strength, and the Greek had exhausted his muscles by driving the ball three times each hole. The Greek could have beaten Rufus without the extra strokes, but had let his desire to win cloud his judgment.

The Greek continued to shank balls, ignoring calls from Marcy Baldwin and the suckers to take a break and rest his weary arms. Then a man wearing loud golf clothes appeared with a sheriff in tow. The man had a sizeable welt on his forehead, and angrily pointed at the Greek. "That's him! He's the one who hit me."

The sheriff told the Greek to stop what he was doing. The Greek ignored him, and continued to shank his drives like a man possessed. The sheriff waited until he'd run out of balls, then arrested him. As the sheriff escorted him away from the hole, Rufus came up from behind, and tapped the Greek's shoulder.

"I win," Rufus said.

42

Valentine drove Gloria back to the clubhouse in a golf cart. Rufus was ahead of them in a separate cart, having collected his winnings from a sobbing Marcy Baldwin. Seeing Rufus win had ignited a spark in him, and Valentine was eager for the tournament to end so that Rufus could play DeMarco in a winner-take-all showdown.

"Can I ask you a question?" Gloria asked.

He glanced sideways at her. "What's that?"

"Will you let me film you when you expose DeMarco?"

Valentine thought about it. It would be an ugly black eye for the tournament, and the governor of Nevada.

"Sure," he said.

She smiled at him. He'd come to the realization that Gloria was about to become a part of his life. He couldn't have asked for a more perfect ending to his trip.

Up ahead, Rufus's cart had disappeared around a curve, and they were alone on the course. It was a flawless morning, the air crisp and clean, and he slowed down so they could stare at the mountains. The sound of an electric horn ripped through the stillness.

He glanced in his mirror. "What's this jackass doing?"

"Who?" Gloria asked.

"The guy behind me. He's driving like a suicide bomber."

She turned around. A cart had come up behind them, and was hugging their tail. She waved for the cart to come around, which it started to do. The trail narrowed, and the cart's driver needed to punch it to pass them.

Only the driver didn't punch it. Instead, he turned his cart into theirs, and pushed them off the trail and down into a steep sand trap. Moments later, their cart hit bottom and slammed onto its side, the wheels still turning.

"Ohhh," Gloria moaned.

She'd eaten the dashboard, and Valentine jumped out of the cart, came around to her side, and pulled her out. He heard footsteps and looked up at the top of the trap. The guy who'd forced them off the road was coming down.

"Can you run?" he asked her.

"I think so."

He gently pushed her forward. "Go get help."

The other side of the trap was not as steep. Gloria ran up it, her hand pressed to her face. She stopped at the top of the trap.

"Tony!"

"Run," Valentine told her.

"But . . ."

"Do as I tell you. Please."

Valentine spun around to face their attacker.

* * *

Little Hands saw Valentine kick off his shoes and square off to face him. For an older guy, he had guts, and Little Hands remembered Billy Jack doing that in a movie instead of running away from a fight with about a dozen guys. On the other side of the sand trap, the blond woman had taken off. The golf course was quiet, and it would be a few minutes before she'd find any help. He came to the bottom of the trap and stopped.

"Remember me?"

Valentine squinted at him in the bright sunlight. "Al Scarpi."

"That's right."

"Thanks for the postcards. You made my Christmas."

"I've been waiting a long time for this."

Valentine threw a handful of sand in his face. Little Hands ducked it, but not the kick that followed. It caught him squarely in the groin. Little Hands went down on one knee, and as Valentine tried to deliver another kick, grabbed his foot out of the air, gave it a twist, and shoved him away. Valentine flew back but managed to stay on his feet. The blonde reappeared at the top of the sand trap.

"I called the police on my cell phone," she called down. "They're coming."

"Run!" Valentine yelled back at her.

"I can't leave you here," she said.

"Do as I say."

Little Hands got to his feet. Valentine went into a crouch, putting himself between the woman and Little Hands.

"They ever figure out what's wrong with you?" Valentine asked him.

Little Hands flexed his arms. "I'm going to mutilate you."

"It was something to do with your mother, wasn't it?"

"Shut up!" Little Hands said.

"Now, I remember. When you were a little kid, you saw her screwing a guy wearing a fireman's hat, and never got over it."

Little Hands charged him. Valentine adroitly stepped to one side and kicked him in the knee. Little Hands went down again. Valentine kept his distance, still crouching.

"I always have sex wearing a fireman's hat," Valentine said.

Little Hands tried to shake the image from his head. His mother on all fours on the bed, the fireman doing her from behind with the red hat perched on his head. Like his mother wasn't worth hanging around for. In the distance, he heard a siren.

He slowly stood up. It occurred to him that he might kill Valentine, but wouldn't get away with it. The police were already too close. He thought of the ninety-seven hundred in the bag, and the new life that awaited him south of the border. Pointing his finger at Valentine, he said, "I swear to God I'll get you one day. And your girlfriend. I'll get both of you. That's a promise you can take to the bank."

Little Hands turned around, and scampered out of the sand trap.

*   *   *

Gloria ran to Valentine's side, and threw her arms around him. "Oh my God, Tony, that's the bravest thing I've ever seen."

Valentine held her while watching Little Hands run. The siren that had driven him away was starting to fade, and wasn't coming their way. He thought about Little Hands's threat and looked at Gloria. "If I ask you to do something, will you do it?"

"What's that?" she asked.

"Stay here until I call you."

"Of course."

He went to the toppled golf cart. There was a driver lying across the backseat, which Rufus had loaned him. He clutched the driver between his hands.

As Valentine came out of the sand trap, he saw Little Hands climbing into his golf cart. The guy had more muscle than anyone he'd ever seen. So much so, that he probably thought nothing could harm him. He imagined Little Hands showing up on his doorstep someday, or worse, on Gloria's doorstep. Showing up and ruining their lives. That wasn't going to happen if he could have a say in the matter.

He ran up to Little Hands's cart just as it started to pull away. Swung the driver like it was a baseball bat and he was trying to knock one clean out of the park. Little Hands glanced sideways at him with a look of disbelief on his face. Like he hadn't expected an old guy to move so fast.

The driver hit Little Hands a few inches above his nose. It snapped his head straight back, and Little Hands jerked the wheel to his right, going off the trail and directly into a palm tree. Little Hands flew out of the cart and hit the tree as well.

Valentine approached him, the driver still clutched in his hands. Little Hands lay on his back, blood pouring out of his ears and nose and mouth. Beside him was a paper bag filled with money. The wind had picked it up, and hundred-dollar bills blew across the golf course. Little Hands's eyelids fluttered; he looked up at Valentine and weakly shook his head.

"I should have quit when I was ahead," he whispered. Then he shut his eyes and died.

43

Karl Jasper was standing on the balcony of George Scalzo's suite, sweating through his five-thousand-dollar Armani suit.

He'd woken up that morning and flipped on the TV to CNN like he always did, then found himself staring at stark images of a gigantic bust taking place in Atlantic City. A perky newscaster had identified those being arrested as "known associates of George Scalzo, reputed head of the New Jersey Mafia" and described the bust as the largest in Atlantic City's history. The newscaster also said that an arrest warrant had been issued for Scalzo. Jasper had run upstairs to Scalzo's suite and found the old mobster flying around in a rage. Scalzo had also seen the news, and they'd gone onto the balcony, and Jasper had tried to talk Scalzo into turning himself over to the authorities.

"Never!" Scalzo screamed at him.

"Come on," Jasper begged.

"Go fuck yourself."

"Do it for the tournament. For me."

Scalzo grabbed Jasper by the throat and thrust his weight against him, and for a moment it had felt like they were both going over the railing. "For you? You think I care about you or your fucking tournament?"

Jasper pushed him away. Other hotel guests were watching from their balconies, and he straightened his jacket and tie. "If you won't do it for me, then do it for your nephew. If they arrest you, the police will want to talk to Skip as well. He'll have to withdraw from the tournament."

"So what?" Scalzo bellowed at him.

"You don't care if your nephew goes down?"

"He's not going down," Scalzo said. "He's leaving with me and Guido. We're getting out of Las Vegas, is what we're doing."

"Have you talked with him about this?"

"Why should I?"

"What if he doesn't want to go? He's the tournament leader."

Scalzo pounded his chest with both fists like a caveman. "Skipper does what I tell him. He's leaving with me. Understand?"

Jasper nodded stiffly. There was no use arguing with a maniac.

"In two hours, I want you to drive me, Skipper, and Guido to a little airport on the outskirts of town," Scalzo said. "We're going to take a charter plane to Los Angeles, and from there, a private yacht to Central America. Just give me two hours to make the necessary arrangements. You drive us to the airport, and we'll disappear."

"At least let your nephew play before you leave," Jasper said.

"Why should I?"

"Because he's a goddamn celebrity, that's why," Jasper said. "The more air time he has, the better the tournament does."

Scalzo stuck his chin out defiantly. "Okay."

Jasper looked at his watch. "I need to run. I'll see you downstairs."

Jasper turned to open the slider. Scalzo's hand came down hard on his shoulder, and he felt the old mobster's breath on his ear.

"You'd better not mess this up," Scalzo said.

Jasper felt himself stiffen. A shift had occurred, and he hadn't even realized it. He was in charge now, with Scalzo's fate in his hands.

"You have nothing to worry about," Jasper said.

At twenty minutes to nine, Skip DeMarco came out of his bedroom. Normally his uncle came to his room before he went downstairs to play, and they went through their little routine. But today his uncle hadn't shown, leaving DeMarco to dress without his uncle appraising his selection of clothes.

"Hey Skipper," he heard a voice say.

"That you, Guido?"

His uncle's bodyguard grunted in the affirmative.

"It doesn't sound like you," DeMarco said. "What happened to your voice?"

Guido's big feet scuffed the carpet as he crossed the suite. "I hurt my nose," he explained.

Guido had been his uncle's bodyguard for twenty

years; a more loyal employee you'd never find. But that loyalty came with a price. When his uncle lost his temper and flew into a rage, Guido's role changed, and he became a whipping boy.

"He smack you in the face again?" DeMarco asked.

"Couple of times," Guido grunted.

"What did you do this time?"

"I woke him up with bad news."

"It must have been real bad."

"The Atlantic City operation got busted last night. Everyone went down."

DeMarco had never heard the full details of the Atlantic City operation from his uncle; all he knew was that it was his uncle's primary source of income, and paid for his house and vacation house and full-time staff and brand-new cars every year.

"Where's my uncle now?" DeMarco asked.

"He's on the phone in his bedroom, talking to somebody," Guido said.

DeMarco asked, "Do you think he can hear us right now?"

"No, the door's shut."

"I want to ask you a question, Guido, and I want you to be honest with me."

"Sure, Skipper."

DeMarco reached out and touched Guido's arm. The muscle beneath the silk shirt was rock-hard. "There's an attorney in Philadelphia named Christopher Russo. He's tried to contact me a bunch of times over the years. My uncle made you keep him away, didn't he?"

"That's right," Guido said proudly. "That guy claimed to be your father. He was nothing but trouble."

"Who told you that?"

"Your uncle. He said Russo was trying to blackmail you. I took care of him."

"What did you do to him?"

"You know, the usual stuff."

"Did you threaten him?"

"Oh yeah," Guido said, getting his bluster back. "I drove to Philly one weekend in the limo and cornered him in the covered parking lot of the building where he worked. I slapped him around a bunch, told him I'd introduce him to pain if he kept trying to see you. I made that bastard promise to leave you alone."

DeMarco felt himself well up and swiped at his eyes.

"What's wrong?" Guido said. "Did he try to contact you again?"

"Yeah," DeMarco said. "He's my father."

44

Valentine was explaining to Bill Higgins and a homicide detective with the Metro Las Vegas Police Department how he'd sent Little Hands to the big craps game in the sky when the cell phone in his pocket vibrated. Pulling it out, he saw it was his son.

"Would you gentlemen excuse me for a minute?" he asked.

Bill and the detective both nodded solemnly. Before being sent away to prison, Little Hands had earned himself a reputation as the most vicious killer in Nevada, and Bill and the detective seemed to be having a hard time accepting that Valentine had managed to beat him in a fight, even though Little Hands was lying beneath a sheet only a dozen feet away. Stepping into the shade of a palm tree, Valentine answered the call.

"Hey, Pop, it's me," his son said.

"You still in Atlantic City?" Valentine asked.

"No, I took a plane out last night and just landed in Las Vegas. I made DeMarco's scam, and figured I'd better fly out and help you put this to bed."

Valentine didn't know what to say. Gerry had beaten

him to the finish line. He'd never felt more proud of his son in his entire life.

"You're a star," he told his son.

"Yolanda helped, and so did Mabel. And you put me on the scent, so you get credit, too," Gerry said. "That's the good news. Now here's the bad. I think DeMarco is being played for a sucker by his uncle. He's being used, Pop, and in a real bad way."

"Used how?"

"This scam is dangerous. Scalzo is putting his nephew's health in jeopardy, and I don't think DeMarco knows it. Matter of fact, I'm sure he doesn't."

Gerry was jumping to conclusions, a bad thing to do in detective work. The facts were the facts and everything else was air. "How can you be sure, Gerry?"

"Because DeMarco could get sterile," his son said.

Valentine had investigated plenty of scams where a member of the gang hadn't been given a complete script of the play. In the end, that person usually got the raw end of the deal, and became a victim.

"Explain this to me," Valentine said.

Gerry explained what he'd learned from the nurse who'd been having an affair with Jack Donovan. As scams went, it was one of the most ingenious Valentine had ever come across, but did contain a significant health risk. It wasn't meant to be used in a tournament, where long-term exposure could be dangerous. Gerry was right. DeMarco probably didn't know the risks he faced.

"That's one heck of a piece of detective work,"

Valentine said when his son was finished. "Maybe I should go to work for you."

"That would be the day," Gerry said. "So what do you think we should do?"

That was a good question. Valentine had been thinking about his conversation with Sammy Mann the day before, when Sammy told him that everyone in Vegas knew DeMarco was cheating, but weren't going to do anything until after the tournament was over. He didn't agree with that rationale, and now realized that he and his son were in a position to fix things.

"Meet me in Celebrity's poker room in forty-five minutes," Valentine said. "We're going to put the screws to Scalzo."

"I'll be there," his son said.

Valentine killed the connection, and walked back to where Bill was standing. The homicide detective had gone off to find the EMS crew he'd called for, and Valentine cornered his friend. "How much trouble are you going to get into if I go back to Celebrity's poker room?"

"Plenty," Bill said. "Why?"

"Because I'm going to go back to Celebrity's poker room, that's why."

"Then wear a disguise. If you get caught, I can say I was in the dark."

Valentine whacked his friend on the shoulder. "Thanks, Bill."

He went to the clubhouse and found Gloria waiting for him, then got the rental and drove back to Celebrity. On the way they stopped at Target, where he purchased a floppy hat several sizes too large, cheap wraparound shades, and a neon green T-shirt that said SCREW THE KIDS—I'M DYING BROKE, which he put on in the store and left hanging out of his pants. To round out the picture, he added a little shuffle to his walk. He showed Gloria the transformation in the parking lot, and she burst out laughing.

"Do you really think that's going to work?" she asked when they were on the road.

"Of course it will work," he said.

"How can you be so sure?"

"There's an old geezer robbing banks in Florida near where I live. He dresses just like this. I think he's up to nineteen banks. They've caught him on videotape every time, but he keeps sticking them up."

"Don't the banks in Florida have security guards?"

"They do," he said. "The old geezer walks right past them, gives the teller a note, takes his money, and leaves. The guards don't pay any attention to him. It would be funny if the guy wasn't breaking the law."

He drove to Celebrity and left his car with the valet. As he and Gloria went through the front door of the hotel, he started to do his shuffle.

"You're moving awfully slow," she said.

"Need to conserve my energy for the buffet line."

"Stop that."

Once they were inside, she pulled him over to a secluded spot and gave him a kiss.

"I'm glad you're not leaving Las Vegas," she said.

Valentine got to test his disguise as he neared Celebrity's poker room. One of the guards who'd escorted him out the day before walked past. Their eyes met, and Valentine touched the brim of his hat. The guard looked through him like he was invisible.

He and Gloria entered the poker room to find a mob of spectators crowded around a table containing the first prize, a whopping ten million bucks stacked like firewood. Shotgun-toting guards stood by the money, their steely eyes roaming the room. It was the biggest prize in professional sports, and according to the electronic leader board hanging over the feature table, DeMarco was the favorite to claim it.

He shuffled up to the feature table. It was bathed in bright lights, with DeMarco's stacks of chips dwarfing his opponents'. DeMarco looked different than he had in previous days, his face drawn and serious, and Valentine wondered if his conscience was eating at him.

"Is that your son over there?" Gloria whispered. "He looks just like you."

He spotted Gerry on the other side of the poker room and decided to give his disguise another test. He walked over to him and, getting no reaction, cleared his throat.

"Didn't I see you on *America's Most Wanted* the other night?" Valentine asked.

His son's eyes went wide. "Pop? Is that you?"

"Keep your voice down."

"Why the disguise?"

"I got banned from the tournament. You ready for a little payback?"

Gerry nodded enthusiastically. He hadn't shaved and his eyes were bloodshot from lack of sleep, but there was a spark in his face that said he was more than ready.

"Good," Valentine said. "Here's the plan. The players are going on break soon, and I'm going to confront

DeMarco, and tell him the little game he's playing is over. See that pretty blonde lady on the other side of the room? She's a newscaster I met. She's going to distract Scalzo and the bodyguard. I need you to cover her back in case something goes wrong."

His son look frustrated. "Why don't you just pull DeMarco off the table, and expose the scam? Then the police can arrest Scalzo."

Valentine drew close to his son. "If I do that, it's going to hurt every casino in Las Vegas, and in the long run, our business as well. Let me handle this my way, okay?"

His son's face softened. "Sure, Pop. Whatever you want."

45

Being the chip leader in a poker tournament was like being king of the world. While the other players were trying to survive, DeMarco could pick and choose his spots, pouncing on players with weak cards when he knew they were bluffing. Letting the other players win a few hands would have made things more equal, but he'd decided it was time to claim his prize and get out of Las Vegas.

The conversation with his father had been eating at him all morning. They hadn't been talking five minutes when his father had told him what a bad person his uncle George was and how DeMarco needed to get away from him. What were his exact words? *You need to escape your uncle's dark shadow.*

DeMarco hadn't liked that. His uncle could be mean and do horrible things, but that didn't negate the treatment DeMarco had gotten from him. His uncle had raised him, and DeMarco wasn't going to run away just because his father didn't like the man.

But his father hadn't let up, and when he and

DeMarco had finally said good-bye, DeMarco had been ready to curse him out.

"There will be a fifteen-minute break after this hand is concluded," the tournament director announced over the public address.

Because DeMarco was not in the hand, he decided to leave the table early. He was not five steps away from the table when his uncle was by his side.

"You okay, Skipper?"

"I'm fine, Uncle George. I just need to hit the bathroom."

DeMarco heard his uncle snap his fingers.

"Guido," his uncle said. "Skipper needs to take a leak. Make sure no one gets near him."

"Yes, Mr. Scalzo."

Guido led him across the poker room to the men's lavatories. As they walked, DeMarco listened to Guido's breathing. Guido's nose sounded broken from the punches he'd received that morning. His uncle had been abusing Guido unmercifully the past few days, and DeMarco was surprised his uncle's bodyguard hadn't walked out on him. They came to the lavatories and Guido stopped.

"Shit," Guido said.

"What's wrong?" DeMarco asked.

"That lady newscaster just cornered your uncle and shoved a microphone in his face. Her cameraman is filming them, too."

"You want to go rescue him?"

"Your uncle told me to keep you company."

"I can take a leak without peeing on my leg. Go help him."

Guido hesitated. DeMarco sensed that he was probably enjoying seeing his uncle in a tight spot. His uncle
had dished out more than he'd taken over the years, and
there was a strange joy in seeing him get paid back.

"Why do you put up with him, Guido?" DeMarco
asked.

"What do you mean?" the bodyguard said.

"My uncle's bullshit. Why do you put up with it?"

"I don't have a choice," Guido said. "A long time ago,
I did something really stupid, and your uncle saved me
from going to prison for the rest of my life. In return, I
agreed to be his bodyguard and do whatever he told me.
That's the deal we struck."

"Oh," DeMarco said.

"Mind if I ask you a question?"

"What's that?"

Guido jabbed DeMarco in the chest with his finger.
"Why do *you* put up with him?"

DeMarco slipped into the men's lavatory. Guido had
sounded just like his father. Why did he put up with his
uncle's nonsense? He guessed it was because he loved
him.

He'd been in the men's room enough times to have the
layout memorized. Stalls on the right, urinals on the left.
He soldiered up to an empty urinal and unzipped his fly.
He'd heard of guys who'd lost monster hands because
they'd had to pee. Thinking about it made him smile,
and at first he did not hear the man occupy the urinal beside him.

"How's that earpiece working?" the man asked.

DeMarco froze. The voice was older, with a heavy Jersey accent. "Excuse me?" he said.

"The inner-canal earpiece you're using to scam the tournament," the voice said. "How's it holding up?"

"I don't know what—"

"It's a modified children's hearing aid," the voice said. "I've got a couple in my collection. They're smaller than regular hearing aids, which lets you stick them way down in your ear so no one will see them, but they also break down easier. Yours working all right?"

"Who are you?"

"Tony Valentine. I was hired by the Nevada Gaming Control Board to investigate you."

DeMarco finished his business, then stepped away from the stall and faced his accuser. "You going to bust me?"

"Not today," Valentine said.

"What's that supposed to mean?"

"It means that you're not going down until I decide to take you down. And that won't happen today."

"Why not?"

"Because the tournament deserves to have a fair outcome."

DeMarco did not know what to say.

"You understand what I'm telling you?" Valentine asked.

"I think so. You're going to let me play."

"That's right. But you have to give me the earpiece."

DeMarco suddenly understood. Valentine was going to let him play, but not cheat. He pulled the earpiece out of his ear and handed it to him.

"There's one other thing I want you to do," Valentine said.

"What's that?"

"Get checked out by a doctor once the tournament is over."

DeMarco heard a toilet flush on the far end of the line of stalls. A man came out, walked past them, washed his hands, and left. "Why should I see a doctor?" DeMarco asked.

"Your uncle hasn't told you how this scam works, has he?"

DeMarco hesitated. For all he knew, Valentine had a tape recorder on him, and was recording every word they said. If he said yes, it was as good as admitting he'd scammed the tournament. Only he sensed that Valentine wasn't trying to trap him. He shook his head.

"That's too bad, kid," Valentine said.

DeMarco reached out and grabbed Valentine's arm. "Tell me," he said.

"Ask your uncle."

"I already did."

"He wouldn't tell you?"

"My uncle said he'd tell me when the tournament was over. Is the scam dangerous?"

"Yeah. You could be sterile. Or worse."

"*What?*"

"The cards at your table have been treated with radio-active iodine, which was stolen from a vault in a hospital," Valentine explained. "Each card has tiny drops of the substance put on the back. The number of drops is based on the card's value and suit, ranging from one drop to fifty-two drops. With me so far?"

DeMarco slowly nodded.

"Once the iodine dries, the cards are covered with a plastic matte similar to what commercial artists use. That seals the iodine into the card, and ensures the iodine won't rub off. The dealer has a dosimeter at the table, hidden inside a cigarette lighter. When the dealer deals, he holds each card briefly over the lighter. The dosimeter reads the dots on the back of the card, then transmits the information to a computer strapped around the dealer's waist. Still with me?"

"Yes," DeMarco said.

"The computer has a program that reads the dots, translates them into Morse code, then tells you through your ear piece what the card just dealt is. The iodine has a half life of eight hours. From the time the iodine is applied to the cards, it starts to break down. Within eight hours it's disappeared, and the cards return to being normal. A perfect scam, except for one thing. It exposes the people handling the cards to radiation."

"Am I going to get sick?"

"You might. Two dealers who were involved with the scam have ended up in the hospital. One of them, who was fighting cancer, died."

"What about the other players at the table?"

"They run less of a risk."

"Why?"

"Two reasons. The tournament director rotates them, and you knock them out so quickly. But you've been at the feature table for most of the tournament, which means you've been exposed to the cards the most. Chances are, you're likely to have problems down the road." Valentine jabbed him in the chest like Guido had done, only with less force. "Now, I'm going to tell you something, kid, and I want you to listen real good."

DeMarco swallowed hard. "I'm listening."

"Your uncle stole the scam from a guy named Jack Donovan, then had Jack murdered. It's never completely made sense to me *why* he had Jack killed. Your uncle could afford to buy the scam from Jack, and murdering people is usually only a last resort. Well, I figured out the reason."

"What's that?"

"Jack Donovan told your uncle that the scam was dangerous, and should be used sparingly. Like in a private game, where you only need to win one pot to come out ahead. The scam was never intended to be used in a tournament. Even though Jack was a scammer, he wasn't a bad guy. My guess is, Jack would have found out what your uncle was using the scam for, and contacted you."

"So Uncle George had him killed."

"That's right."

Outside the lavatory DeMarco could hear the sounds of the other players approaching. He thought back to what his father had said that morning. *You need to escape your uncle's dark shadow.* He'd never known how dark that shadow was, until now.

46

The men's lavatory quickly filled up. DeMarco felt Valentine's hand on his sleeve.

"I want one more thing out of you," Valentine said.

DeMarco could hear other players swirling around them, the slamming of the stall doors, the loud banter of the players still remaining in the tournament. "What's that?"

"Level the playing field between you and your opponents."

"I don't understand what you mean."

Valentine drew close to him, put his mouth a few inches from DeMarco's ear. "Lose a few hands so that everyone at your table has about the same amount of chips."

"Why should I do that?"

"Because then the tournament will be even," Valentine replied.

It was DeMarco's turn to whisper. "Why should I do that, if you're going to have me and my uncle arrested?"

"Because I'm not going to have you arrested," Valentine whispered back.

"You're not?"

"No."

DeMarco gazed at the floor. "I really appreciate this."

Valentine squeezed DeMarco's arm so hard that he winced in pain. "I'm not letting you go because I like you," the older man said.

"Then why?" DeMarco asked.

"Just because you and your uncle cheated this tournament doesn't mean you have the right to ruin it. I want the World Poker Showdown to end fairly, with a clean winner. Understand?"

DeMarco took a deep breath and squared his shoulders. His arm was singing with pain where Valentine had squeezed it. "Yeah, I understand," he said.

"Good," Valentine said. "Now get the hell out of here."

DeMarco walked out of the men's lavatory to find Guido waiting for him. When his uncle's bodyguard got excited, his breathing accelerated, each breath sounding like a short pant. He was doing that now and said, "Skip, your uncle needs to talk to you."

"That's nice."

"What's that supposed to mean?"

"I don't want to talk to him. Walk me back to the table."

DeMarco stuck his arm out, and Guido took it and escorted him back.

"How many players are left in the tournament?" DeMarco asked.

"Only ten," Guido said. "A bunch of guys got knocked

out in the last hand. They're down to the final table. Look, Skip, I don't know how to tell you this—".

"Then don't."

"—but your uncle has decided to leave Las Vegas right away. The situation in Atlantic City is bad. Karl Jasper has a private plane waiting for us at an airport just outside of town."

"Us?"

"Yeah, you, me, and him."

DeMarco stopped. They had reached the feature table, and he could hear the TV people adjusting their equipment and talking about the lighting. He could also hear gamblers in the crowd setting the odds on the remaining ten players in the tournament. They were calling him the favorite. "I'm not going," he said.

"Say what? Your uncle—"

"Tell my uncle to call me, and I'll meet up with him later."

"Skip, that's not such a good idea. Your uncle—"

"—isn't running the show anymore," DeMarco interrupted. "I am. I'm the tournament chip leader, and everyone expects me to play. So I'm going to play."

"Don't make me do this, Skip."

DeMarco turned so he faced his uncle's bodyguard. "Do what? Drag me across the room by my collar? I'll have you tossed out of here so fast it will make your nose bleed. I'm in charge of my own life, not you, and not Uncle George. Now say good-bye."

"Say good-bye?"

"Yes. Say good-bye, and then go take care of my uncle. He's going to need it."

"Who's going to take care of you?"

"I am."

"You sure you're ready for that?"

DeMarco didn't know if he was ready to run his own life, or not. But the only way he was going to find out was by trying. "Yeah, I'm ready."

Guido's fast-paced breathing returned. So fast, in fact, that DeMarco thought he might have a stroke. Guido had always been there for him, and he reached out and touched the bodyguard's stomach the way he'd done as a little kid. "You're a good guy, Guido. Thanks for everything you've done for me."

"Just doing my job," the bodyguard said.

DeMarco took his seat at the feature table. He could hear the dealer riffle-shuffling the cards, the fifty-two pasteboards purring like a cat. He'd been exposed to radiation for five days, and realized the dealers who were bringing radioactive cards to the table had known the health risk as well. To themselves, and to him.

"Drink, sir?" a female voice asked.

"Get me a Coke and a pack of cigarettes," he said.

The cocktail waitress came back a minute later with his order, putting the drink and pack in front of him. He removed his wallet, pulled out a bill. He hadn't paid for a thing since coming to Las Vegas. He supposed now was as good a time as any to start.

"How much do I owe you?"

"Eight dollars."

"How much is this bill worth?" he asked.

"A hundred dollars," she said.

"Keep it."

She thanked him and departed. He tore open the pack

of smokes, stuck one in his mouth. To the dealer he said, "Give me your lighter, will you?"

"Excuse me, sir?"

"The lighter sitting next to you. Give it to me. I want to light up my smoke."

The dealer didn't know what to say. DeMarco rose from his chair, grabbed his drink, and leaned forward a little too quickly. He sent the drink in the dealer's direction and heard the dealer squawk. "Did I soak your cards?" DeMarco asked.

"Yes," the dealer said angrily.

"Good. Now get out of here," DeMarco said under his breath.

"What?"

"You heard me. Take your trick lighter and leave."

The dealer said, "*Shit*," under his breath, then pushed back his chair and left the table. DeMarco sat down. Moments later the tournament director came up behind him.

"Where did the dealer go?" the tournament director asked.

"He felt sick and left," DeMarco said.

The tournament director spoke into a walkie-talkie, and asked for someone to clean up the table, and for a new dealer. When he disconnected, DeMarco asked, "Would you mind telling me the chip count for each of my opponents?"

"Sure," the tournament director said.

Each player's chip total was on the electronic leader board hanging over the table, and the tournament director read the totals to him. He was first, followed by seven players with roughly the same amount of chips, followed by the last two players, who were two million shy of the others. He would have to lose a couple of hands to the last two. That would make everyone at the table equal.

"Thanks," he told the tournament director.

A new dealer came, and the other players returned. DeMarco felt the bright lights of the TV cameras come on. It was showtime.

47

"**H**ow dare Skipper disobey me," Scalzo said, standing with Karl Jasper and his bodyguard on the curb in front of Celebrity. "You should have made him come with you."

"How was I going to do that?" Guido asked.

"You should have put the heavy on him."

"There were too many people standing around."

"Keep making excuses and I'll smack you in the fucking mouth," Scalzo snapped.

Guido wanted to tell his boss to calm down, there were bigger problems to worry about. He'd spoken to one of their people in Atlantic City, and the news was getting worse by the hour. Forty-two members of the blackjack gang had been arrested last night, and now one had turned state's evidence and told the cops that Scalzo had masterminded the scam. Other members were certain to do the same, and point the finger at the boss. Cheating a casino was a serious crime, but conspiring to cheat a group of casinos was much worse. If his boss didn't get out of the country, he was screwed.

A white Mercedes pulled up to the curb and a valet

jumped out. Jasper gave the valet his stub. "Put the suit-cases in the trunk," Scalzo barked.

"Yes, sir," Guido said.

Guido dragged his boss's suitcases to the back of the car. The trunk was locked, and Jasper came around, holding the keys he'd gotten from the valet. Jasper popped the locking mechanism and the trunk opened by itself. Guido hoisted the first suitcase off the ground, then froze. Inside the trunk was a leather satchel. The mouth of the satchel was wide open, exposing a half dozen bundles of hundred-dollar bills, all of them new. The suitcase slipped out of his fingers and hit the ground.

"What the hell are you doing back there?" Scalzo yelled, having climbed into the passenger seat. "Hurry up."

"Yes, sir."

Guido lifted the suitcase off the ground while contin-uing to stare at the money. A slip of paper lay on the bundles with handwriting on it. He glanced at Jasper, who'd gone to the driver's side but hadn't gotten in, then pulled the slip out and read it.

There's more where this came from.

Guido dropped the note into the satchel. He didn't know what was going on, then noticed a dark blanket lying inside the trunk. Something was lying beneath it, and he pulled the blanket back to have a look. A shovel.

"Need some help?"

Guido looked up. Jasper stood by the driver's door, watching him. Their eyes briefly locked, and the look in

Jasper's eyes was unmistakable. It slowly dawned on Guido what was going on. Then he made a decision.

"I'm fine," Guido said, and resumed putting the suitcases into the trunk.

"Scalzo's getting away," Gloria said, standing with Valentine and Gerry by the front door. Valentine had come out of the men's lavatory after confronting DeMarco and walked right up to Scalzo, Jasper, and his bodyguard, in the hopes of eavesdropping on their conversation. When the three men had beaten a path out of the casino, he'd decided to follow them, and grabbed Gloria and his son.

As Jasper's Mercedes drove away, Valentine took out his cell phone and called Bill Higgins. He got a busy signal and felt Gloria tug his arm.

"Come on," she said.

"Where are we going?"

"To my car. We're going to follow them."

Gloria's rental was parked with several expensive foreign cars near the entrance. She'd bribed the valet attendant to park it there, and had told Valentine it was a common trick with reporters, in case they needed to run down a story. She got her keys from the guy manning the key stand, and Valentine turned to his son.

"I want you to stay here. Someone needs to watch DeMarco, and make sure he doesn't continue to cheat the tournament."

His son started to protest, then bit his lip. "Okay, Pop. But you've got to promise me you'll stay out of trouble. You scare me sometimes."

There was real concern in his son's voice. Valentine gave him a hug then jumped into Gloria's car.

In a hurry to get out of her spot, Gloria ran over the curb and burned rubber pulling away. At the bottom of the exit she hit the brakes and looked both ways.

"Which way did they go?" she asked.

Valentine hopped out of the car, climbed on the hood of the rental, then got back in and pointed to his right. "That way."

She gunned the accelerator and the rental flew down the road. Celebrity was on the southwest side of Las Vegas in an area that had not yet felt the wrath of bulldozers and earthmovers. It was still desert and sage brush; the land stretched out like an artist's canvas. Gloria got a quarter mile behind the Mercedes and slowed the rental to sixty-five. Valentine tried Bill again, and got another busy signal.

Several miles passed. Then a sign for a regional airport popped up.

"He must have a plane waiting for him," Gloria said.

She sped up. The Mercedes pulled into the airport entrance, but instead of driving toward the main cluster of buildings, took a dusty gravel side road. Gloria followed, the rental lurching like a carnival ride. The Mercedes went a mile up the gravel road, then disappeared behind a mold-colored hangar.

"Park next to the hangar," Valentine said.

"Shouldn't I follow them?"

"No. They might have guns."

She parked and they hopped out, went to the corner of the hangar, and stuck their heads around. Several hundred yards away, the Mercedes was parked beside a deserted runway, with Jasper, Scalzo, and the bodyguard standing in the tall grass, a sharp wind blowing in their faces and making their hair stand on end.

"Where's the plane?" Gloria asked.

"They must be waiting for it to land. I wish I could see their faces."

Gloria went to the rental, and returned holding a camera with a zoom lens. "It's Zack's," she explained.

He took the camera and extended the lens, then looked across the field. Scalzo was shouting at Jasper and looked like he wanted to kill someone. Valentine remembered running Scalzo out of Atlantic City years ago, and the ugly scene Scalzo had made while being escorted out of town. Scalzo was a monster when things didn't go his way.

"There it is," Gloria said, pointing at the sky.

A small plane circled the airport, throwing an elusive shadow over the men. Grabbing a suitcase, Scalzo walked to the end of the runway and stared up at the sky, shielding his eyes with his hand. The plane did another pass, then flew away and disappeared in the clouds.

Scalzo turned and shook his fist at Jasper, like it was his fault the plane hadn't landed. Jasper drew a silver-plated gun from his sports jacket and pointed it at the mobster. Scalzo looked to his bodyguard, as if expecting him to deal with Jasper. Only the bodyguard had turned his back and was looking in the opposite direction.

Jasper fired three times, the explosive sound swallowed up by the wind. The bullets hit Scalzo squarely in the chest and blew holes in his shirt. Scalzo staggered backward and brought his hand up to his heart. He touched himself, came away with a bloody hand, then looked up at the sky and punched the air. Crumpling to the ground, he lay motionless on his back.

"Oh my God," Gloria said. "Is he dead?"

Valentine watched as the bodyguard removed a blanket from the Mercedes' trunk and covered his boss. Then the bodyguard took a shovel from the trunk and started to dig a hole. "It sure looks that way. You'd better get back in the car."

The bodyguard was covered in sweat by the time he'd finished digging. He dragged Scalzo across the ground by his ankles, then laid him in the hole and covered him with dirt. Finished, he smoothed the ground with the shovel's edge. Jasper did not help, but leaned against the Mercedes and smoked a cigarette while staring at the ground.

The bodyguard stood over the grave and crossed himself. Valentine put the camera down and started to walk away. As he did, a shiny glint caught his eye. It came from the other side of the field, next to a storage shed with pieces of plywood nailed across its windows. He lifted the camera and had a look.

Two men stood in the building's long shadow. Both were tall and in their late thirties, with short-cropped hair and dark, off-the-rack suits. They had law enforcement written all over them. A car was parked beside them, and sunlight had crept over the building's roof and caught the car's windshield. Valentine adjusted the camera lens and read the car's license plate. He memorized it, then hustled over to Gloria's rental and hopped into the passenger seat.

"Time to get out of Dodge?" she asked.

"Yes," he said.

Gloria made the tires spin on the gravel. Soon they were traveling down the highway and heading back toward Celebrity. She chewed her lower lip as she drove, the memory of Scalzo's murder not easy to digest. Valentine took out his cell phone and again tried Bill's number. This time the call went through.

"Higgins here."

"I need a favor," Valentine said.

"Name it," Bill replied.

"I need you to check out a license plate number for me. ZH1 4L7. I think the plate might be government issued."

"How soon do you need this?"

"As fast as you can," Valentine said.

Bill hung up and Valentine did the same. Gloria was looking in her mirror, and he spun around in his seat. There was no one behind them.

"I'm just a little paranoid," she said.

"Nothing wrong with that," he said.

Two minutes later his cell phone vibrated and he stared at its face. It was Bill.

"Find anything?" he said by way of a greeting.

"You were right," Bill said. "The car belongs to the FBI's office in Las Vegas."

"Thanks, Bill. Thanks a lot."

He hung up. Gloria drove for another few miles in silence, then said, "Are you going to call the police, and tell them that you saw George Scalzo get rubbed out?"

That was a good question. Two FBI agents had watched Scalzo die, and he suspected that the small plane they'd seen circling overhead was also law enforcement. Sammy Mann had said the cheating at the World Poker Showdown would get cleaned up after the tournament ended, and he suspected the people in town who ran things had decided that the process should be sped up.

"They already know," he said.

48

Gloria did not feel well as she pulled into a roadside bar and grill. They went in and Valentine took a seat at the bar, while she searched for a restroom. Two sunburned guys sat at the other end of the bar, their rugged faces bathed in the artificial light of video poker games. He ordered coffee and stared at the TV perched above the bar. It was tuned to the cable channel showing the World Poker Showdown. A commercial for an on-line gambling site was on.

The coffee was good and strong. He drank it black and felt it warm his insides. He'd come to the conclusion that everyone on the planet had an addiction. His was caffeine. It got his heart going and made him think more clearly. He hadn't wanted to see Scalzo get whacked, but wasn't going to lose any sleep over it. He believed in the rule of law, and considered cops and law enforcement people who broke the law in order to put criminals away to be rogues. But he also understood that sometimes the rule of law didn't work, and people took matters into their own hands. The world was a better place with George Scalzo gone.

His phone vibrated in his pocket. He pulled it out and looked at it. Gerry. There had been times in his life when he hadn't looked forward to calls from his son. He was happy that had changed. "What's up?"

"Where are you?" his son asked.

"In the middle of nowhere," Valentine said. "Scalzo is out of the picture. Case closed."

"No, it's not," Gerry said.

Valentine put his coffee cup down. He sensed his son knew something that he didn't. "What do you mean? Why isn't the case over?"

"Because DeMarco just won the World Poker Showdown," Gerry said.

"You're kidding me, right?"

"Afraid not. He started out losing a few hands, and everyone at the table was equal in chips. DeMarco looked beatable. Then he came back strong and wiped his opponents out."

"Was he cheating?"

"No, Pop. There was a new dealer at the table and a new deck of cards. DeMarco played the final table on the square. It was really something to watch."

Gloria came out of the ladies' room looking pale. She sat next to him at the bar and ordered a sparkling water. Valentine asked, "What do you mean, Gerry?"

"DeMarco took a lot of chances, even bluffed a couple of times. I hate to say it, Pop, but he's a helluva poker player."

"You think so? He didn't just get lucky?"

"Luck had nothing to do with it," Gerry said. "Pop, I need to beat it. They're about to give DeMarco his prize, and I want to hear what he has to say."

Valentine said good-bye and folded the phone. On the TV, the commercial was over, the tournament back on. DeMarco sat at a table surrounded by his ten-million-dollar prize. Dangling off his wrist was the sparkling diamond and platinum bracelet that came with winning the event. Beside him sat the CEO of Celebrity, a ham-faced guy with a loose smile and a loud tie. Clutched in the CEO's hand was a microphone.

"So, champ," the CEO said, "how does it feel to beat the best poker players in the world?"

"It feels pretty good," DeMarco admitted.

"You predicted you'd win the tournament, and you did. Did you come here believing you were the favorite?"

"If I did, I was mistaken," DeMarco said.

The CEO lifted his eyebrows in mock surprise. "Really?"

"There were plenty of players in the event who could have won."

"Sounds like winning has humbled you."

DeMarco tilted his head almost imperceptibly.

"One of the players you knocked out called you a cheater and challenged you to play heads up," the CEO said. "His name is Rufus Steele, and you agreed to play Steele if he could raise a million dollars. I'm told that Steele has raised the money and is itching to take you on. Are you still up for playing him?"

DeMarco straightened in his chair and his face turned expressionless. He'd just beaten the best players in the world, and adrenaline was pumping through his veins. But Steele was a different animal. Steele didn't want his money. He wanted revenge.

"Bring him on," DeMarco said, the swagger returning to his voice.

"When?"

"How about right now?"

"You sound ready for a fight," the CEO said.

"No disrespect, but Rufus Steele is past his prime, and I'm entering mine," DeMarco said. "I'll play him any-time, anywhere."

"Eieee!" Gloria said, jumping up from her chair at the bar. The color had returned to her cheeks and her eyes were blazing. "This is my story! Come on!"

They were speeding down the highway toward Celebrity when Valentine's cell phone started vibrating. He'd been the last person he knew to buy a cell phone, and now he couldn't live without one. He stared at the phone's face. CALLER UNKNOWN.

"Valentine here," he answered.

"Hey pardner," Rufus Steele's voice rang out. "You anywhere near the hotel?"

"I'm about five minutes away."

"Good," Steele said. "I just agreed to play that punk DeMarco. I threw in a little stipulation, just to keep things honest."

"What kind of stipulation?"

"You're the dealer," Steele said.

49

Gloria Curtis hadn't lasted twenty-five years as a newscaster by being a wallflower. Upon reaching the hotel, she cornered the tournament director and convinced him to let her announce DeMarco and Steele's showdown, then persuaded the hotel's general manager to let the event be played in the poker room. Once that was arranged, she hit every bar and restaurant in the hotel, rustled up a few dozen well-known players still hanging around, and talked them into sitting ringside.

"You really know how to set a stage," Valentine said, shuffling the cards at the table where the match was to be held.

Gloria stood beside him with a pencil stuck between her teeth, studying the room. Removing the pencil, she said, "There's something still missing."

"What's that?"

"Steele will be dressed up, and so will DeMarco. I think you need to be dressed up as well."

With the tournament now over, he'd switched out of his geezer disguise and was wearing his last clean shirt and sports jacket. "What do you want me to change into?"

"A dealer's uniform," she said.

A dealer's uniform consisted of a white ruffled tuxedo shirt, a black bow tie, and a black vest. It was a monkey suit, sans the jacket.

"You're going to be on television and need to look the part," she added.

"You're the boss," he said.

He left the table and found the tournament director, and got directions to the employee dressing rooms, which were at the far end of the lobby behind an unmarked door. He knocked loudly, and a male dealer opened the door. The dealer was about his size but heavier, and Valentine asked him if he'd be interested in renting his uniform. The dealer seemed amused by his request.

"You doing this on a bet?" the dealer asked.

"To impress a woman," Valentine said.

"I figured it was one or the other. Sure, I'll rent you my uniform."

Valentine paid the dealer a hundred bucks, and the dealer took him to his locker, where a fresh set of clothes hung. Valentine stripped and put the dealer's clothes on, then looked at himself in a mirror. The vest was too large, the shirt too tight, and the bow tie made him look silly. Otherwise, it was perfect.

"Thanks a lot," he told the dealer.

He returned to the poker room tugging at his collar. Gerry was standing by the doorway waiting for him, and appraised his new wardrobe.

"Table for two, please," his son said.

"Very funny," Valentine said.

"You'd better hurry. They're ready to start."

Valentine went to the table and stood behind his chair. Close to fifty spectators had ringed the table with chairs, and he spied the Greek, Marcy Baldwin, and several suckers whom Rufus had fleeced sitting front row. The rest of the crowd consisted primarily of old-timers with chiseled faces who'd come to cheer Rufus on.

Steele stood at one end of the table, puffing away on a cigarette. He wore a scarlet United States Cavalry shirt buttoned diagonally from waist to shoulder, and his Stetson sported an ostrich feather in its band.

"Hey pardner," he said. "Glad you could make it."

"Wouldn't miss it for the world," Valentine replied.

DeMarco stood at the other end of the table dressed in a bilious gold shirt, opened to the middle of his hairless chest, and black designer slacks. He'd rolled back his right sleeve, exposing his champion bracelet.

Gloria stood directly between the two participants, mike in hand. She did a sound check with Zack, then began. "Good afternoon, everyone. This is Gloria Curtis, coming to you from the poker room in Celebrity Hotel and Casino in Las Vegas. To my right stands Skip DeMarco, newly crowned champion of the World Poker Showdown. To my left, Rufus Steele, one of the greatest players in the history of the sport. These two gentlemen are about to play for two million dollars. Before we start, I'd like to ask each participant to give us a few words."

Gloria moved toward DeMarco, shoving the mike beneath his chin. "Skip? Would you care to say something?"

"Age before beauty," DeMarco said.

Everyone in the room laughed, including Steele, the smoke billowing out of his nostrils like dragon's breath. Gloria moved down to his end of the table and stuck the mike in the old cowboy's face. "Rufus? How about a few words?"

"I've been playing poker for my entire life," Rufus said. "I believe the game exemplifies the worst aspects of capitalism which have made our country so great. I am looking forward to beating my opponent like an ugly stepchild."

More laughter from the crowd. DeMarco appeared to bristle. When Gloria returned to his end of the table, he said, "Rufus, how much money do you have?"

" 'Bout a million and a half," Rufus replied.

"Let's play for that," DeMarco suggested.

"Winner-take-all?"

"Winner-take-all," DeMarco said.

"You're on, son."

Gloria faced the camera and flashed a brilliant smile. "There you have it, folks. Skip DeMarco has upped the ante against Rufus Steele. Three million dollars, winner-take-all, the new kid versus the old warrior. This is one you're not going to want to miss." Then she stepped away from the table, and the contest began.

The two participants took their chairs, and Valentine explained the rules. The game was No Limit Texas Hold 'Em, and would be played until one man had the other's money. The blinds would be $20,000 and $40,000, which guaranteed that each starting pot had a minimum of $60,000. After a player bet or called or raised, his opponent had thirty seconds to respond, or would automatically fold his hand. Valentine would be the timekeeper.

"Agreed?" he asked.

"Sounds good to me," Rufus said.

"Me, too," DeMarco said.

Valentine then riffle-shuffled the cards seven times. A famous mathematician had proven that a true random order could only be obtained after seven shuffles. It was work, but he wanted the contest to be as fair as possible. Finished, he cut the cards, burned one, then dealt two cards to each man.

"Good luck," Valentine said.

After ten hands, Rufus was up $540,000.

Valentine had never seen anyone play Texas Hold 'Em the way Rufus played it. In a normal game of Hold 'Em, each player received two cards, then there was a round of betting, followed by three community cards, called the flop, being dealt face up on the table, followed by another round of betting. Then two more cards, called Fourth Street, or the turn, and Fifth Street, or the river, were dealt face up, with a round of betting after each. The five community cards were common to both players, who used them in combination with their own cards to form the strongest possible hand.

That was how Hold 'Em was usually played. But it wasn't how Rufus played it. He beat aggressively before any community cards were dealt, putting DeMarco into a corner. It was an unusual ploy, and it forced DeMarco to make an immediate decision. Eight times DeMarco had folded. The other two times he'd called Rufus's bet only to have Rufus go over the top and go "all in," pushing every chip he had into the pot. Both times, DeMarco had wilted and dropped out of the hand.

"Having fun?" Rufus asked as the eleventh hand was dealt.

"It isn't over yet," DeMarco shot back.

Rufus looked at the crowd. "I love these kids."

DeMarco brought his two cards up to his face and studied them. Placing the cards down, he paused for a few moments then pushed two hundred thousand in chips into the pot. His body language had changed, and Valentine sensed that he'd gotten good cards. Rufus glanced at his own two cards, his face as tight as a bank vault.

"I'm going to raise," Rufus said.

DeMarco leaned back in his chair. Valentine sensed that DeMarco had set a trap he was about to spring.

"How much are you raising?" DeMarco asked.

Rufus played with his stacks of chips. "Half a million."

"I'm all in," DeMarco fired back.

Rufus peeked at his cards stonily. "How much you got left, son?"

DeMarco counted his chips. "Nine hundred and eighty thousand."

Rufus pushed back his Stetson and rubbed his face, then stood up from the table. He shifted from foot to foot like a horse sensing bad weather. "What the heck. I'll call you."

DeMarco jumped out of his chair. Picking up his two

cards, he slapped them face up decisively on the felt. He had a pair of aces, the strongest starting hand.

"What have you got?" DeMarco asked.

Rufus flipped over his two cards. There was a mass sigh from the crowd.

"What does he have?" DeMarco asked again.

"The ten of diamonds and six of diamonds," Valentine told him.

"You called my bet with *that*?" DeMarco asked incredulously.

"Sure," Rufus said.

"But those are lousy cards."

"Son, I came here to gamble."

Valentine burned the top card, then dealt the flop, calling the values aloud for DeMarco's benefit. The three community cards were the four of diamonds, ace of clubs, jack of diamonds. DeMarco had flopped three of a kind, Rufus four cards to a flush. DeMarco was the odds-on favorite to win and let out a war whoop.

"No diamonds," he begged.

Valentine burned the top card and dealt Fourth Street. The card was the queen of spades, which helped neither player. DeMarco was jumping up and down. He was one card away from winning. It didn't seem right, but gambling rarely was. Out of the corner of his eye, Valentine glanced at Rufus. The old cowboy looked like he was enjoying himself.

Valentine burned the top card, then paused dramatically before turning over Fifth Street, and calling out its value.

"Two of diamonds," he said.

DeMarco stopped jumping. Valentine slid the two of diamonds down to his end of the table, and DeMarco picked the card up, and held it in front of his face.

"Jesus Christ," he whispered.

Rufus had made his diamond flush and beaten DeMarco's three of a kind. A hush had fallen over the room. Facing the crowd, Rufus took off his Stetson and bowed deeply from the waist. Then everyone in the room, including the Greek, Marcy Baldwin, and the suckers, gave him his due, and broke into long and hearty applause.

DeMarco stood frozen in place, his face pained and astonished. Gloria appeared by his side, and with Zack's camera whirring, asked, "Skip, what happened?"

DeMarco spent a moment regaining his composure, and the crowd grew quiet. Even Rufus seemed interested in what he had to say.

"Mr. Steele was the better man today," he said quietly.

"Were you surprised by how aggressively he played?" Gloria asked.

"Yes. I've never played anyone like him. He's really good."

"So the old man taught you a few things," Gloria said.

DeMarco winced. When he spoke again, his voice was subdued. "I'm sorry for the disparaging remarks I made about him earlier in the tournament. I was out of line."

"Apology accepted," Rufus called out.

DeMarco nodded solemnly, then placed his hand on the table edge, and used it to guide him to Rufus's end. Stopping, he stuck his hand out, which Rufus warmly shook. It was the way contests were supposed to end, and Valentine rose from his chair, and joined in the applause. As it subsided, Gloria edged up beside him and squeezed his hand.

"You see," she said. "Sometimes the good guys do win."

Poker Protection Tips

Cheating at poker may well be the largest unchecked crime in the United States. It takes place on all levels—private games, tournaments, the Internet, and in casino card rooms. As any pro will tell you, the best protection is to understand the various forms of cheating so you can look out for them when you play. Here are some of the most common forms of cheating taking place today, and what you can do to stop them.

MARKED CARDS

Recently, a poker book appeared on the market stating that marked cards are rarely used by cheaters. The author claimed that cheaters don't use marked cards because it was too easy for players to spot them. Nothing could be further from the truth. Marked cards (also called paper or paint) are a favorite weapon among poker cheaters. Magic shops and gambling supply houses sell tens of thousands of marked decks a year for "amusement purposes only." They are easy to obtain. And they are easy to use.

Marked cards give cheaters an unbeatable edge. They can be used in a variety of different games, especially those where cards are dealt face down on the table, then turned over one at a time. Here's what you need to look for.

Professionally Marked Cards

Cheaters know dozens of different ways to mark cards, many of which are undetectable to the untrained eye. Some favored methods are called juice, block out, humps, white ink, shade, flash, white-on-white, and sorts. Sounds confusing? It is. I've been shown cards marked by all of these methods, and I could not spot the marks until they were pointed out to me. The only sure-fire way to prevent marked cards from showing up in your game is by doing the following:

- Bring new decks to the game every time you play. Use established brands from the U.S. Playing Card Company. Do not use promotional cards. They are often inadvertently marked by the manufacturer.

- Make it a different player's responsibility to bring the cards for each game. This rotation will ensure that one player doesn't continually cheat the game by bringing marked cards.

- Open the cards in front of the other players. The cards should still be in the box, and have the plastic wrapping and seal on them.

- Spread the cards face up on the table after they're opened. Make sure they're all there, then check the pip configuration on the ace of spades, ace of clubs, and ace of hearts, plus the center pips on the threes and fives of the same suits. The pips should all be pointing in the same direction (top of the box when first removed). If not, someone has tampered with them.

- Do a riffle test. This is still the best way to detect most marking systems. Hold the deck face down just below eye level, and riffle them while staring at the backs. Do this several times. Shift your eyes, and look at different areas of the cards. Most marking systems will jump out when this test is performed.

- Always perform these tests. If a cheater is trying to bring a marked deck to your weekly poker game, this will convince them to find another game.

Cards Marked at the Table

Some cheaters prefer to mark cards during the course of a game. There are three ways to accomplish this. The first is to use a foreign substance to mark the cards. Favorite substances include nicotine and ash from cigarettes and cigars and water. Pros will use a substance called daub, which is normally kept behind the ear, or in a shirt button. The second method of marking is to put bends or warps in the cards during play. The cheater accomplishes this while handling the cards. After six or seven hands, it's not hard to put bends or warps in the majority of high cards in the deck. The third method is nicking. This is done with a sharpened fingernail. Nicks are put in the short ends of the cards. Cheaters read nicks when the cards are lying face down on the table, or when the deck is held in preparation for the deal. Some cheaters can read nicks when they are several cards down from the top. A famous cardshark named Walter Scott was able to read nicks halfway down in a deck.

Protection Tips: Keep ashtrays and drinks off the table. Encourage players in your games not to bend the cards. Most important, examine the deck between hands. If the cards are starting to look dirty or bent, throw them away. The cost to replace them is far less than getting swindled out of a pot.

Factory Marked Cards

During the famous California Gold Rush of the 1850s, thousands of Americans went west to seek their fortunes. Many found gold, and subsequently lost it in the gambling halls that sprung up in and around gold mining towns. One of the most notorious scandals of this period was the fact that over 200,000 decks of playing cards that had been printed in Mexico were marked, and were being read by cheaters. As a result, gamblers refused to play with cards that were not manufactured in this country, a situation that continued until a few years ago.

At the present time, factory marked cards are being manufactured in China, and used to cheat unsuspecting players. These cards are thin and cheaply made, with marks on the back specifying suit and color. These cards have turned up in discount stores and other places that sell playing cards in the United States.

Protection Tip: Whenever possible, play with cards manufactured by the United States Playing Card Company in Cincinnati, Ohio, which follows the strictest guidelines when it comes to ensuring the quality of its products.

COLLUSION

Collusion between players is the single biggest threat to the individual player in both private games and professional card rooms. It has been going on since the beginning of time, and is more prevalent today than ever before. Sadly it is a subject that is rarely talked about, although everyone knows it goes on. Casinos that have poker rooms are also lax in tackling the issue. Since the house makes its money from raking the pot, it does not scrutinize poker games as thoroughly as it should. As a result, you're as likely to get cheated by collusion inside a casino card room as you are in a private game.

Playing Top Hand

Playing Top Hand is one of the strongest forms of collusion known. Two players get together before a game, and agree upon a simple signal. It might be scratching the nose, or lighting a cigarette. This signal means that the player has "the nuts" (a cinch hand), and wants the other player to raise the betting when it's his turn. This effectively brings more money into the pot, while taking the heat off the player with the best hand.

Cheaters call this "getting value for your cards." After the game is over, the two players will get together, and chop up the winnings.

Playing Top Hand can also serve another purpose. Let's say the game is Texas Hold 'Em, and the signals being used are more complex. Two fingers on the wrist means two aces, while two fingers on the elbow means two kings. Player A signals to Player B that he has two aces. Player B, who has two jacks, folds. Another player wins the hand with a straight. This player has been cheated. He won Player A's money, but not Player B's money.

Protection Tips: This scam is difficult to detect, and difficult to stop. Knowing the people you play with is a good start. If you notice that one player always raises, and another player always wins, then you may have two players using this scam. Further confirmation would come from the fact that these players never act against each other. If you catch two players doing this, you have two choices. Warn them, or bar them.

Local Courtesy

When a player is willing to bet against certain players but not others, it's called Local Courtesy. I have seen this countless times in Las Vegas card rooms. The locals (who account for over 50 percent of the players) don't mix it up with each other. They reserve their action for tourists. This makes the game extremely one-sided. More often than not, the tourists leave as losers. The truth is, most players have done this at one time or another. It's psychologically harder to bet against a friend than a stranger. It's one thing if it's subconscious, another entirely if it's deliberate.

Protection Tip: If you're playing in a poker room, find out who the locals are. Watch their betting. If they avoid playing against each other, find another game. You can also complain to management.

Speaking in Tongues

A friend recently told me of playing in a game in a poker room in Gardenia, California, and how several players spoke Vietnamese to each other. My friend seemed astonished that he lost all his money to these guys. Wonder what they were talking about?

Whipsaw

Two players raise and reraise each other while forcing out a middle player. This works best in the early stages of a game such as Texas Hold 'Em or Seven Card Stud, and allows the players to steal the blind.

Protection Tips: Limit the number of bets in the early rounds. It's also wise to make the players show their hands after a bet and call.

LOCATION

Location is one of the most sophisticated card scams around. It requires no sleight-of-hand, just a good memory and some practice. Two players are involved. For the sake of explanation, let's call them A and B. A sits to the right of B. A deals the game. He drops out, and so does B. While the other players are finishing the game, A and B show each other the hands they folded. This is common among players and is called rabbit hunting. A and B secretly memorize their hands. If the game was five-card draw, they will memorize ten cards. These cards are thrown in the center of the table (the muck). As other hands are folded, they are thrown on top of these cards. The deck now goes to Player B. He shuffles the cards, but does not disturb the memorized cards on the bottom. He presents the deck to Player A, who cuts the memorized cards to a known position. The cut doesn't have to be perfect, but it needs to be close. The purpose is to position the memorized cards so they will fall after the first sixteen cards are dealt.

B announces he's going to play Texas Hold 'Em and deals two cards to each of the eight players in the game. A and B now have two advantages. First, they know that their ten memorized cards will make up the River, Turn, and Fifth Street. If none of the memorized cards help them, they fold. Second, after the River is dealt, they will be able to work forward in the memorized stack and know what cards the Turn and Fifth Street will be.

Protection Tips: Discourage rabbit hunting in your games. Once a player folds, don't let him show the cards he folded to another player. You should also watch each player as he shuffles, and make sure that *all* the cards are mixed.

DEALING WITH CHEATERS

Most of us are hesitate to confront someone we think is cheating. Cheaters know this, which is another edge they have over honest players. Frank Garcia, a gambling expert, once explained to me how a cheater deals with being confronted. It goes something like this: The cheater is dealing off the bottom of the deck. Another player starts yelling, and says she saw the cheater. The cheater throws the deck onto the table, pushes his chair back, and in a loud voice says, "Are you calling me a cheater? Who the hell do you think you are?" The cheater has effectively neutralized the situation. He's turned the accusation into something personal and confronted his accuser head-on. By doing so, he's removed the other players from the conflict.

One of two things will now happen. Either the accuser will back down and the game will resume. Or the accuser will hold firm and the cheater will leave the game in a huff. Either way, the cheater has saved his neck.

There is a better way to deal with this situation, and it's something all cheaters fear. It's called forming a posse. If you suspect someone of cheating, mention it to the others during the break, when the cheater is out of earshot. Then start watching the cheater. Figure out what he is doing, even if it takes several sessions. Once you know the scam, confront the cheater as a group. This is one scenario a cheater can't worm his way out of.

Be careful when playing with a group of players you don't know, especially if there are high stakes involved. If there is cheating going on, 99 percent of the time two or more players are involved. Don't try to be clever and turn the tables on the cheaters. The results can be disastrous. The best thing to do is leave the game.

Then there is the problem with being cheated in a casino or a card room. If you suspect foul play, file a complaint with the management, and make sure you have corroboration from another player as to what happened. Do this immediately after you've been swindled. If management brushes you off, write them a letter documenting what happened. Include the date, time, and where you sat. Be sure to copy whatever governing body regulates them. Don't forget to mention that the casino or card room "looked the other way" when you lodged your complaint. The governing body will follow up on your complaint, either by letter or phone. If other letters are on file, they'll probably pay the establishment a visit.